VILLAGE DIARY

Books by Miss Read

VILLAGE SCHOOL
VILLAGE DIARY
STORM IN THE VILLAGE
THRUSH GREEN
FRESH FROM THE COUNTRY
WINTER IN THRUSH GREEN
MISS CLARE REMEMBERS
COUNTRY BUNCH
OVER THE GATE
VILLAGE CHRISTMAS
THE MARKET SQUARE
THE HOWARDS OF CAXLEY
FAIRACRE FESTIVAL
MISS READ'S COUNTRY COOKING
NEWS FROM THRUSH GREEN
TIGGY
EMILY DAVIS
TYLER'S ROW
THE CHRISTMAS MOUSE
FARTHER AFIELD
BATTLES AT THRUSH GREEN
NO HOLLY FOR MISS QUINN
VILLAGE AFFAIRS
RETURN TO THRUSH GREEN
THE WHITE ROBIN
VILAGE CENTENARY

VILLAGE DIARY

BY 'MISS READ'

ILLUSTRATED BY J. S. GOODALL

London
MICHAEL JOSEPH

First Published by
MICHAEL JOSEPH LTD
44 Bedford Square,
London, WC1
OCTOBER 1957
SECOND IMPRESSION DECEMBER 1958
THIRD IMPRESSION NOVEMBER 1960
FOURTH IMPRESSION JUNE 1964
FIFTH IMPRESSION JULY 1968
SIXTH IMPRESSION SEPTEMBER 1972
SEVENTH IMPRESSION AUGUST 1975
EIGHTH IMPRESSION JUNE 1980

ISBN 0 7181 0407 2

Printed in great Britain by
Hollen Street Press Ltd at Slough
and bound by James Burn at Esher, Surrey

To JILL
the first reader

CONTENTS

January 9

February 31

March 53

April 75

May 97

June 115

July 139

August 157

September 177

October 197

November 217

December 237

JANUARY

As I have been given a large and magnificent diary for Christmas—seven by ten and nearly two inches thick—I intend to fill it in as long as my ardour lasts. Further than that I will not go. There are quite enough jobs that a schoolmistress just *must* do without making this one a burden.

Unfortunately, the thing is so colossal that I shan't be able to carry it with me, as the adorable Miss Gwendolen Fairfax did hers, so that she 'always had something sensational to read in the train.'

It was a most surprising present for Amy to have given me. When we first taught together in London, many years ago, we exchanged two hankies each, I remember; and since she cropped up again in my life a year or so ago, it has been bath salts on her side ('To make you realize, dear, that even if you are a school teacher there is no need to let yourself go completely') and two-hankies-as-before on mine.

When Amy handed me this present she remarked earnestly, 'Try to use it, dear. Self-expression is such a wonderful thing, and so vital for a woman whose life is—well, not exactly abnormal, but restricted!' This smacked of Amy's latest psychiatrist to me, but after the first reaction of speechless fury, I agreed civilly and have had over a week savouring this *bon mot* with increasing joy.

Mrs Pringle, the school cleaner, told me yesterday that Miss Parr's old house at the end of the village has now been turned into three flats. The workmen have been there now for months; they arrived soon after her death, but I hadn't realized that that was what they were doing. A nephew of Miss Parr's now owns it, and has the ground floor. A retired couple from Caxley evidently move into the top floor this week, and a widower, I understand, has the middle flat.

'A very nice man too,' Mrs Pringle boomed menacingly at me. 'Been a schoolmaster at a real posh school where the boys have to pay fees and get the cane for nothing. Not in his prime, of course, but as Mrs Willet said to me at choir practice, there's many would jump at him.' Mrs Pringle eyed me speculatively, and I can see that the village is already visualizing a decorous wooing, culminating in a quiet wedding at Fairacre Church, with my pupils forming a guard of honour from the south door, with the aged couple hobbling down the path between them.

I said that I hoped that now that the poor man had retired,

he would be allowed to rest in peace, and went out to clean the car. This is my latest and most extravagant acquisition—a small second-hand Austin, in which I hope to be able to have wonderful touring holidays, as well as driving to Caxley on any day of the week, instead of relying on the local bus on Tuesdays, Thursdays and Saturdays as heretofore. So far I have not been out on my own as I am still having lessons from an imperturbable instructor in Caxley, who thrives on clashing gears, stalling engines and a beginner's unfortunate confusion of brake and accelerator. Miss Clare, that noble woman, who taught the infants at Fairacre for many years, says that she will come out with me 'at *any* time, dear, whether you feel confident or not. I am quite sure that you can master anything.' Am touched, but also alarmed, at such faith in my powers, and can only hope that she never meets my driving instructor.

Miss Clare spent the evening with me recently and our conversation turned, as it so often does, to life in Fairacre in the early years of this century, when Miss Clare was a young and inexperienced pupil-teacher at this village school. I love to hear her reminiscing, for she has a tolerant and dispassionate outlook on life, born of inner wisdom and years of close contact with the people here. For Miss Clare, 'To know is to forgive,' and I have never yet heard of her acting in anger or in fear, or meting out to a child any punishment that was hastily or maliciously devised.

Her attitude to those who were in authority over her is as wide and kindly as it always was to the small charges that she taught for forty years.

We were talking of Miss Parr, who had died recently. She had been a manager of Fairacre School since the reign of King Edward the Seventh, and was a stickler for etiquette. It appears that one day she met Mrs Willet, now our caretaker's wife, but then a child of six, in the lane, and was shocked to find the little girl omitted to curtsy to her. At once she took the child to its mother, and demanded instant punishment.

'But surely——' I began to protest. Miss Clare looked calmly at me.

'My dear,' she said gently, 'it was quite understandable. It was customary then for our children to curtsy to the gentry, and Miss Parr was doing her duty, as she understood it, by correcting the child. No one then questioned her action. "Other days, other ways" you know. It's only that now, sometimes, looking back—I wonder——' She put down a green pullover she was knitting and stared meditatively at the fire.

'When you say that no one questioned the actions of his superiors, do you mean that they were automatically considered right or that verbal protestations were never made, or what?' I asked her.

'We recognized injustice, dear,' answered Miss Clare equably, 'as clearly as you do. But we bore more in silence, for we had so much more to lose by rebellion. Jobs were hard to come by, in those days, and no work meant no food. It was as simple as that.

'A sharp retort might mean instant dismissal, and perhaps no reference, which might mean months, or even years, without a suitable post. No wonder that my poor mother's favourite maxim was "Civility costs nothing." She knew, only too well, that civility meant more than that to people like us. It was a vital necessity to a wage-earner when we were young.'

'Was she ever bitter?'

'I don't think so. She was a happy, even-tempered woman, and believed that if we did our best in that station of life to which we had been called, then we should do well. After all, we all knew our place then. It made for security. And here, in Fairacre, the gentry on the whole were kindly and generous to those they employed. You might call it a benevolent despotism, my dear—and, you know, there are far worse forms of government than that!'

Miss Clare's eyes twinkled as she resumed her work and the room was filled again with the measured clicking of her knitting needles.

Tuesday was a beast of a day; foggy and cold, with the elm trees dripping into the playground. Two workmen arrived from Caxley to see to the school skylight over my desk: it must be the tenth time, at least, that it has received attention since I came here just over six years ago. Usually, it is Mr Rogers, from the forge, who has the job of clambering over the roof, but the managers decided to try the Caxley firm this time, hoping, I imagine, that it might be better done by them. The village, of course, is up in arms at this invasion of foreigners, and Mr Rogers wears a martyred expression when he stands at the door of his smithy. I am confident that he will soon be in a position to smile again, as the skylight has defied all comers for seventy-odd years—so the school log-books say—and I doubt whether any workmen, even if hailing from the great Caxley itself, will vanquish it.

One man, in Mrs Pringle's hearing, said loudly that 'it was a proper bodged-up job,' so that, of course, will inflame passions further. Mrs Pringle, who was scrubbing out the school dustbins at the time, drew in her breath for so long, and with such violence, that I thought she would burst; but only her corsets creaked under the strain.

Tea, at Miss Clare's, was the bright spot of the day. We had a lardy cake which was wonderfully hot and indigestible, and conversation which was soothing, until I was putting on my coat when Miss Clare shattered me by asking if I had yet met a very nice man, a retired schoolmaster, who had come to live in Miss Parr's old house.

I am beginning to feel very, very sorry for this unfortunate man, and have half a mind to ring him up anonymously, advising his early removal from Fairacre if he wishes to have an undisturbed retirement.

The last day of the holidays has arrived, and, as usual, half the jobs I intended doing have been left undone. No marmalade made, no paint washed down, only the most urgent mending done, and school starts tomorrow.

It all looks unbelievably clean over there. I staggered back with the fish tank and Roman hyacinths, all of which have sheltered under my school-house roof for the past fortnight. Miss Gray—Mrs Annett, I mean—will have a smaller class this term, only sixteen on roll, while mine will be twenty-three strong.

The stoves are miracles of jetty brilliance. Mrs Pringle must have used pounds of blacklead and enough energy to move a mountain to have produced such lustre. Woe betide any careless tipper-on of coke for the next few days!

Term has begun. Everyone is back with the exception of Eileen Burton, who has, according to the note brought by a neighbouring child, 'a sore throat and a hard, tight chest.' Can only hope these afflictions are not infectious.

The workmen have found it necessary to remove the whole frame of the skylight, so that, having had a clear two weeks to do the job undisturbed, they now tell me that we must endure a flapping and smelly tarpaulin over the hole in the roof, while a new window-frame is made in Caxley. Straight speaking, though giving me some relief, dints their armour not at all as blame attaches, as usual, to other members of the firm 'higher-up and back in

Caxley, Miss,' so that I can see a very comfortable few days ahead.

The children appeared to have forgotten the very elements of education. Five-times table eluded them altogether, and my request to write 'January' on their own, met with tearful mystification. Having walked round the class and seen such efforts as 'Jamwy,' 'Ganeree' and 'Jennery' I wrote it on the blackboard with dreadful threats of no-play-for-a-week for those who did not master its intricacies immediately.

The vicar called, just before we went home, in his habitual winter garb of cloak, biretta and leopard-skin gloves. Surely they can't stand another winter? I only wish I had such a serene outlook as Mr Partridge's. He greeted us all as though he loved every hair of our heads, as truly I believe he does. I see that he has 'Jesu, Lover of my Soul' on the hymn list this week, but haven't the heart to tell him that I think it painfully lugubrious and quite unsuitable for the children to learn.

I invited him over to the school-house to tea and ushered him into the dining-room, where the clothes-horse stood round the fire bearing various intimate articles of apparel and a row of dingy polishing rags which added the final touch of squalor. Not that he, dear man, would have worried, even had he noticed the things—but that clothes-horse was whisked neatly into the kitchen in record time!

I have just returned from a day out with Amy. She rang me up last night to say that there was a wonderful film on, which I must see. It would *broaden* me. It was about Real Life. I said that I'd looked through the *Caxley Chronicle* this week, but I thought that both cinemas were showing Westerns.

'Caxley?' screamed Amy down the wire. Did I think of nothing but Caxley and Fairacre? When she thought of what promise I had shown as a girl, it quite upset her to see how I'd gone off! No, the film she had in mind was to be shown in a London suburb—the cinema specialized in revivals, and this was a quite wonderful chance to see this unique masterpiece. She would pick me up at 10.30, give me lunch, and bring me back to the wilds again.

I mentally pulled my forelock and said that that would be lovely.

Amy's car is magnificent and has a fluid fly-wheel, which as a gear-crashing learner, filled me with horrid envy. We soared up the hills, passing everything in sight, while Amy told me that life, even for a happily married woman, was not always rosy. James, although utterly devoted of course, was at a dangerous age. Not that he was inattentive; only last week he gave her these gloves—she raised a gargantuan fur-clad paw; and the week before that these ear-rings—I bent forward to admire a cluster of turquoises—and this brooch was his Christmas present, and was fantastically expensive—but she found she was beginning to suspect the *reason* for so many costly presents, especially when he had been away from home, on business, so frequently lately.

I said: 'Why don't you ask him if there is anyone else?' Amy said that was so like me—it wasn't surprising that I had stayed single when I was so—well, so *unwomanly* and *unsubtle*. No, she could handle this thing quite skilfully, she thought, and in any case it was her duty to stick by dear James through thick and thin. Unworthy thought crossed my mind as to whether she'd stick so nobly if James suddenly became penniless.

We arrived in the West End; Amy had no difficulty in finding a car park with an obsequious attendant who directed our footsteps to the hotel where Amy had booked a table. I was much impressed by the opulence of this establishment and said so. Amy shrugged nonchalantly: 'Not a bad little dump,' then, scanning the menu, 'James brings me here when he wants to be quick. The food is *just* eatable.'

We ordered ham and tongue, with salad, which Amy insisted on having mixed at our table, supervising the rubbing of the bowl with garlic (which I detest, but could see I must endure) the exact number of drops of oil, etc. and expressing horror that the whole was not being turned with wooden implements.

I would much rather have had my salad fresh and been allowed to ask for Heinz mayonnaise, in constant use at home, but realized that Amy was enjoying every minute of this worldly-woman-taking-out-country-mouse act, and would not have spoiled it for her for worlds.

Over lunch, Amy continued to tell me about James's generosity, and disclosed the monthly allowance which he gives her. This, she said, she just manages on. As the sum exceeds easily my own modest monthly cheque as a headmistress, I felt inclined to remind her of our early days together, teaching in a large junior school not many miles from this very hotel, when we thrived cheerfully on a salary of just over thirteen pounds a month, and visited the theatre, the cinema, went skating and dancing, dressed attractively and, best of all, were as merry as grigs all the time. As Amy's guest, however, I was bound to keep these memories to myself. As I watched her picking over her salad discontentedly I remembered vividly a meal we had had together in those far-off days. It must have been towards the end of the month for I know we spent a long and hilarious time working out from the menu which would fill us up more for eightpence—baked beans and two sausages, or spaghetti on toast.

The cinema was rather hard to find, in an obscure cul-de-sac, and the film which Amy had particularly come to see had just begun. It was so old, that it seemed to be raining all the time, and even the bedroom scenes—which were far too frequent for my peace of mind—were seen through a downpour. The women's hair styles were unbelievable, and quite succeeded in distracting my grasshopper mind from the plot; either puffed-out at the sides, like the chorus in *The Mikado*, or cut in a thick fringe just across the eyebrows, giving the most brutish aspect to the ladies of the cast. Waist lines were low and busts incredibly high evidently when this film first saw the light.

The supporting film was of later vintage, but, if anything, heavier going. Played by Irish actors, in Irish countryside in Irish weather, and spoken in such a clotted hotchpotch of Irish idiom as to be barely intelligible, it dealt with the flight of a young man from the cruel English. Bogs, mist, mountains, girls with shawls over their heads and bare feet splashing through puddles, open coffins surrounded with candles and keening, wrinkled old women, all flickered before us for an hour and a half—and then the poor dear was shot in the end!

We emerged into the grey London twilight with our eyes swollen. Drawn together by our emotional afternoon we had tea in a much more relaxed mood than lunch, and drove back in a pleasantly nostalgic atmosphere of ancient memories shared.

It was good of Amy to take me out. A day away from Fairacre in the middle of January is a real tonic. But I was sorry to see her so unhappy. I hope that I am not so wrong-headed as to blame Amy's recent affluence for her present malaise. As anyone of sense knows, money is a blessing and I dearly wish I had more—a lot more. I should have flowers in the classroom, and my house, all the year round, buy a hundred or so books, which have been on my list for years, and spend every school holiday travelling abroad—just for a start. I think the truth of the matter is that Amy feels useless, and has too little to do.

She used to be a first-class teacher and was able to draw wonderful pictures on the blackboard, that were the envy of us all, I remember.

School has now started with a vengeance, and I have heard all Mrs Annett's infants' class read—that is, those that can. She has done wonders since she came a year ago. The marriage seems ideal and Mr Annett has lost his nervous, drawn look and put on quite a stone in weight. He brings her over from their school-house at Beech Green, each morning, and then returns to his duties there as headmaster. I was glad that the managers persuaded her to continue teaching. She intended to resign last September, but we had no applicants for the post, and as the Annetts had had a good deal of expense in refurnishing she decided to work for a little longer. The children adore her and her methods are more modern than Miss Clare's were. She has a nice practical grasp of infant-work problems too, as an incident this morning proved. I was sending off for more wooden beads for number work. 'Make them send square ones,' she said. I looked surprised. 'They don't roll away,' she added. Now, that's what I call intelligent! Square they shall be!

Joseph Coggs appeared yesterday morning with a brown-paper carrier bag. Inside was a tortoise, very muddy, and as cold and heavy as a stone. It was impossible to tell if it were dead or only hibernating.

'My mum told me to throw an old saucepan on the rubbish heap at the bottom of our place,' he told me, 'and this 'ere was buried under some old muck there.' He was very excited about his find and we have put the pathetic reptile in a box of leaves and earth out in the lobby—but I doubt if it will ever wake again. The children, I was amused to hear, were hushing each other as they undressed.

'Shut up hollering, you,' said Eric in a bellow that nearly

raised our tarpaulin, 'that poor snail of Joe's don't get no rest!'

The weather is bitterly cold, with a cruel east wind, which flaps our accursed tarpaulin villainously. (The frame 'has been a bit held-up like, miss. Funny, really.') Scotland has had heavy snow, and I expect that Fairacre will too before long.

The vicar called in just before the children went home to check up numbers for our trip to the Caxley pantomime on Saturday. Two buses have been hired as mothers and friends will come too, as well as the school managers who generously pay the school-children's expenses. It is the high-light of dark January.

Mr Annett called to collect his wife—she won't be coming with us to the pantomime—and the vicar remarked to me on their happiness, adding that, to his mind, a marriage contracted in maturer years often turned out best, and had I met that very pleasant fellow—a retired schoolmaster, he believed—who had come to live at Miss Parr's?

An almost irresistible urge to push the dear vicar headlong over the low school wall, against which he was leaning, was controlled with difficulty, and I was surprised to hear myself replying politely that I had not had that pleasure yet. Truly, civilization is a wonderful thing.

I met Mr Bennett as I walked down to the Post Office the other evening. He is the owner of Tyler's Row, four thatched cottages at the end of our village. The Coggs live in one, the Waites next door to them, an old couple—very sweet and as deaf as posts—in the next, and a tight-lipped, taciturn woman, called Mrs Fowler lives in the last.

Mr Bennett had been to collect the rent from his property.

Each tenant pays three shillings a week and parts with it with the greatest reluctance.

'I gets to hate coming for it,' admitted poor Mr Bennett.

He is beginning to look his seventy years now, but his figure is as upright and trim as it was when he was a proud soldier in the Royal Horse Artillery, and his waxed moustache ends still stand at a jaunty angle. He has his Old Age Pension and lives with a sister at Beech Green, who is ailing and as poor as he is.

'Every door's the same,' went on the old soldier. ' "Can't you set our roof to rights? Can't you put us a new sink in? Come and look at the damp in our back scullery. 'Tis shameful." And what can I do with twelve bob a week coming in? That's if I'm lucky. Arthur Coggs owes me for three months now. He's got four times the money coming in that I have, but he's always got some sad story to spin.'

The old man took out a pipe and rammed the tobacco in with a trembling finger.

'I shall have to give this up, I s'pose, the way things are. I went to get an estimate from the thatcher over at Springbourne about Tyler's Row roofs. Guess how much?'

I said I imagined it would cost about a hundred pounds to put it in repair.

'A hundred?' Mr Bennett laughed sardonically. '*Two* hundred and fifty, my dear. There's nothing for it, it seems, but to sell 'em for about a hundred and fifty while I can. Mrs Fowler would probably buy 'em. She's making a tidy packet at the moment. Pays me three bob, my dear, and has a lodger in that back bedroom who pays her three pound!'

'But can she?' I asked. 'Didn't you have a clause about sub-letting?'

'No. I didn't. When Mrs Fowler first come begging, all pitiful as a widder-woman, to have my cottage, I was that sorry for her I let her have the key that day. Now the boot's on the other foot. She earns six pounds a week up the engineering works in Caxley, gets three off her lodger, and greets me with a face like a vinegar bottle. "Proper hovel," she called my cottage, just now, "I sees you don't give me notice though, my dear," I says to her, "and, what's more, that's a real smart TV set you got on the dresser there." Ah! she didn't like that!'

The old man chuckled at the thought of his flash of wit, and blew out an impudent dart of smoke from under the twirling moustaches.

'I've just met Mrs Partridge,' he added. 'She asked me if I'd like to give something towards the Church Roof Fund. I give her a shilling, and then I couldn't help saying: "If I was you, Ma'am, I'd call along Tyler's Row for donations. There's something in the nature of forty or fifty pounds going in there each week. You should get a mite from that quarter."'

He leant forward and spoke in a conspiratorial whisper.

'And you know what she said to me? "Mr Bennett, I'm afraid their hearts don't match their pay packets!" Ah, she sees it all—she and the vicar! Times is topsy-turvy. There's new poor and new rich today, but one and all has got to face responsibility, as I see it. You can't take out of the kitty and not put in, can you, Miss?'

The bus to Beech Green and Caxley drew up with a horrible squeaking of brakes. The driver, a local boy, from whom no secrets are hid, shouted cheerfully to Mr Bennett above the din.

'Been to collect them rents again? Some people has it easy, my eye!'

The old soldier cast me a quizzical glance, compounded of despair and amusement, mounted the steep step, and vanished among the country passengers.

I have been inflicted with a sudden and maddening crop of chilblains and can scarcely hobble around the house. No shoes are big enough to hold my poor, swollen, tormented toes and I am shuffling about in a pair of disreputable slippers which had been put aside for the next jumble sale, but were gratefully resurrected. A very demoralizing state of affairs, and can only put it down to the unwelcome appearance of snow.

The pantomime was an enormous success. Both buses were full, and Cathy Waites, looking very spruce in her new High School uniform, sat by me and told me all about the joys of hockey. 'I'm right-half,' she told me, eyes sparkling, 'and you have to have plenty of wind, because if you're right-half you have to mark the opposing left-wing, and she's usually the fastest runner on the field.' There was a great deal more to the same effect, and in answer to my query about her prowess in more academic subjects, she said: 'Oh, all right,' rather vaguely, and went on to tell me of the intricacies of bullying-off.

Jimmy, her little brother, who sat by his mother opposite, was eating a large apple as he entered the bus, and in the six miles to Caxley consumed, with the greatest relish, a banana, a slab of pink and white nougat, a liquorice pipe, a bar of chocolate cream, and a few assorted toffees. This performance was only typical of many of his companions.

Joseph Coggs sat by me when we settled in the Corn Exchange. The pantomime was 'Dick Whittington,' and he was over-awed by the cat, whose costume and make-up were remarkably realistic.

'How does he breeve?' he asked, in a penetrating whisper.

I whispered back. 'Through the holes in the mask.'

'But he don't have no nose,' objected Joseph.

'Yes he does. It's under the mask.'

'Well, if it's under the mask, how does he breeve?'

We were back where we started, and I tried a different approach.

'Do you think he's holding his breath all this time, Joseph?'

'Yes, he must be.'

'Then how can he talk to Dick?'

Still not persuaded of the cat's 'breeving,' or half-believing it to be a real cat all the time, Joseph subsided. He loved every minute of the show—which was an extraordinarily good amateur performance—and nearly rolled out of his seat with excitement, when I pointed out Linda Moffat to him on the stage. She was a dazzling fairy queen, in a creation of her clever mother's making, and her dancing was a pleasure to watch. I was glad that Mrs Moffat, with her friend Mrs Finch-Edwards, had been able to come with us this afternoon to witness Linda's success.

Several of the cast were known personally to the Fairacre children and storms of clapping greeted the appearance of anyone remotely known.

'Look,' said Eric, on my other side, clutching me painfully, 'there's the girl what drives the oil-van Tuesdays.' And he nearly burst his palms with rapturous greeting.

When we emerged, dazzled with glory, into the winter twilight, the snow was falling fast. Queen Victoria, on her lofty pedestal wore a white mantle and a snow-topped crown. The lane to Fairacre was unbelievably lovely, the banks smooth as linen sheets, the overhanging beech trees already bearing a weight of snow along their elephant-grey branches, while the prickly hawthorn hedges clutched white handfuls in their skinny fingers.

St Patrick's clock chimed half-past five when we stepped out at Fairacre, after our lovely afternoon. Our footsteps were muffled, but our voices rang out as clear as the bells above, in the cold air.

Mrs Pringle asked me as we got off the bus if I had ever tried Typhoon tea? I successfully curbed an insane desire to ask her if it brewed storms in tea-cups? I enjoyed this *bon mot* all through my own tea-time.

* * *

A most peculiar thing happened today. A very loud knocking came at the door of my classroom, while we were chanting the pence table to 100, in a delightful sing-song that would make an ultra-modern inspector's hair curl—and when I opened it, a strange young man tried to push in. I manœuvred him back into the lobby, shut the classroom door behind me, and asked what he wanted. He was respectably dressed, but unshaven. He said could he come in as he liked children? Thinking he was an eccentric tramp on his way from the Caxley workhouse to the next, I told him that he'd better be getting along, and shooed him kindly into the playground.

An hour later Mrs Annett came in from P.T. lesson, somewhat perturbed, because the wretched creature had hung over the school wall throughout the lesson making inane remarks. At this, I went out to send him off less kindly. By now, he had entered my garden and was drawing patterns on the snowy lawn with a stick.

When I asked him what he was supposed to be doing, he flummoxed me by whipping out a red, penny note-book and saying he'd come to read the gas meter. As we have no gas in this area, this was so patently silly that I made up my mind at once to get the police to cope with the fellow.

As I opened my front door he tried to come in with me, whining: 'I'm so hungry—so hungry,' and grinning vacantly at the same time. By now I was positive I had a madman on my hands, and very devoutly wished that I had not seen a gripping film about Jack the Ripper in Caxley recently, the horrider parts of which returned to me with unpleasant clarity.

'Go to the back porch,' I ordered him, in a stern schoolmarmish voice, 'and I will give you some food.' Luckily he went, and I sped inside, locked front and back doors, and rang Caxley police station in record time. A reassuring country voice answered me, and I began to feel much better as I described the man, until the voice said, in a leisurely manner: 'That'd be the chap that ran off from Abbotsleigh yesterday'—our local mental home.

'Heavens——!' I began, squeaking breathlessly.

'He wouldn't hurt a fly, miss,' went on the unhurried burr, 'he'll be scared stiff of you. Just keep him there if you can and we'll send a car out—it'll be with you in a quarter of an hour.'

I didn't know that I cared to be told that the man would be scared stiff of me, but I cared even less for the suggestion that I cherished him under my roof. Nor did I like the thought of the forty children, of tender years, for whom I was responsible, not to mention Mrs Annett, whose husband I should never dare to face, if aught befell her. All this I babbled over the telephone, adding: 'I'm just going to give him a drink and some bread and cheese, in the back porch, so please try and get here while he's still eating.'

'Car's gone out already. Never you fear, miss. Treat him like one of your kids,' said my calm friend, and rang off. I handed a pint of cider, half a loaf, and a craggy piece of hard cheese through the kitchen window, and with subtle cunning of which I was inordinately proud, supplied him with a small, very blunt tea-knife which should slow up his progress considerably. I couldn't make up my mind whether to dash back to the school and warn Mrs Annett, or whether to hang on in the house until the police car came. In the end I stayed in the kitchen, watching the meal vanish all too swiftly and edging my mind away from that pursuing film.

After the longest ten minutes of my life, the car drew up. Two enormous, cheerful policemen came to the back porch, and asked the man to come for a ride with them.

He went, without a backward glance, still clutching the plate and mug. Once inside the car he finished his cider, and I emerged from the front door and collected his utensils, wishing him a heartfelt good-bye into the bargain.

The policeman said: 'Thank you, miss, thank you!' and drove off, still beaming.

When I caught sight of myself in the mirror in the lobby I was not surprised. The most scared schoolmistress in the United Kingdom crawled thankfully back to her noisy class, and never breathed a word of reproach to the dear souls.

I really believe that my chilblains have finally gone, and wish I knew what had cured them—if anything particular, apart from Time-the-great-healer, I mean.

The various suggestions for their rout have ranged from (1) calcium tablets (Mr Annett); (2) painting with iodine (Mrs Annett) which I tried, but found tickly to do and so drying that the poor toes started to crack as well as itch; (3) treating with the liquid obtained from putting salt in a hollow dug in a turnip (Mr Willet, the caretaker); and (4) thrashing with a sprig of holly until the chilblains bleed freely (Mrs Pringle). Needless to say I did *not* attempt the last sadistic assault on my suffering extremities.

I am very worried about Joseph Coggs. His mother was taken to hospital last week with some internal trouble connected with the recent baby. Mrs Pringle, who usually describes any ills of the flesh in the most revolting detail, has seen fit on this occasion to observe an austere reserve about Mrs Coggs' symptoms, taking up the attitude that there are some things that the great army of married women must keep dark from their less fortunate spinster sisters. The twins, who usually adorn the front desk in Mrs Annett's room, and a toddler brother, have been sent to Mrs Coggs' sister in Caxley; but as she has no room for Joe he is living a hand-to-mouth existence with his father (who is completely useless) and with Mrs Waites, the next-door neighbour, 'Keeping an eye on him.'

It all sounds most unsatisfactory to me. The child is not clean, has not had his clothes changed since his mother's departure, and looks frightened. Mr Willet told me more this morning when he came to fill the two buckets for the school's daily drinking-water, from my kitchen pump.

'I don't say nothing about Arthur Coggs' drunkenness,' announced Mr Willet, with heavy self-righteousness. 'Nor don't I say nothing about his hitting of his wife now and again—that's his affair. Nor don't I say nothing about an occasional lift round the ear for his kids—seeing as kids must be brought up respectful—but I *do* say this. That's not right to leave that child alone in that thatched cottage with the candle on, while he spends the evening at the "Beetle and Wedge." Why, my wife and I we hears him roaring along home nigh on eleven most nights.'

'But the candle would have burnt out by then,' I said, horror-struck. 'Joe would be alone in the dark.'

'Well, I don't know as that's not a deal safer,' said Mr Willet, stolidly. 'Better be frightened than frizzled. But don't you upset yourself—Joe's probably asleep by then.'

'I thought Mrs Waites was looking after him.'

'Mrs Waites,' said Mr Willet, with a return to his pontifical manner, 'is well-meaning, but flighty. Never room for more than one thought at a time in her head. Maybe she takes a peep at him, once in a while; maybe she don't.'

Discreet questioning of Joseph, later in the morning, revealed that the state of his home affairs was even worse than suspected. The candle *does* go out, Joseph is too terrified to get out of bed, so wets it, and Arthur Coggs on his return from the pub shows his fatherly disapproval by giving the child what Joe calls 'a good hiding with his belt.' (On seeing my appalled face, Joe added, reassuringly, that 'he didn't use the buckle end.') Joseph's stolid acceptance of this state of things was rather more than I could bear, and I went to Mrs Waites' house during the dinner hour to see what could be done.

She was sensible and helpful, offering to let Joe share her little Jimmy's bed downstairs. This sounded ideal, and I promised to see Arthur Coggs about the scheme after tea. He—great bully that he is—was all smiles and servility, and confessed himself deeply grateful to Mrs Waites, as well he might be.

Luckily, Mrs Waites, who is a confirmed novelette-reader, has just read in this week's number, she told me, a story about a friendless child who later becomes heir to a dukedom and landed estate (no taxes mentioned), and suitably rewards kindly woman who befriended him in his early years. This has sweetened her approach to young Joe considerably, and though I can't see a dukedom looming up for him, he will doubtless never forget his own neighbour's present kindness. Flighty, Mrs Waites may be, but thoroughly sweet-natured, and I can quite see how she has fluttered so many male hearts.

I seem to be more than usually financially embarrassed, and when I had paid the laundry man this morning, found I was left with exactly two shillings and sevenpence. Mrs Pringle brought me my weekly dozen eggs this afternoon, and I had to tip out my threepenny bits which I save in a Coronation mug, and make up the balance.

That's the worst of being paid for December and January just before Christmas! I shall have to take my Post Office Savings Book into Caxley on Saturday morning and withdraw enough to keep me going until the end of the month. It would be more than my reputation's worth to withdraw it here in the village. Mr Lamb, our postmaster, and brother to Mrs Willet, would fear I was either betting or keeping two homes. Meanwhile I must just embezzle the dinner money.

We have had pouring rain all day and—miraculously—the new skylight seems weatherproof.

I gave my class an arithmetic test. Linda Moffat did exceptionally well, and should go on to Caxley High School in two years' time if she keeps on at this rate. She grows prettier daily, and will doubtless become a heart-breaker.

All goes well with Joseph, thank heaven, and the child is cleaner than I've ever seen him. He and Jimmy are great friends and I can see that Mrs Annett is going to have to squash those two young gentlemen before long.

Joe's tortoise seems to have turned round in his box. At my suggestion that perhaps somebody lifted him round, there were hot denials, and I apologized hastily. He certainly looks less dead.

Jim Bryant, our postman, brought our cheques today. He was never more welcome. I gave Mrs Pringle and Mrs Annett theirs, but could not find Mr Willet. However, he had a noisy coughing attack in the lobby this afternoon, which reminded me of his rightful dues.

'There now,' he said, when I gave the cheque to him, 'this is a real surprise!'

Bless him, if anyone ever earned his humble wage it's Mr Willet! He copes with coke, water, dead leaves, dustbins, snow, intruding animals varying from Mr Roberts' cows to black beetles—not to mention the buckets from our primitive lavatories—with unfailing cheerfulness. May he endure for ever!

FEBRUARY

THE village is agog. The engagement has been announced in *The Times* and *The Daily Telegraph* of John Parr—our Miss Parr's nephew, who now owns her house here in Fairacre. His bride, unfortunately, is not to be a Fairacre girl—what a wedding that would have been at St Patrick's—but lives somewhere in Westmorland. Mrs Pringle was somewhat disapproving this morning.

'Young enough to be his daughter! Man of his age—fifty-odd—with one foot in the grave, as you might say, to enter into 'oly wedlock with a kittenish bit like that! Don't seem respectable to me. A decent body, much the same age now, why, that's quite a different kettle of fish! I said as much to Mr Willet—which reminds me—that schoolmaster what lives on top of Mr Parr was in the Post Office yesterday. Looked lonely to me.'

We are all anxious to read about the engagement in 'The real paper,' the *Caxley Chronicle*, where we are bound to learn more details. For, anyone in the news, who has the remotest connection with Caxley or its environs, must expect to face a detailed account of himself in the local paper.

In John Parr's case I think there will be some shortage of material, as he has lived almost all his fifty years in Hendon, only visiting his aunt at Fairacre as a child, until he took over her property recently. Still, it's a challenge to the paper and I shall look forward to next Tuesday, when it appears, as keenly as the rest of the village.

This avid interest of the countryman in his neighbours is a most vital part of country living, and is the cause of both pleasure and annoyance. I suppose it springs from the common and pressing need for a story. Books supply the panacea to this fever for those who read; but for the people who find reading distasteful, or are too sleepy after a day's work in the open air to bother with books, then this living drama which unfolds, day by day, constitutes one long enthralling serial, with sub-plots, digressions, flash-backs and many delicious aspects of the same incident as seen through various watchers' eyes.

The countryman, too, has more time than his town cousin, to indulge in his observations and speculations. To the lone man ploughing steadily up and down a many-acred field, the sporadic activity of the dwellers in the cottage on the hill-side acquires an enormous importance to him. He will see smoke coming from the wooden shed's chimney, and surmise that it is washing day. He will watch the old woman cutting lettuce from her garden and speculate on such things as cold meat for midday dinner—it all fits in. Later, as the garments billow on the line he will recognize the checked shirt that young Bill was wearing, American fashion, at the pub on Saturday night and wonder if his missus's first has arrived yet. And it may well be that it is he who first sees the brave white fluttering of new nappies and night-gowns which semaphore the tidings that a new soul has arrived to join in the fun and feuds of Fairacre.

Of course it is irritating at times to find that all one's personal affairs are an open book to the village, but, personally, I have two ways of mitigating the nuisance. The first is to face the fact that one has no real private life in a village and so it is absolutely necessary to comport oneself as if in the public gaze the whole time. The second is to let people know a certain amount of one's business so that their minds have a nice little quid, as it were, to chew on. There is then a sporting chance that any really private business may be overlooked. On no account, in a village, can one begin a sentence with: 'Don't let it go any further, but——' One has to face this consuming interest squarely. It doesn't worry me now, though it did in my early days here as headmistress; but I have reminded myself many times, that either—none must know, or all.

The vicar called in and said what delightful news it was about John Parr. A man needed companionship, particularly as he grew older, and would I be able to go to tea at the Vicarage one day next week (he had a note somewhere from his wife, but it seemed to have vanished—at times he half believed in poltergeists) to meet that charming fellow who lived above Parr? I said that I should look forward to it immensely.

I drove alone, for the first time today, to Caxley to do a little shopping. As I approached the bus stop, I overtook Mrs Pringle stumping along, black shiny shopping bag on arm, and offered her a lift.

'Most likely flying in the face of Providence,' she remarked morosely, as she settled her bulk beside me. 'I'll never forget going out with my old aunt the first time she took her car out alone. Phew! That was a nightmare, I can tell you! She started learning late in life, like you, and never had no consecration, if you follow me.'

I said I didn't, edging round a disdainful cat that was washing its legs in the road.

'Well, couldn't never do two things together like. Come she put one pedal down, she hadn't got consecration enough to put the other.'

'Is she all right now?' I asked—foolishly enough.

'Oh no!' said Mrs Pringle, with the greatest satisfaction, 'she lost the use of her right arm as a result of the accident. Not that the doctors didn't TRY, mark you. Speak as you find, I says, and it was months afore they really give her up. Pulleys, massage, deep-ray, X-ray, sun-ray——'

'Hooray,' I said absently, but luckily Mrs Pringle was well launched.

'Why, she was in that hospital for nigh on three months, and the doctors said theirselves that they'd never come across a woman what bore pain so brave before. Of course, she was only driving very slow at the time. Say she'd been driving this pace, now, she'd very like have killed herself outright. Having no consecration, you see, she couldn't stop quick.'

I was glad to reach Caxley and drop the old misery outside the Post Office.

I bought a very dashing pair of tan shoes, which cost far

more than I can really afford, but I consoled myself with the thought that February is a short month—a specious piece of reasoning, which I shall not delve into. Also managed to get a new book from the library, much praised by the critics.

I felt rather wobbly on the drive home—probably lack of consecration—and so horribly tired this evening that I went to bed early with hot milk and the book.

I spent most of Sunday in bed, with what I can only think is a particularly unpleasant 'flu germ. My only nourishment was four oranges and about a gallon of lemon water, the thought of anything else anathema.

The book, of which I had read such glowing reports, I hurled from my bed of pain about 11 a.m., when the heroine—as unpleasant a nymphomaniac as it has been my misfortune to come across—hopped into the seventh man's bed, under the delusion that this would finally make her (a) happy, (b) noble, and altruistic, and (c) interesting to her readers. Could have told the wretched creature by page 6, that, spinster though I am, this is not the recipe for contentment.

I am heartily sick of books from Caxley library—all termed 'powerful' by their reviewers, (and in future I shall steer clear of any with this label) which give the suffering reader a detailed account of the bodily functions of their main characters. If the author has such a paucity of ideas that he must pad out his 300 pages with reiterated comments on his hero's digestive, alimentary and productive systems, I am sorry for him; but I don't see why he should be encouraged.

To have a heroine who does nothing but climb, regularly every thirty pages, from one bed into another, is, to my mind, not only inartistic. It is worse. It is tedious.

I spent the evening huddled over the fire, refreshing myself mentally with *The Diary of a Country Parson*, and physically with sips of lemon water. On opening the larder door, I nearly had a relapse, by being faced with a leering joint of fatty beef, some cold cooked sausages embedded in grease, and a pot of cod liver oil and malt.

Retired early to bed, and felt the greatest sympathy for James Woodforde who found 'Mince Pye rose oft' sometime in the 1790s. I lay awake for several hours and noticed, not for the first time, how peculiarly significant inanimate objects, such as chairs and tables, become when one's energy is low. It is almost as though they have some life of their own, a silent, immobile, waiting one, rather sinister—as though they were saying: 'Yes, we were here before you came. And we'll still be here, standing and watching when you—poor ephemeral creature—have gone.'

I suppose the logical reason is that all these things are used and taken for granted, and hardly noticed, as one bustles about with all sorts of plans to occupy one's mind. But when illness comes, then one becomes conscious of their presence, and imbues them with more power than is really theirs. I had worked out this interesting theory at about 2 a.m., and was toying with the idea of writing a letter to the *Caxley Chronicle* about it—with a rather well-turned aside, about the Romans' Lares et Penates—when I must have dropped off.

This has been Black Monday. The telephone rang at 8 a.m. and Mr Annett, who sounded quite beside himself with worry told me that Mrs Annett had a high temperature and was too ill to come to school.

'I'm so sorry,' I said, 'it's probably this ghastly 'flu.'

'Don't expect her this week at all,' said the harassed husband, 'I am insisting on her staying in bed for at least three days. She can't be too careful at a time like this.'

I should have liked to ask Mr Annett to explain this last remark. Did he mean, I wondered, that Mrs Annett was expecting a child? Or did he mean, simply, that at this time of year one must take reasonable precautions? I forbore, as a respectable maiden lady, to cross-question the poor fellow, contenting myself with sending my love to the patient and a message to the effect that we should manage very well.

The distance from my house to the school is about fifty yards, but it seemed like half a mile to my shaky legs.

Mrs Pringle was nowhere to be seen and the stoves were unlit. Luckily they were laid and soon burnt up well, but the school was terribly cold.

Jim Bryant brought a note from her which read:

I am laid by with gastrick, and a flare-up of my leg. The doctor is comeing today and will let you know what he say.

Matches is hid behind bar soap on top shelf. Mr Willet makes free otherwise. Hope you can manige.

Mrs Pringle.

Only ten of Mrs Annett's children arrived, so that with my own I had a class of twenty-nine—not too bad. Evidently this germ is fairly widespread in the village.

I felt too wobbly to do much active teaching, and the children worked cheerfully enough, from books, and the infants brought in their own number apparatus and reading books and got on very well.

Dinner turned out to be neck of mutton stew and mashed potatoes, which I served out with much nausea and as little lingering as possible. Figs and custard completed this—to me—revolting meal, but the children returned again and again for helpings, with true Fairacre appetites.

Mr Willet brought a message from Mrs Pringle during the afternoon, to the effect that Doctor Martin recommended a week off, maybe more, and that her niece 'over to Springbourne' would oblige while she was 'laid by.' Mr Willet, after looking sadly at me for a long time, said that I looked a bit peaky to him, and suggested that I had a 'glass of stout and something substantial, like a good thick wedge of pork pie' for my supper. It was only the comforting support of the school fire-guard at my back that kept me from collapsing at the dear soul's feet.

Nevertheless, did manage to imbibe a glass of hot milk and two digestive biscuits, before going to bed, and felt very much better.

There appears to be no hope of getting a supply teacher while Mrs Annett is away. Mrs Finch-Edwards is fully occupied with her young baby and Miss Clare is nursing her sister, who is really very ill with this same wretched complaint.

Luckily, in a day or two, I felt perfectly fit again, and as there are so many absentees my class is not overwhelmingly large. The age range makes it rather difficult to choose a story that will interest them all, but the 'Ameliaranne' books are proving a great standby.

The *Caxley Chronicle* today carried an account of John Parr's engagement. As his fiancée is second cousin to a duke, the *Caxley Chronicle* has thrown poor John Parr to the lions with a casual 'who has always given generous support to the local branch of the League of Pity,' and concentrated on his bride-to-be's more glamorous connections. I foresee that Fairacre and particularly Mrs Pringle, will feel slighted.

Mrs Pringle's niece is doing her scatter-brained best to fill her aunt's place, but she is a sore trial. She has bright, rusty-red locks, very erratically cut, with no parting, and the back view of her head resembles a particularly tousled floor mop. Her eyes are of that very light blue, peculiar either to fanatics or feather-brained individuals, and her large mouth is curved in a constant mad grin. I don't mind admitting that I find her unnerving.

She wears a long, mauve hand-knitted woollen frock, which has been sketchily washed and pegged by the hem, so that it undulates in a remarkable fashion round her calves.

While I was looking out our morning hymn, before school, she dusted round me, and kept up a febrile chatter which I allowed to go in one ear and out of the other. However, she caught my attention suddenly by saying proudly: 'I've just had my third!' I had heard something about one moral slip, and had been inclined to take the usual tolerant village line, that it was regrettable, but might not perhaps be the girl's fault. When it comes to two, we villagers are not so sympathetic; and so, when Miss Pringle announced her third to me, I probably looked as taken aback as I felt.

'I said I've just had my third!' repeated the girl. I made no comment; and, probably, sensing from my lack of enthusiasm that all was not quite well, she added apologetically: 'I can't think how it happened!'

Amy rang up 'for a cosy chat' last night, just as I was going to bed. James had been called away on urgent business (unspecified) which would keep him engaged until Sunday. Amy said that he hated going, and couldn't tell her much about it as it was 'top-level and frightfully hush-hush.' (What 'top-level-hush-hush' stuff a director of a cosmetic firm meddles in, is no affair of mine, but it doesn't stop me thinking.)

I told her about the 'flu and no supply teachers, quite innocently, and was amazed when she offered to come and help.

I had to ring the education office to get official consent,

but as Amy has excellent qualifications, she was welcomed with open arms in this plague-stricken time.

She arrived in the luscious car, and I heard the children debating who it could belong to.

'That must be an inspector. Too posh for an ornery teacher. Look at Miss Read's car now!'

'More like the new head nurse—except there ain't no jars of head-stuff in the back.' (Luckily Amy was out of earshot.)

It was very cheering to have her here and we both enjoyed working together. She will stay until the end of the week.

I was to have gone to tea at the vicarage today, but Mrs Partridge rang up at morning play-time to say that we must postpone our tea-party as poor Mr Lawn (Pawn? Prawn? Line crackling badly as the 'Beetle and Wedge' is having a telephone installed at the moment) has succumbed to prevailing sickness. I expressed sincere sympathy.

I had a Thurberesque conversation with the mad Miss Pringle after school, about the third child of shame, which is to be christened on Sunday.

'Mr Partridge's coming over to Springbourne. I told him when he brought the hymn list this morning, I thought of Lance-a-lot Drick, for the baby's name.'

'Drick?'

'Like Bogarde. Drick Bogarde. But vicar said Not-Too-Fanciful, but I think it's too much of a mouthful. So I said make it Huge and Call-it-a-Day.'

Much shaken I said Hugh was a good name, and gave her five shillings for the baby. I have no doubt that it will buy a purple lipstick for its mother.

It will be a relief to see Mrs Pringle's glum countenance back on Monday.

I drove to Caxley after school, and met Mrs Martin, our

doctor's wife, coming out of Boots', and enquired after his health.

'He's been run off his feet, poor dear, and now he's gone down with this horrible 'flu himself.'

I said I was sorry and was he a good patient?

'A fiend incarnate!' his wife assured me solemnly. 'But he must be in a really bad way.' She looked furtively about her, came very close to me, and dropped her voice to a conspiratorial whisper. 'He's been driven to taking his own cough mixture! That'll show you how bad he's been! He's just sent me in for a bottle from Boots', that doesn't taste quite so evil!'

On Monday we were all back at our posts. Mrs Annett arrived swathed in rugs and was supported to her room by her attentive husband. She assured me, when he had departed, that she was as fit as a fiddle.

Mrs Pringle's outraged expression when she saw the state of her beloved stoves, was a real tonic.

'That Minnie Pringle!' she breathed menacingly. 'Black-lead and elbow-grease don't mean nothing to her!'

The weather had turned delightfully warm and spring-like. The lilac buds in my garden are as fat as green peas, and crocuses, daffodils and tulips are pushing through. Even the grass is beginning to smell hopeful again, as one walks on it.

Mrs Annett and I celebrated this return of joy by taking the whole school out for a nature walk in the woods, at the foot of the downs. They belong to Mr Roberts, the farmer, who lives next door to the school and is one of its most energetic managers, and he lets us go there whenever we please. This is a great privilege, for, like most country schools, Fairacre has a small playground with a stony, uneven surface, which means that any really riotous games in this confined space lead to skinned knees and hands. We consider ourselves very lucky to be able to use Mr Roberts's woods, and his meadow too, and so enjoy a wider world now and again.

The frogspawn was rising in the pond near the 'Beetle and Wedge.' The boys were anxious to take off their shoes and socks and wade in to fetch some for the classroom; but knowing the collection of tins, pieces of bedstead and other household junk which litters the bottom, I forbade this project.

The woods were awe-inspiringly quiet. Even the children hushed their sing-song chatter as they scuffled along in the beech leaves. Signs of spring were everywhere. The honeysuckle is already in small leaf, the primrose plants are sturdy rosettes, and we saw several birds with dry grass or feathers in beak, and a speculative glint in the eye.

At the edge of the wood is a small field, which is one of my secret joys. It always looks lovely. At this time of year it has a soft dewy greyness, which the line of pewter-coloured willow trees, at its boundary, enhances. Today a wood-pigeon, as soft and opal as a London twilight, winged across, and made the picture unforgettable. I once saw this field at eight o'clock on a fine May morning, when it was gilded with buttercups. A light breeze shivered the young willow leaves, and everything vernal that Geoffrey Chaucer and Will Shakespeare ever wrote was caught alive here.

We let the children run, while we sat on a dry log and rested. Mrs Annett, with her gaze fixed bemusedly on a cluster of heart-shaped violet leaves between her brogues, told me, in a dreamy tone in keeping with this enchanted place, that she was to have a child in August.

I said how very pleased I was, and we continued to sit, propped together, on the dry log in comfortable silence, savouring the niceness of this most satisfying affair.

Joseph Coggs' discovery of a very dead grey squirrel and his request for 'a lend of my penknife' to cut off the poor creature's tail in order to claim a shilling, brought this idyll to a close. We returned in great good spirits to Fairacre School.

Although we had had quite a long walk I was amazed to see how fresh and lively the very young children were on our outing. The longer I teach, the more I am convinced that it is wrong for children in their first year at school to have to attend school for the whole day.

Perhaps, before long, morning school only for the five, and even six year olds, will be the order of the day, and I am sure it would be welcomed by mothers, teachers and children. Most children have a big adjustment to make when they start school. The numbers alone are tiring, and new surroundings, new voices and a new, and perhaps more rigid, discipline all make for strain.

Before he went to school, the child probably had a rest before or after lunch, when, even if he did not sleep, he had a quiet period, on his own, with his feet up. After his rest, during the afternoon, he had his walk, when all the pleasures and richness of the outdoor world impinged on his young mind.

In a small country school it is difficult to provide a rest-time after school dinner for these really small people. It is not surprising that they frequently nod off to sleep in the afternoon, and I for one am only too pleased to let them. A refreshing nap will do them far more good than making a batch of plasticine crumpets—enthralling though that may be with the aid of a really sharp matchstick—and I am only sorry that I can't make them more comfortable, when I see a tousled head resting on two fat arms on the unsympathetic hard wood of an ancient school desk.

A new chant to the psalms had us all bogged down, at church today, and I enjoyed watching the different methods of attack. My neighbour in the pew, Mr Lamb from the Post Office, preserved an affronted silence. Mrs Willet gobbled up three-quarters of each phrase on one uniform and neutral note, and then dragged out the last quarter in a nasal whine, somewhere near the printed notes. Mrs Pringle mooed slowly and heavily, a few beats behind the rest, but with an awful ponderous emphasis in the wrong places; while the vicar, with a sublime disregard for the organist's accompaniment, sang an entirely different chant altogether, and did it very well.

I drove to Caxley to have tea with Amy and James. She talked quite wistfully of her few days' teaching, and, I believe, would jump at the chance of coming again some time. She was perturbed about a rash which has come out on her face. I must confess that I could only see it when my eyes were two inches from her cheek. I suggested that the Caxley water which is villainously hard, might be responsible, and why didn't she use rainwater for a few days?

'Water?' screamed Amy. (If I had said vitriol, she couldn't have sounded more horrified.) Did I realize that she hadn't touched her face with *water* for over five years? Only the very blandest and most expensive complexion milk was dabbed on—with an upward movement—thrice daily, with an occasional application of an astringent lotion which was prepared in Bond Street to her own prescription. Her beauty specialist had forbidden—positively forbidden—the use of water on such a very sensitive skin.

I could only feel that layers of complexion milk over the years, had probably formed a light cheese over Amy's face, which accounted for the rash; but as I was eating her delicious sponge-cake at that moment, was obliged, in common courtesy, to keep these thoughts to myself.

I am now the somewhat bewildered possessor of an

engaging kitten. It all began with Jimmy Waites asking if he could go home during the dinner hour to fetch two kittens.

'So as Linda can choose which one she likes,' he said. Mrs Moffat had asked if Linda might keep it at school during the afternoon, and return home, with the pet of her choice, in time for tea.

This all seemed very agreeable, and the infants were delighted to hear that they would be entertaining two kittens for the afternoon session, and spent most of the morning preparing the doll's cradle for these much more exciting occupants. The doll, a cherished Edwardian beauty, from the vicarage nursery, was propped up on the cupboard, and surveyed her wanton young masters and mistresses with a glassy stare.

Mrs Annett had the greatest difficulty in persuading the children to drink their morning milk, but finally discovered that they were all hoarding it for the kittens' dissipation later. At length a bottle was put up on the cupboard, beside the slighted beauty, for the guests, and the milk bottles emptied rapidly.

Excitement ran high when Jimmy Waites entered with his basket. Mrs Waites had prudently tied a blue-checked duster over the top, and when this was removed two pretty kittens peered out from a nest of straw.

Linda Moffat, as pretty as a kitten herself, took the business of choosing her pet very seriously, and was given much unsolicited advice from her companions.

'Don't you take that black and white 'un, Lin. See his paws? Allus be filthy, them white paws.'

'I reckons he looks the best.'

'He do seem to stand up stronger, don't he? More push, like.'

'That other's the prettiest,' and so on.

The infants, who were in my room, milling round with their elders, while this great decision was being made, became querulous, for they were dying to put both to bed in the waiting cradle.

'Buck up, Linda.'

'They's both nice, Linda. Don't matter which one!'

Linda's troubled eyes met mine.

'I wish I could have them both. The other's got to be drowned.'

There was a shocked silence. I looked at Jimmy Waites.

'That's right, miss,' he said, his underlip quivering.

'My dad drowns them,' volunteered Joseph Coggs, with some pride. 'He does all the kittens down our end of the village.' He was stroking a fluffy head with a black stubby finger. He looked up into my face. What he saw there must have called forth his sympathy.

'He uses *warm* water,' he assured me earnestly.

'Can't you find a home for the other one, Jimmy?' I asked turning aside hastily from all the disturbing implications of Joseph's kindly remark.

'Mrs Bates up by the Post Office was going to have it, but she've got a puppy now, that Bill Bates give her for her birthday. No one else don't want it.'

'Who thinks they could have it?' I canvassed. The whole of Fairacre School instantly raised eager hands.

'Well,' I temporized, 'you'll have to ask your mothers, of course. Meanwhile, Jimmy, I'll keep the other one, and if someone wants it I will hand it over.'

At this happy outcome the noise was terrific. The infants showed their joy by jumping heavily, fists doubled into their stomachs, on to the resounding floor-boards. The older ones cheered and banged their desk lids, and we were all but deafened. Mr Willet, entering at this moment said: 'Mafeking relieved?' and was so taken with his own shaft of wit that he broke into gusty laughter, and I began to wonder if order would ever be restored.

The kittens, with remarkable composure, sat in the straw and washed their paws elegantly, despising disorder—and death itself—with the same fastidious good breeding that the French aristocrats showed in the shadow of the guillotine.

'Sweets for quiet children!' I roared above the tumult. It worked, as always, like a charm. The infants fled into their own room—being careful to leave the dividing door open so that I could see their exemplary demeanour—my own children melted into their desks, crossed their arms high up on their chests, put their sturdy country boots decorously side by side, and glared ahead at 'The Angelus' behind my desk, with unblinking gaze. Only when the sweet tin was in Patrick's grasp, and the fruit drops were being handed round, did they relax and breathe again.

There are some foolish and narrow-minded theorists who would condemn the use of a sweet tin in schools, dismissing this valuable and pleasant adjunct to discipline with such harsh words as 'bribery' and 'pandering to animal greed.' I stoutly defend the sweet tin. If the good Lord has seen fit to provide sweets and children's tastes to match them, then let us take advantage of the tools that lie at hand.

Linda carried the basket to the other room and introduced the kittens to their new bed.

'I think I'll have the tabby one,' she said, as she returned and closed the dividing door behind her. She brushed a straw from her immaculate grey flannel pinafore frock and resumed her place. The important business of the afternoon now over, we addressed ourselves to 'Poetry,' at the silent, but stern, behest of the time-table on one side and the school clock on the other.

I met Doctor Martin as I was going to the grocer's after

school. He said that he had quite recovered from his illness. I wondered if his own, or Boots', cough mixture was responsible for his return to health, but did not say this aloud.

He was just off, he said, to pay six calls on people he supposed he would find in better health than he was himself. He had never known his surgery so besieged. After he had rattled off, in his disreputable old car, I went on my errand, pondering, not for the first time, on the remarkable self-flattery of most doctors. Do they honestly think—always excepting the five per cent of humanity that is incorrigibly neurotic—that some people go to see them for pleasure? Do they seriously imagine that sensible men and women subject themselves to the miseries of doctors' waiting-rooms, of cold medical implements, and of colder medical fingers, with the further possibility of such horrors as injections and enemas to come, for the fun of the thing—or, as one would be led to believe from comments dropped by some doctors, for the express purpose of adding to the burden that already breaks the doctor's back? When one hears such a cheerful and sturdy medical man as our beloved Doctor Martin talking in this fashion, it poses a number of unanswerable questions.

On Saturday, the village was shocked to hear of the death of young Peter Lamb. He was killed in a motor-cycle accident on the way home from a football match in Caxley in the afternoon. He was seventeen, and the only child of the Lambs, who keep the Post Office. The motor-cycle was their present to him on his last birthday. He spent hours polishing the gleaming monster on the lawn at the side of their house. I taught him for only a year, as he went on to Mr Annett at Beech Green at eleven, but I remember him as a very happy boy.

Mr Willet told me this ghastly news after morning service.

He was pacing among the graves on his melancholy sexton's business of choosing a site for the grave he must dig.

'Terrible business,' he said, blowing out his ragged moustache with a sigh. 'The old slip away, and there's some left to grieve, but often their friends that would have taken it hardest have gone before. But a young fellow like this—well, miss, 'tis not just his own that loses him, 'tis every mortal in the village.'

('Send not to know for whom the bell tolls,' whispered a voice in my head, as Mr Willet echoed John Donne across the centuries.)

'Take the cricket team. Long stop he was. We've got no one like him to fill that place. I suppose, when it comes to it, John Pringle will have to move over from deep field and that lily-livered young Bryant that flinches at mid-on will have what he's always wanted and be put out in the field.' Mr Willet stepped round a tomb-stone. 'Take the bell-ringers. More shifting round to train up a new chap for Peter's place. Hard work for us all, you'll see. Ah! He'll be missed sadly!' ('It tolls for thee!')

Nowhere do John Donne's words, 'No man is an island' more poignantly apply than in a small community like a village. As a pebble in a pond spreads its ripples far about, so has this blow affected us all.

'Peter used to mend my bike for me,' nine-year-old Eric said, emerging from the vestry, where he had been blowing the organ.

'He always took my wireless batteries into Caxley to be re-charged,' said old Mrs Bates, among the knot of villagers at the church gate.

'He was going out steady with that girl at Beech Green. She'll take it hard, I don't doubt,' said another.

As the vicar said later, from the pulpit: 'We are indeed members one of another.'

But there was more to all this sober mourning than grief for one young man. The village was robbed, and we were all—every soul in Fairacre—the poorer for it.

Miss Clare came over to tea and spent the evening. The little cat, still with me—and, I imagine for good now—rolled ecstatically on the hearth-rug in the warmth of the fire. Miss Clare was knitting a green pullover and the ball of wool had to be rescued every now and again.

We had talked, naturally, of poor Peter Lamb and Miss Clare surprised me by saying that the pullover had been intended for him.

'He always dug over my vegetable patch every spring and autumn, and I could never get him to take any money. Sometimes he'd take cigarettes, but this time I thought I'd get on with the pullover for next winter.'

'What will you do with it now?' I asked.

She looked across at me with her wise calm gaze.

'I shall finish it,' she said composedly. 'A lot of work has gone into it, and I shall finish it as well as I can and give it to the cricket club.' She smoothed it lovingly. 'It will make a nice prize for their Whist Drive next winter when they raise money for the club.'

This eminently sensible and realistic approach I could not help but admire. So, surely, should all life's buffets be met—with dignity and good sense, but how many of us have Miss Clare's courage?

'I can't think what to call this kitten,' I said, to lighten our solemnity a little. 'What do you suggest?'

Miss Clare addressed herself to this problem with as much thought as she had to the right disposal of Peter's pullover.

'I have always called mine one after the other, plain "Puss",' she admitted, frowning with concentration, 'but you could think of something more interesting.'

I went on to enlarge on the difficulties of naming a cat.

I abhorred the idea of anything—as dear Eric Blore (in 'Top Hat,' I think) said with a divine exhalation of breath—'too *whumsical.*' None of your 'La Belle Fifinella' or even 'Miss Bertha Briggs' for my respectable Fairacre cat!

'And because he's black and white I'm not sinking to such obvious nonsense as "Whisky" or "Magpie,"' I went on, now well launched. 'Nor do I like Tom, Dick, Harry, Jane, Peggy, Betty, or anything, for that matter, which sounds as though I'm talking about a lodger, to people who don't know my circumstances.'

'It certainly is difficult,' Miss Clare agreed, and let her knitting needles fall into her lap.

We lapsed into silent thought. By the firelight I could see that Miss Clare was deep in meditation. Her face was so wistful that I imagined that her mind had strayed back to the all-pervading sadness of young Peter's death. Perhaps she too, I thought, is feeling the penetrating truth that Donne summed up for us.

She raised meditative eyes and looked earnestly at me.

'Come to think of it,' she said slowly, 'I did have *one* cat called Tom.'

Oh lovely, lovely life that can toss us from horror to hilarity, without giving us time to take breath! No matter how dark it may be, yet, unfailingly, 'Cheerfulness breaks in.'

MARCH

MARCH has come in like a lion, with a vengeance, this year. The wind has whipped round to the east again, and hail-storms have been frequent and heavy. A number of the children were caught in one on the way to school and Joseph Coggs and his two small sisters were in tears with the painful rapping they had taken. Their clothes were quite inadequate—not a thick coat between them, and the two little girls in skimpy cotton frocks and layers of dirty jumpers and cardigans on top. Of course their legs are mauve with cold and they look chilled to the marrow.

It always surprises me to see how many of the mothers fail to clothe children consistently. The little things come to school in the winter with, perhaps, a snug woollen bonnet and scarf, a thick coat, and then there comes a long expanse of cold mottled legs, terminating, more often than not, in minute white cotton socks. Mrs Moffat makes Linda neat tailored leggings, and of course a few of the children go into sensible corduroy dungarees for winter wear, but the common feeling seems to be that if they are muffled up above the waist, their legs can take care of themselves. The number of messages I get in the cold months explaining absences due to 'stummer-cake' or 'a chill inside' does not surprise me.

The battle of the wellingtons continues to rage through this bad spell. I will not allow the children to wear them all day in school and insist that a pair of slippers, or failing that, a thick pair of old socks, are brought to school to wear indoors.

'But my dad wears his all the time,' they protest. 'My mum says what's good enough for my dad's good enough for me!' One can hardly retort that the anti-social condition of dad's feet is only one of the reasons for insisting on changing one's rubber boots, but gradually, by dint of hygiene lessons and fulsome praise for those good children who do bring slippers as requested, we are slowly getting an improvement in this direction.

Mrs Annett has given in her notice, which means that she leaves Fairacre School at the end of April. We shall all miss her sorely. The vicar has already started drafting an advertisement for insertion in *The Teacher's World*, and is almost in despair about finding suitable lodgings for the new teacher in the village.

'I shouldn't cross that bridge yet,' I told him. 'We may not get any applicants for the post.'

'Oh my dear Miss Read! Please, please!' protested the poor man, beating his leopard-skin gloves together and creating a light shower of moth-eaten fur in the classroom. 'I cannot bear to think what the future holds for Fairacre School. Whatever happens it *must* not close! It shall not close!' Here the vicar looked and sounded as militant as Uncle Toby in Tristram Shandy when he too faced the extinction of a body much-beloved. 'But, sometimes, I wonder—poor Springbourne, you know. I hate to pass that little empty school, with its dreadful blank windows. And dear Miss Davis, they tell me, is finding that large school in Caxley much too much for her, and is struggling with nearly fifty six-year-olds!'

I said how sorry I was for her. She is an elderly gentle woman, who smoothed the path of her little flock at Springbourne for many years. The bustle of Caxley, as well as a tiresome bus journey must exhaust her considerably.

'And I have heard,' added Mr Partridge, with horror darkening his benevolent countenance, 'that some of those children—young as they are—as Openly Defiant!'

He looked round at our own meek lambs who were busy colouring border patterns in a somnolent way, and his expression softened. I hoped that he would not notice the pronounced bulge in Ernest's cheek, which, I guessed, harboured a disgusting lump of bubble-gum. His eye travelled lovingly over the class, and he sighed happily.

'How fortunate we are here!' he said, 'they are dear, good children, all of them!' And, heavy with bubble-gum guilt, as some of them obviously were, I could not help but agree with him.

It would indeed be a tragedy if Fairacre School were to close, but I do not think it will happen here, as we maintain a steady number of about forty, which makes a good workable two-teacher school, with Mrs Annett taking the infants, and the juniors being taught by me, until the age of eleven. But alas! Springbourne's fate has been shared by several others in the neighbourhood, and more are scheduled to close within the next few years.

This closing of small village schools is a controversial and debatable problem. There is no doubt that some of the really small schools of, say, eighteen, or fewer, children on roll, under the sole charge of the head teacher, should be closed for several very good reasons. The biggest difficulty in these one-teacher schools is the age-range from babes of five years old to children ready for secondary education at the age of eleven. Conscientious teachers who have tackled this type of school single-handed, year after year, realize how impossible it is to do justice to every child. A newly admitted baby of five, homesick and mother-sick, can demand vociferously, urgent and immediate attention, for perhaps a week or more before he really settles in to his new environment. It is disconcerting, to say the least of it, to the rest of his schoolmates, some of whom may have the added anxiety of the eleven-plus examination hovering over them.

It is well-nigh impossible too, to organize team games, which junior children so much enjoy, and which will play so great a part in their later school life. Stories, poems and songs, broadcast programmes, films and classroom pictures must be chosen with the interests of five as well as eleven-year-old children in mind; but perhaps greater than all these teaching problems is the human one. It can be a very lonely life for a teacher, and the care of even such a tiny band of children can be a responsibility, which in some cases becomes too heavy to be borne. It is small wonder that these lonely women, devoted and conscientious, are often the prey of nervous disorders such as rheumatic pains, headaches and neuralgia. Maybe the cross-draughts that play so merrily between Gothic doors and ecclesiastical windows have something to do with it, but the mental strain is always there, and it takes a particularly robust and cheerful woman to cope successfully, and alone, for years on end, with these fascinating but exacting little schools, that are so much a part of our English village life.

The upkeep of some of these tiny places is, of course, out of all proportion to the number of children taught, which accounts for the transfer of pupils to one nearby, but it seems to me equally improvident to overcrowd one school by bringing busloads of children from others, and this may well happen.

Probably the ideal rural school is the three-teacher one, with a teacher for the infants, one for the younger juniors of seven to nine, and the head teacher taking the rest up to the age of eleven. (Though why the head teacher should not take the infants, I don't know. The longer I teach, the more positive I am that it is the first three years of the child's school life that really matter most). But village populations are not made to order, and local education authorities are not to be envied as they deal with children, parents, managers, rate-payers, the church and the Ministry of Education.

However, at a time like this, when harassed and nerve-wracked individuals rush to the countryside at every opportunity, there to revive their flagging energies and to find that 'balm of hurt minds,' fresh air and country sounds and scents—it seems decidedly odd to do away with village schools which are the very essence of country education. What a child may learn on his daily walk to school along a country lane will never be forgotten; and to know intimately the changes that come to plants and trees, to birds and insects, as the full cycle of the four seasons turns, is a source of joy and wonder to the child who is the father of the man.

I have seldom had a more exasperating day. I began by smashing a Wedgwood coffee-pot, as I tried to hurry with the washing-up, which I had left in the most slatternly way, from last night, before going over to school.

At play-time Patrick fell heavily, took the skin from both knees, and worse still, a corner off a front tooth—his second, naturally. I was washing his knees in the school-house when the telephone rang, and an underling at the Caxley Education Office peremptorily demanded the return of a form 'with no delay.' This asinine document was devoted to the number, size, material, age, etc. of the various types of desk in Fairacre School, and as we have a motley collection it took me the rest of the morning, crawling round, ruler in hand, to measure the wretched things.

Mrs Crossley, 'the dinner lady' left two canisters of swedes, which the children abominate, and no gravy. I wonder what Beech Green School thought of two lots of gravy and no swedes! Mrs Pringle, rather more disgruntled than usual, reminded me so often of the combustible nature of her leg—'proper flared up last night, no better today' that I would have welcomed her resignation, and said so. She retaliated by crashing the cutlery about in a deafening manner, all through my geography lesson.

I was thankful to get back to the peace of the school-house at tea-time, and decided to make some grape-fruit marmalade. Just as I was engrossed in a tricky bit of mental arithmetic about pounds of sugar and the weight of three grape-fruit, and waiting for my tea-kettle to boil, a knock came at the front door. A strange man stood on the doorstep holding a sheaf of tracts. I could hear the kettle's lid rattling in the kitchen, and knew, from bitter experience, that the floor would be swamped.

The strange man asked me, in a sepulchral tone, if I had found the Lord, thrusting a tract into my hand at the same time.

'Thank you, thank you! Yes indeed!' I answered, backing inside and shutting the door firmly. I returned to my swamped kitchen and began to mop up the floor in a very bad temper.

Really, Fairacre people must have a name for utter godlessness, judging by the number of earnest souls who present themselves at our doorsteps! Nothing puts me into a more unchristian state of mind than these unsolicited visitors, and yet I haven't the heart to tell them not to come again.

While I was regaining my composure over the tea-tray I noticed with horror that the tract was priced at sixpence. I could only hope that my cavalier and grasping behaviour would discourage further attentions; but, on the other hand, would not have been surprised to hear the stranger returning to demand his payment.

I was very glad indeed to climb into the sanctuary of my bed, and shelve life for nine hours.

The postponed tea-party at the Vicarage has taken place and I have at last met John Parr's tenant, about whom I have heard so much.

His name is Henry Mawne—' "H. A. Mawne," ' the vicar enlarged, and smiled hopefully at me. Seeing that I was still unenlightened, he added, 'Of the *Caxley Chronicle*,' and I remembered then that the Nature Notes have appeared recently over this name. I told Mr Mawne that I cut his notes out and put them up in the classroom for the children to read, and he was obviously delighted.

He is tall and very thin, and seems a pleasant, unassuming

man. Since his retirement he has spent most of his time fishing and bird-watching, and is collecting material for a book about downland birds. He seems very well able to look after himself, and will no doubt continue to do so, despite village gossip to the contrary.

'What I particularly like about Fairacre people,' he said to the vicar, 'is their acceptance of a newcomer without a lot of unnecessary comment. I've found everyone so friendly, but not a bit inquisitive.'

I could not help feeling that Mr Mawne's ear must have been singularly far from Fairacre's bush telegraph, which has fairly hummed with such pertinent questions as:

Is Mr M. a widower? If so, what did his wife die of? And when? Is he a bachelor? How old is he? Who will he marry? And when? How much would his pension be from teaching? Would he have an old-age pension as well? How long has he known Mr Parr? What does he do with those field-glasses? Why is he always 'skulking about up the downs'? And much more, to the same effect.

He was very interested in the village school, and asked if he might call in to see the children. I said that we should love to see him, and if he would like to give us a nature talk sometime, we should look forward to it immensely. It is good for our Fairacre children to hear someone else speaking in their classroom—heaven knows they have little enough variety. It is equally good for me to sit back and see a lesson taken by an expert in his subject.

At six o'clock Mrs Partridge took me upstairs to her bedroom for my coat. There is a wonderful view from the windows there, of the gentle swell of the downs beyond and the wooded hollow where Fairacre shelters. The spire of St Patrick's dominates the foreground, with the stubby little bell-tower of my school thrusting bravely up beside it.

On the bedside table lay a red leather-bound copy of the

Bible and a photograph of an elderly man, with a mop of white hair, who smiled vaguely from his silver frame.

'Gerald's father,' said Mrs Partridge following my gaze, 'Gerald always says "He was a saint—if only I could do half as well!" '

The thought of our good vicar, whose life is as blameless as is humanly possible, sorrowing for his short-comings, made me wonder in what adverse light my own behaviour is thrown. I looked back, in that one swift moment, on innumerable child-slappings, hard words, black thoughts and a thousand back-slidings, and went downstairs in a sober mood.

Mr Mawne was examining a light horse-whip on the hall wall.

'My father used one like that on us on special occasions,' he said cheerfully.

'Really?' answered the vicar. 'Now, my father always shut us up in a dark cupboard under the stairs——'

I decided that values are strictly relative, and felt much more hopeful of my own shaky claims to divine mercy.

I decided to let the children write a poem about the spring. They have learnt Robert Bridges' 'Spring Goeth All in White' and Thomas Nashe's 'Spring, the Sweet Spring' recently, and I thought it would be interesting to see what sort of attempts these most unbookish children would make. Their faces, when I suggested this mental exercise, were studies in stupefaction.

'What—rhyming and that?' asked Eric, appalled.

'Yes, rhyming,' I answered ruthlessly. There was a shocked silence. Linda Moffat was the first to find her breath.

'How many verses, Miss Read?'

'As many as you can think of.'

Patrick then piped up.

'Do us have to make it go thumpety-thumpety like that "Half a league, half a league" bit you read us?'

I said that rhythm would be expected, and they delved into their desks for their pens and English exercise books, with the doomed look of those that face the firing squad.

For half an hour the room was quiet, broken only by the solemn tick of the ancient wall-clock, and the sighs and groans of spirits in poetic travail. After the first few minutes, I had softened so far as to suggest that they could begin with:

In the Spring

and go on from there. As drowning men clutch at straws, so did these Fairacre children clutch at these three words which could be copied from the blackboard.

After thirty minutes I collected their efforts and sent them tottering out to play. Never had their young minds been so sternly exercised, and the results were highly entertaining.

For sheer brazen effrontery and gross idleness, I think Ernest's takes the prize. He had shamelessly lifted, intact, a verse from one of the tombstones in the neighbouring churchyard. In his painstaking copperplate he had written:

In the spring
She drooped and died.
Now she sleeps
By Jesu's side

There is not one spelling mistake. Nor should there be, considering that we pass and repass this inscription a dozen times a day.

Linda Moffat had very cunningly covered the maximum of paper with the minimum of effort. Her poem ran:

In the spring
The swallows wing
In the spring

In the spring
The flowers bring (What? I wonder)
In the spring

In the spring
We all do sing
In the spring

Perhaps the most engaging poem was Eric's. He is a 'growler,' unable to sing in tune and incapable of keeping in step in dancing and other rhythmic work. Written in an appalling hand, with, apparently, a crossed nib dipped in black honey, his poem said:

In the spring
I has my birthday and usually a hice
cake which my gran makes. It is on March 20th

I rather liked the gentle reminder about a fortnight before the great day, and felt inclined to give him a couple of extra writing lessons as a present.

But for brevity and charm, for a little snatch that reminds one of William Barnes's simplicity and use of dialect, I think the attempt of young bandaged-kneed Patrick takes the prize. His poem read thus:

In the spring
It comes on worm (sic!)
Us likes the spring
Us has no storm

Poor dears, how hard I made them work! Truly the mastering of one's own language is a major operation!

The kitten is still with me, and I hope that I shall never have to part with him. He answers to the deplorably plebeian name of 'Tibby,' while I still rack my brains daily for some other more inspired cognomen.

Now that the weather is warmer he plays outside and yesterday afternoon he ventured across the playground and found his way into the classroom, much to the children's delight. He settled himself in a patch of sunlight on the needlework cupboard, and I foresee many more such excursions to school, as he is a most companionable animal.

In any case, I see no reason why a good-tempered, steady-going cat should not be included in a country classroom. It adds a pleasantly domestic touch to our working conditions.

Amy came to tea and brought her sister, who is staying with her, as well. She is one of those people—all too common, alas!—who bore one to death with accounts of their important acquaintances. Never was a conversation so sprinkled with lords, ladies, admirals, generals, and what not, until I thought I should be driven to deriving a game about them all, in order to keep my sanity. It could be done with points, I told myself, my glazed eyes on my visitor and a fixed smile on my lips. Two points, say, for peers of the realm and their ladies, and for top-ranking people in the services. One point for friends mentioned, who were working in:

(a) The Foreign Office
(b) Embassies
(c) B.B.C. and
(d) 'Little' shops in Bond Street;

and none, I decided, as I dropped sugar into my guest's cup, for nephews who had just written:

(a) an enchanting collection of obscure verse—published privately,
(b) a powerful novel or
(c) a script for Midland Region.

However, she made a great fuss of dear Tibby, and didn't flinch when he ran cruel claws into her beautiful sheer nylons, so that I forgave her for her harmless delusions of grandeur, and made her a present of a pot of my grapefruit marmalade when she left. How far this generosity was prompted by my guilty conscience I should not like to say.

It has been a real spring day. The wind has turned due west and is as warm and soft as can be. I have a few crocuses out among the clumps of snowdrops, and there are fat buds on the japonica by the wall, which is all most heartening.

Mrs Pringle, to whom I made a blithe comment about the fine weather, did her best to turn the world sour for me.

'See the moon last night? Lying on its back?'

I said that I had. I had noticed it from my landing-window as I went to bed—an upturned silver slice, supporting the shadowy completion of its circle.

'Know what that means?' enquired Mrs Pringle, arms akimbo, and her voice heavy with foreboding.

Mr Willet, who was screwing up the catch on the wood-shed door, and had been listening to our conversation, now shouted across:

'Well, you tell us then. Seems you want to!'

'The moon on its back,' said Mrs Pringle, with much emphasis, 'is a sure sign of rain. "Moon on her back, with water in her lap." Ever heard that? You see—we'll have a tempest before night—a proper downpour!'

She looked across to my garden where two pairs of stockings and two tea-towels danced in the breeze.

'You've chose the wrong day for washing,' she added, and returned into the lobby to scour the sink.

Mr Willet puffed out his moustache with disgust.

'Never heard such nonsense,' he said to me, in a carrying whisper, 'real old wives' tale that, about water in its lap. The ignorance! The stuff some of these folk believes, in the twentieth century! Lives in the dark ages some of 'em.'

He screwed another turn or two, grunting with effort.

At length he ceased, and wiped his brow with the back of his huge hand. He still looked disgruntled.

'"Moon on her back. Water in her lap,"' he quoted disgustedly. 'A downpour! Lot of nonsense! Why, any fool knows it means a high wind!'

Mrs Partridge called after tea to tell me about great goings-on in the W.I. world. Although I am a member of the Fairacre W.I., I can rarely attend the meetings, as they are held in the afternoon; but Mrs Partridge, who is President, keeps me *au fait* with the news.

Evidently the county as a whole is to stage a pageant. Each Institute, or group of Institutes, will have an historical scene to act, and the whole will tell the story of the people who have lived in this county, through the ages.

'When do we start?' I asked.

'As soon as we've had another meeting,' answered Mrs Partridge.

'No, I mean, at what stage of history do we begin? The Norman Conquest, or the Ice Age, or what?'

'For the life of me,' said Mrs Partridge, much perplexed, 'I don't know, but the County Office will send further particulars, I don't doubt.'

Neither did I, having seen some of the lengthy documents that flutter from that quarter every month.

'Do we choose which scene we like?' I asked. I was mentally casting Mrs Pringle as the seventeenth-century witch who was dumped in the horse-pond somewhere near Beech Green. My tone, I noted with regret, was eager.

'Now I come to think of it,' said Mrs Partridge, closing her eyes the better to 'consecrate,' 'the Drama Committee have drafted out so many scenes, about a dozen, I fancy, and the groups will draw for them. So much fairer, of course. After all, most women will prefer becoming costumes, and would plump for Stuart times with all those delicious silks and laces.'

'I rather fancy the Plantagenets,' I replied, wondering if Mrs Moffat could run me up a wimple. Really the whole project had endless possibilities for fun.

'Ah! now that *is* a good idea,' agreed Mrs Partridge. 'I've always had a feeling that I could wear long plaits with pearls entwined.'

We went off into a quiet reverie about wimples and plaits, until Tibby (name still evades me) brought us to earth by jumping through the window, knocking over a jar of catkins *en route*.

'Well, dear,' said Mrs Partridge, rising to her feet, and becoming her usual bustling self, 'that's how it is. The children, of course, will take part. It is to be held on a Saturday, in the grounds of Branscombe Castle; and I'll call an evening meeting for one day next week. We shall know then which scene we're to do and can arrange rehearsals and so on.'

'When is it to be?' I asked. Mrs Partridge spoke patiently, as to a tiresome child.

'I've told you, dear. One evening next week.'

I began to feel that Fairacre's vicar's wife and its schoolteacher might easily go on the halls in the near future as a pair of cross-talk comedians, Partridge and Read.

'No, no! The pageant. When does it come off at Branscombe Castle?'

'Oh, I'm sorry. In August, I understand.'

'Supposing it rains?'

'My dear,' said Mrs Partridge, with the utmost firmness, 'it will not rain! You should know by now, dear, that if one starts to take rain into consideration in village life—well—there just wouldn't be any village life!'

When she had gone I pondered over this direction of

village activities which Mrs Partridge does so well. It is interesting to be living in this transition period between local, and in Fairacre's case enlightened, squirearchy, and whatever communal form may evolve in a village which is, perforce, part of a welfare state.

The older people, like Miss Clare and Mrs Pringle, shake their heads sadly over the departure of 'the good old days,' when the gentry did so much for the village, sparing neither advice nor practical and financial help. They looked to the families in the three or four large houses, not only for employment, but for guidance in matters spiritual and temporal; and now that death or the cold hand of poverty has removed this help, the older generation seems rudderless, and at times resentful, for the stability has gone from their lives.

'Why, when my father was working as gardener, up at the Hall,' said Mrs Pringle, one day, 'he broke a leg, falling out of the apple tree in the kitchen garden. And for all the weeks he lay up in our front room, regular as clockwork there came a basket of groceries sent down from the Hall kitchen. That's what I call being looked after.'

In vain was it to point out that an all-embracing state insurance has superseded this earlier happy relationship.

'All forms and stamps,' snorted Mrs Pringle, unimpressed, 'and some jumped-up jack-in-office in Caxley telling you how to get back what's been taken from you! Give me the old days!' It is the personal touch that these older people miss so sorely, the discussion of problems over a fireside, the confession, perhaps, of follies come home to roost, and the comfort of friendly advice and practical guidance. To have to board a bus, and sit, perplexed, as it rattles six miles into Caxley, to find an answer to one's personal problems at an office or a bureau or a clinic, comes hard to these people; and to be passed from the supercilious young lady in the outer office, from hand to hand, until the right person is encountered, means that the older countryman, more often than not, arrives even more tongue-tied than usual. How much simpler it all was, he will think dazedly, as he stares at the ledgers and typewriters and the man who waits with sheaves of forms in front of him, when he walked round to the kitchen door at the Hall, with his troubles, confident that he'd be home again within half an hour, with his course set plain before him.

As Miss Clare put it: 'I know it's a great comfort, dear, to feel that one will never starve, and that sickness and madness and death itself are looked after. For an old woman in my position, the welfare state is a blessing. This national health scheme, for instance, has taken a great load off my mind. But I miss the warmth of sympathy—foolish perhaps, but there it is. It did both of us good—the one who told his trouble, and the one who tried to help—for, I suppose, we were both united in overcoming a problem and in sympathy with each other.'

I suggested that the present system might eventually be better. After all, advice from the Hall might be bad as well as good, depending on the mentality and disposition of the owner at any given time.

'Yes,' agreed Miss Clare, 'in the long run, I think each man will think out his own problems; but it is going to take him a very long time to realize that the machinery for coping with those personal problems is set up by his own hands. We in a village, my dear, can understand a small-community government—it's not much more than a family affair and we all appreciate our relationship. But when it comes to a nation—with ministries and councils and departments taking the place of the parish clerk and parish priest and squire—well, naturally, we're a little out of our depth, just at the moment!'

* * *

I had a wasted morning in Caxley trying to buy a lightweight coat for the summer.

As I was roaming round the coat department at Williams's, which styles itself 'Caxley's leading store,' followed by an assistant staggering under an armful of coats already rejected by me, I bumped into Amy.

'You look a wreck!' she said truthfully but unkindly.

'I *am* a wreck!' I replied simply, and went on to tell her of my hopeless quest.

'My dear, we are of the race of Lost Women,' said Amy dramatically. The wilting assistant stopped to listen to any more interesting disclosures. 'Clothes there are—beautiful clothes, magnificent clothes, inspired clothes—for those with thirty-six- or even thirty-eight-inch hips! For the forty-four inches and over there is a good range of comfortable garments, obviously designed by kind-hearted men who take pity on large problem-women. But for us, dear, for you and me—for you, with your forty-two hip measurement——' (she gave me no time to protest that I was only forty. Amy, in full spate, brooks no interruption).

'And for me,' she continued, 'with my forty—well, thirty-nine really, but I prefer to be comfortable—what do we get?'

She waved a hand at the departing assistant who was returning a dozen or so coats to their show-case.

'Nothing?' I ventured.

'Nothing!' agreed Amy emphatically. Suddenly, her eye became fixed intently on my red frock that Mrs Moffat had made me.

'Turn round,' she commanded. 'Hmph! A zip right down to the waist, eh? That accounts for the fit. And that panel over the midriff is cut on the cross, I see. Who made it?'

I told her that Mrs Moffat designed and made it.

Amy continued to prowl round me, occasionally peering more closely at a particularly interesting seam. She even started to undo the zip 'to see how the back was faced,' until I protested.

'She's a marvel,' announced Amy, at length. Now Amy knows about clothes, and is an expert needlewoman as well as an astute buyer of really beautiful garments.

'Do you think she'd make for me?' she asked.

I said that I would ask her. I had to go for a fitting in the afternoon for two cotton frocks that she was making.

'But I'm having them buttoned down the front,' I told Amy. 'You can't believe how difficult it is for a woman living alone to cope with a zip down the back.'

'What you want,' said Amy, 'is a husband,' and without pausing to take breath added, 'How's Mr Mawne?'

I suggested, a trifle tartly, that coffee might restore both of us to our senses, and the question remained unanswered.

I had been invited to stay to tea at Mrs Moffat's bungalow after my fittings. I found Mrs Finch-Edwards, as handsome and exuberant as when she had taken charge in the infants' room over a year ago, sitting in the trim little drawing-room, while her baby daughter kicked fat legs on the rug at her feet.

She was an adorable baby, chubby and good-tempered, and Mrs Finch-Edwards had had her christened Althea.

'And she sleeps right through the night!' Mrs Finch-Edwards assured us. 'My hubby and I don't hear one squeak from six till six the next morning!'

'You just don't know how lucky you are,' Mrs Moffat answered, as she poured tea. 'Now Linda——' and the conversation became a duet compounded of such phrases as gripe-water, dreadful dummies, picking up, lying on the right side, kapok pillows, down pillows, no pillows—until it was enough to turn an old maid silly.

Mrs Moffat said that she would be delighted to make dresses for Amy, and I explained that, as she now lived at Bent, just the other side of Caxley and drove her own car, she could come whenever it was convenient for Mrs Moffat to have her. Mrs Finch-Edwards and Mrs Moffat, I know, have high hopes of opening a shop one day, showing dresses that they have designed and made. In time they hope to have a substantial business, with a workroom of first-class sewing girls, while they attend to the designing and organization. They should make a success of such a venture, I feel sure, for they are both energetic, ambitious and particularly gifted at this type of work.

'I've made several children's frocks for that new shop in Caxley,' Mrs Finch-Edwards told me, 'but of course I can't do much while Althea's so young—but just wait!'

'Just wait!' echoed Mrs Moffat, and her eyes sparkled as she met the equally enthusiastic glances of her friend across the tea-cups.

The *Caxley Chronicle* today published a short article of mine about Lenten customs in Fairacre and other neighbouring parishes. This is my first appearance in the paper, and I must say it all looked very much more impressive in neat newsprint, than it did in pencil in a half-filled spelling-book from school.

The vicar began this project by showing me accounts in parish magazines of the last century, and Mrs Willet also told me of many interesting things that her father and mother did during Lent. The reaction to my appearance in print has been most amusing, and Mrs Pringle addressed me with something like awe this morning. To be 'in the papers' at all, is something. To be 'in The Paper,' is everything at Fairacre.

Less welcome were such comments as:

(a) 'It is a real gift.' (The Vicar)
(b) 'I suppose it just flows out.' (Mrs Willet)
(c) 'If it's in you, I suppose it's bound to come out.' (Mr Willet, rather morosely)
(d) 'Wonderful, dear, and so effortless.' (Amy, on the telephone)

As I had spent six evenings at the dining-room table sitting on a hard chair with my toes twisted round its legs, chewing my pencil to shreds and groaning in much the same anguish as had my class when they composed their recent deathless verse, I found all these comments particularly souring.

On thinking over Mr Willet's gloomy comment I have come to the conclusion that he looks upon any kind of artistic urge as a sort of poison in the system, which is 'better out than in.' Perhaps this theory is more widely held than we realize, I thought to myself, as I knitted busily up the front of a cardigan this evening; in which case matters become very profound.

Instead of praising and envying artists, perhaps we should be sorry for them—victims as they are of their own pains. Is all art involuntary? Is it, perhaps, a bad, rather than a good thing? I paused to study the front of my cardigan, and found that I had decreased at both armhole and front edge, giving a remarkably bizarre effect to the garment, and involving two inches of careful unpicking.

I decided suddenly that literary fame had gone to my head, that the obscurer motives behind artistic impulses were beyond my comprehension, that a glass of hot milk would be a really good thing, and bed the best place for a bemused teacher.

APRIL

In a week's time Fairacre School will have broken up for the Easter holidays. I, for one, am always glad to see the end of this most miserable of terms. In it we endure, each year, the worst weather, the darkest days, the poorest health and the lowest spirits. But now, with Easter in sight, and the sun gaining daily in strength, the outlook is much more heartening.

The return of the flowers and young greenery is a perennial miracle and wonder. The children have brought treasures from hedge, garden and spinney; and coltsfoot and crocus, violet and viburnum, primrose and pansy deck our classroom, all breathing out a faint but heady perfume of spring-time.

How lucky country children are in these natural delights that lie ready to their hand! Every season and every plant offers changing joys. As they meander along the lane that leads to our school all kinds of natural toys present themselves for their diversion. The seedpods of stitchwort hang ready for delightful popping between thumb and finger, and later the bladder campion offers a larger, if less crisp, globe to burst. In the autumn, acorns, beechnuts and conkers bedizen their path, with all their manifold possibilities of fun. In the summer, there is an assortment of honeys to be sucked from bindweed flowers, held fragile and fragrant to hungry lips, and the tiny funnels of honeysuckle and clover blossoms to taste. Outside the Post Office grow three fine lime trees, murmurous with bees on summer afternoons, and these supply wide, soft, young leaves in May, which the children spread over their opened mouths and, inhaling sharply, burst with a pleasant and satisfying explosion. At about the same time of year the young hawthorn leaves are found good to eat—'bread and cheese' some call them—while the crisp sweet stalks of primroses form another delicacy, with the added delight of the thread-like inner stalk which pulls out from the hairier outer sheath.

The summer time brings flower games, the making of daisy chains, poppy dolls with little Chinese heads and red satin skirts made from the turned-back petals, 'He-loves-me-he-don't' counted solemnly as the daisy petals flutter down, and 'Bunny's mouth' made by pressing the sides of the yellow toadflax flowers which scramble over our chalky Fairacre banks. And always, whatever the season, there is a flat ribbon of grass blade to be found which, when held between thumbs and blown upon, can emit the most hideous and ear-splitting screech, calculated to fray the nerves of any grown-up, and warm the heart of any child, within earshot.

How fortunate too are country children in that, among all this richness, so much appeals not only to their senses of taste and smell, but to that most neglected one—the sense of touch. As they handle these living and beautiful things they run the gamut of texture from the sweet chestnut's bristly seedpod to the glutinous, cool smoothness of the bluebell's satin stalk. They part the fine dry grass to probe delicately with their fingers for the thread-like stalks of early white violets; and yet to pluck the strong ribbed stems of the cow parsley, they must exert all the strength of wrist and hand before its hollow tube snaps, with a rank and aromatic dying breath.

They leap to grasp the grey rough branch of the beech tree that challenges their strength near the school gate, and legs writhing, they feel the old rough, living strength of that noble tree in the very palms of their hands. Alas for their brothers in town who respond to the same challenge from a high brick wall! At its best it can but offer a dead stony surface, filthy with industrial grime, and, at its worst, the cruel shock and horror of vicious broken bottles.

For the most part country children say little of the joys that surround them. These are, rather naturally, taken for granted, and in the case of the boys they would think it vaguely effete to comment on the flowers and plants around them. The girls are less monosyllabic, and chatter interestedly about their latest finds. They enjoy finding the earliest violets—particularly a pinkish one that grows not far from 'The Beetle and Wedge'—and it is they who bring most of the contributions to the nature table. Their sense of touch is more sensitive and affords them greater satisfaction, and I remember Sylvia Burton's bunch of wild flowers, presented proudly one morning, with the comment: 'They've all got square stalks, miss. I've felt them.' Sure enough they had—it was a most satisfactory bouquet formed by members of the natural order *labiatae*.

The vicar called in to give his weekly talk. This time, as well as a little discourse on everyday Christianity, he told the children about Palm Sunday and the Easter festival, as is his wont before the school breaks up for the Easter holiday.

When he asked for pussy-willow to decorate the church, Joseph Coggs raised an eager, if grimy, paw.

'I can get a whole lot,' he said, eyes agleam. 'If I wriggles through the hedge down the bottom of Miss Parr's place, there's a pond and a pussy-willow tree.'

The vicar looked slightly taken aback.

'But I'm afraid that's a private tree, Joseph,' answered the vicar. 'It belongs to the people who live in the flats there.'

Joseph looked bewildered.

'But they never picks it,' he assured the vicar, 'and they'd never see me get in.'

The vicar drew in a sad breath, and very kindly and patiently gave an extra little homily about the sanctity of other people's property, and the promptings of one's own conscience, and the eye of the Almighty which is upon us all, even those who are but six years old and are wriggling on their stomachs through the long Fairacre grass. It was nicely put, and Joseph appeared to understand the vicar's words, but it was quite apparent to me that the principles behind the little homily were at war with the words of Joseph's feckless father, whose favourite maxims are

'Finding's Keepings' and 'What the eye doesn't see etc.,' principles which, unconsciously, Joseph has imbibed. There is no doubt that innocent children, from such a slack and neglected home as Joseph's, need most positive guidance in right behaviour, frequently and firmly, if they are not to slide willy-nilly, into the clutches of evil companions and so to drift into the ranks of criminals.

This evening the meeting of the Women's Institute was held to hear more about the forthcoming pageant. We had had a heavy shower after tea, and the approach to the village hall, which stands not far from Mrs Moffat's spruce new bungalow, was very muddy. Someone's tractor had made deep squelchy ruts, which were full of rain water, and the women clucked their tongues with disgust, as they tried to wipe their shoes free of mud on the grass at the side of the door. Loudest in her protestations was Mrs Pringle.

'No need for all this muck,' she boomed, as she arched an elephantine ankle and poked mud from her instep with a stick. 'Time this place was built you could buy a load of good gravel for a few shillings—but it never was done. Now look at it. A pity poor old Sir Edmund's passed on. He'd have put down a good path for us.'

'I suggest we all put a shilling towards a load of gravel,' I said. Mrs Pringle snorted, and turned on me a glance so hostile that it was a wonder that I did not fall, withered, at her feet.

Inside the hall were about forty women, many of them with toddlers and young babies.

'My husband said fat chance he'd have of getting down to "The Beetle" if he had the children to look after—so I brought 'em too.'

'Ah!' agreed her neighbour comfortably, 'The men don't like the kids round 'em. 'Tis only natural, I s'pose!'

This charitable remark was endorsed by other women around, who, in the kindest and most indulgent tones, recounted various incidents of male selfishness, which made me feel very glad that, as a single woman, I was not called upon to endure such affronts to common justice.

'Oh, mine's very good,' said another, 'He never minded me coming up here this evening. "I'll have a sit and look at the paper," he says, as nice as you like, "and you can wash the dishes when you comes back, if you're a bit late now." Oh, he's easy!'

The murmuring grew in the hall as the late comers arrived. The usual flicking of switches went on, as someone tried to find the best method of lighting the hall, with the few bulbs remaining that worked.

The hall was erected about thirty years ago, and is a useful but ugly building of corrugated iron painted a dark red, which has, over the years, faded to a depressing maroon. The roof is also made of iron, and in very hot weather the building becomes stiflingly hot. If it rains heavily, the noise of the water drumming on the roof can successfully drown any speaker. If it is cold, the place is sketchily heated by means of four oil stoves, which frequently smoke and decorate the room, and its occupants, with black floating smuts which play havoc with clothes and complexions.

The lavatory, of the bucket variety, is housed, at some distance from the building, in a bower of elder trees, and is a constant annoyance to our Mr Willet, as he is frequently asked to look after it. Actually, Arthur Coggs is supposed to do it, but more often than not he forgets his duties. As he is away all day in Caxley working as a builder's labourer, and Mr Willet is on the spot here in Fairacre, it so happens that the urgent and outraged cries for help are answered by our school caretaker.

The hall itself is a fairly large building, with its inside

walls lined with the sticky, ginger-coloured match boarding so beloved by our forbears. The First Fairacre Scout Troop, comprising about fifteen boys, holds its meetings here, and on one wall hang diagrams showing how to tie knots, a copy of Scout rules, a chart showing birds and their eggs and various other fascinating documents.

A little further along, hanging somewhat askew, are several photographs of past football teams. There is not one smile among the many grim countenances here displayed, but the biceps, forced up by judicious folding of the arms, are a wonder to behold. The manly forms of some thirty or forty years ago appear to have been much more corpulent than those of today, but perhaps there were more staunch and bulky garments underneath the red and white striped Fairacre jerseys then.

On the door, thoughtfully placed, is a small white card, on which is printed in uneven capitals:

HAVE YOU SWITCHED OF THE LIGHT?

The missing F tweaks at my schoolmistress's sensibilities so severely that I itch to be alone in the hall one day, when I shall give myself the exquisite satisfaction of adding the F. As it is, with possibly the perpetrator himself, or at least 'his sisters and his cousins and his aunts' all about me, I can do nothing, unless I am prepared to face a hornets' nest of buzzing family umbrage.

On the platform sat Mrs Partridge, our president, with Mrs Pratt, once Mrs Annett's landlady, beside her as secretary. The ink-stained deal table was covered with a magnificent cream linen cloth, embroidered by members of the institute. After each meeting it is folded into a clean piece of sheeting and borne away to Mrs Pratt's house and put safely into the first drawer of her sideboard, until it is time for it to see the light of day again. Mrs Pringle views this cloth, with something of the low churchman's disapproval of the high churchman's elaborate ceremony.

'Made an idol of, that there cloth,' she told me once. 'I said at the time it was too fanciful and would show the dirt. What's more, I offered my mother's best tablecloth that she used year in and year out in her front parlour for as long as I can remember. As fine a piece of red chenille, with a good deep fringe to it, as ever you see in a day's march. A mite faded maybe, but that's no call for making personal remarks about my mother's care of it. Mondays and Thursdays that was hung on the line and brushed lightly with an old clothes-brush dipped in cold tea. Come up beautiful. But no! 'Twasn't good enough for the W.I., so this fal-lal has to be made instead!' Mrs Pringle bridled at the memory of this rebuff to her offer, and I attempted to comfort her.

'Never mind. You must be glad that you've still got it at home.' Of course I had put my foot in it yet again.

'In a foolish moment,' began Mrs Pringle heavily, 'and believing that the girl would treasure it, I let that Minnie Pringle over at Springbourne have it for a Christmas present.' She paused, drew in a long and sibilant breath, and thrust her face within two inches of mine.

'And you know what? A fortnight later, as sure as I stand here and may I be struck down if I don't tell the truth of it, I saw that very same cloth on her aunt's table up the road. Called there one day I did, to give her my club money, and there was MY tablecloth on HER table. "Where d'you get that, pray?" I asked her. Civil, mark you, but cool. "Our Min she give it me," she said. "Why?" I told her, and you know what? She just laughed! *Just laughed!* I was proper wild, I can tell you. Never said nothing more to her, of course. Wouldn't demean myself. But when I next saw that Minnie Pringle, I give the rough side of my tongue—the hussy!'

At last Mrs Partridge rose behind the tablecloth which had caused Mrs Pringle so much heart burning, and the meeting began. The minutes were read, approved, signed and, as nothing arose from them, Mrs Partridge came straight to the point and told us the latest news of the pageant.

'The draw has been made,' she told us, 'and it is Fairacre's privilege to open the pageant. Ours is the first scene.' A gratified murmur arose from the hall, and proud smiles were exchanged. Mrs Partridge, astute in the handling of these affairs, allowed us to bask in this glory for a few happy seconds, before releasing the cold shower.

'It is a wonderful thing, of course,' she proceeded smiling expansively, 'and we are very lucky to get this scene. It also means that our part will be over first, and we can relax and enjoy the rest of the pageant. So less tiring for the children too.'

'I just ain't gonna be in it,' said an audible but obstinate toddler to his mother, at this juncture. Mrs Partridge continued without batting an eyelid.

'And now you'll want to know the title of Fairacre's scene.'

Mrs Moffat caught my eye across the room and mouthed the word 'Wimples' at me. I smiled back.

'It is "The Coming of the Romans",' went on Mrs Partridge.

'*Romans!*' said the members in one outraged breath. If they had been called upon to be earwigs, they could not have sounded more affronted. Mrs Partridge gathered us up again.

'The Roman soldiers' costume will be most effective, of course. A lot can be done with gilt paint and good stout cardboard.'

After the first shock of losing wimples, pearls-in-plaited-hair, ruffs, buckled shoes and other flattering accoutrements, the meeting came round to the idea of even earlier times and their sartorial possibilities. Seizing her opportunity Mrs Partridge continued glibly.

'The scene opens with the native people of this country—Ancient Britons then—busy about their everyday work. The men shaping flints for tools, dragging logs back for the fire and so on, and the women nursing their babies and cooking over an open fire. After a time, there are sounds of distant voices and marching, and one of the Ancient Britons runs into the camp, pointing dramatically into the distance. A Roman cohort approaches—the natives flee terrified, but gradually creep back. The Romans give them small gifts, and we see that the regime of Roman rulers and British vassals will soon be set up.' Mrs Partridge paused, at the end of this swift résumé of our forthcoming task, and there was an ominous silence. At last Mrs Pringle broke it, in a voice heavy with foreboding.

'Madam President,' she began, becoming suddenly a stickler for etiquette, 'and fellow-members. Does this mean that some of us here have to be Ancient Britons?' Before her relentless gaze even Mrs Partridge quailed a trifle.

'But naturally, Mrs Pringle,' she replied, doing her best to answer with easy grace. 'Some will be Ancient Britons, and others Romans.'

'Humph!' snorted Mrs Pringle. 'And what, may I ask—if anything, I mean—do Ancient Britons wear?'

It was an anxious moment. You could have run a satisfactory heating system with the electricity generated in the hall at that quivering instant. Mrs Partridge, with the knowledge of past crises overcome and the rarefied blood of a vicar's wife beating in her veins, rose gamely to the challenge.

'We shall wear,' she said steadily, 'furs—probably mounted on old sacks.' There was a gasp from Mrs Moffat.

'And our hair,' she continued remorselessly, 'will be as rough and as dirty as we can make it.'

Mrs Pringle sat down with a jolt that made her companions on the bench shudder in sympathy. For once, she was speechless.

Mrs Partridge pressed home her attack.

'And our feet,' she said, with a hint of triumph, 'will be *bare*!'

There were faint sounds of dismay among the ranks before her, and the shuffling of feet clad, at the moment, in comfortable, if muddy, footwear. At this despondent moment, when dissension might so easily have reared its ugly head and wrecked our future revels, Mrs Moffat, a comparative newcomer to Fairacre, rose to her feet. Very pretty, very smart, an incomparable dress-maker and not much of a mixer as yet, she is still looked upon with a slightly suspicious eye by the old guard in the village.

'I don't know whether you want volunteers for the Ancient Britons,' she said, pink with her own temerity, 'but if you do, I'd like to be one of them.' It was a courageous statement, and made at a most strategic moment of the campaign. Moreover, it was a particularly noble one, when one considers that Mrs Moffat well knew that her own good looks would be hidden under sacks and old fur bits, which in themselves must be anathema to her sensitive clothes-loving soul. This unselfish gesture did not go unnoticed. There were sounds of approval, and one or two encouraging nods.

'Come to think of it,' said another woman, slowly, 'I don't mind being an Ancient Briton myself. I got a nice bit of ol' hearth rug——'

Mrs Partridge clinched the matter by saying: 'I'm looking forward to being one myself. For one thing the costume will be so easy to contrive.' Then with consummate generalship she drew her ranks of broken women together, at this precise moment which, she realized, would be the most propitious that she could hope for in these adverse conditions.

'I'm sure we shall be able to arrange Ancient Britons and Romans quite happily among ourselves; and I don't think we'll go any further with our plans tonight. It's getting late, and I know some of the mothers want to get these young people off to bed. I propose that we have a first rehearsal and allot parts one day next week. Shall we say at the vicarage?'

There were murmurs of assent, as people rose to their feet.

'Wednesday afternoon?' shouted Mrs Partridge above the noise.

'Clinic!' bellowed someone.

'Thursday then?' persisted Mrs Partridge, in a stentorian tone.

'Market day,' shrieked another.

'Monday?' bellowed Mrs Partridge indefatigably. The noise of scraping chairs and forms was unbelievable.

'Washday!' said someone; but she was howled down, by a self-righteous group near the door with lungs of brass.

'Did ought to be finished that by midday!'

'I gets mine done by eleven. And eight to wash for, my girl!'

'You can get there Monday afternoon, if you gets a move on!'

At last Monday afternoon was decided upon. The children would have broken up by then, and those that could be press-ganged into the pageant's service would be able to join their mothers in the fun at the vicarage.

Mrs Pringle, picking her way over the puddles, as we emerged in a bunch from the hall, voiced her feelings on the proceedings.

'Heathenish lot of nonsense!' boomed the familiar voice through the darkness. 'Furs and old sacks and bare feet!

Why, my mother would turn in her grave to think of me tricked out so common. We was all brought up respectable. Our feet never so much as saw daylight except at Saturday bath-night and getting into bed. Catch me exposing my extremities to the gaze of all and sundry, and as like as not getting pneumonia into the bargain!'

In the brief pause for breath which followed this diatribe a would-be peace-maker broke in.

'Perhaps you could be a Roman soldier, Mrs Pringle.'

The snort that this meek suggestion brought forth, would have done credit to an old war-horse.

'And what would my figure look like hung round with a few bits of gilt cardboard?' demanded Mrs Pringle majestically.

It seemed best to assume that this question was rhetorical and to be grateful for the merciful darkness which hid our faces.

The last day of term is over. It was spent in the usual jubilant muddle of clearing desks, tidying cupboards, searching for lost books and taking down pictures and charts from the schoolroom walls.

The last part of the afternoon was devoted to drawing a picture about Easter. Each child was given a very small piece of rough paper and a pencil, as everything else was packed securely away for three weeks, and had to do the best he could with this meagre ration.

I expected a spate of Easter eggs, chicks and the like, but was surprised by the various reactions to the word 'Easter.' The most striking use of paper and pencil came from Patrick, who had carefully folded his paper in half to form an Easter card, which he finally presented to me. It showed three large tombstones with crosses, and the letters R.I.P. printed crookedly across them, and inside was neatly printed

'Happy Easter.' I accepted this gloomy missive as gravely as I could. It had taken the artist half an hour and a good quarter of an inch of blacklead pencil to execute it.

When the pencils too had to be yielded up to the cupboard, we were reduced to the game of 'Left and Right,' that incomparable standby of empty-handed and busy teachers. Linda Moffat supplied a hair-grip and called upon Anne, her desk-mate, to guess which fist it was secreted in. She guessed correctly, took Linda's place, and the game followed its peaceful course with little attention from me, as I was engrossed in adding up the attendances for the term in the register. This wretched record does not hold the same fears for teachers these days, as it did when I was a girl, but it still exercises a baneful influence over me, and early memories of trips to my first headmistress with a wrongly-marked register in my trembling hand and instant dismissal hovering over me, have set up a horrid complex towards registers as a whole.

At the end of the afternoon we made our special farewells to Mrs Annett, and one of the Coggs twins presented her with a bouquet of daffodils, tulips, Easter daisies and narcissi, which the children had brought from their gardens. We shall miss her sorely. It has been decided by the managers to wait until after the summer holidays for the permanent appointment, when the newly-trained young teachers will be out from the colleges. Meanwhile, I was delighted to hear from the vicar that Miss Clare will be with us for next term. This is good news indeed.

I spent a very pleasant evening with the Annetts, after pottering happily about all day enjoying the freedom from school duties. I have turned out the cupboard under the stairs—one mad jumble of brooms, dusters, primus stove, and might-come-in-useful collection of pieces of brown paper, cardboard, carrier bags and the like—and feel much elated. From the schoolroom came sounds of Mrs Pringle at work scrubbing the floor-boards. Above the clanking of the pail and the groaning of heavy desks being shunted across the room, Mrs Pringle's carrying contralto voice could be heard raised in pious song, ranging from *A few more years shall roll* to *Oft in danger, oft in woe*.

It was very pleasant to take my time over tea and dressing. The little car goes well now, and gone are the days when I imagined knots of children playing marbles in the middle of the road round each corner, and held my breath when another car approached. In fact I felt quite a dashing driver as I swept into Beech Green school's empty playground, and slammed the car door shut, only to realize that I had left my keys inside. Luckily, the other door was unlocked, so all was well; but I went in a more humble mood across to the school-house next door.

It is very much more comfortable now that Mrs Annett is there to run the house, and I remembered my first visit there, when Mr Annett was officially looked after by a house-keeper, and how I had noticed the general neglect.

Now the furniture gleamed and fresh flowers scented the house. In the corner Mrs Annett's violin stood beside Mr Annett's 'cello. They are both keen members of the Caxley orchestra, but Mrs Annett will probably not be able to take part next season, when she has a young baby to look after. Their radiogram is a great joy to them and we played Mr Annett's new records until supper-time.

After supper we fell to talking about country schools and I was interested to hear that Beech Green is developing the practical farming side with even more vigour.

'If I have to have the children here until they are fifteen,' said Mr Annett, 'and I have no woodwork shop, no place for metal work and mighty little other equipment, then I must find something that is worthwhile for them to do, and from which they learn. Otherwise they'll be bored and surly. Luckily we've plenty of land here, enough for a large vegetable plot, and we've got permission to keep hens, ducks and pigs as well.'

I knew that Beech Green school had sent garden produce to Caxley market for some years, but the livestock was something quite new.

'We've been given a small grant from the county,' he went on, 'and our profit from the market has helped. The boys have made really fine coops and runs, which have involved quite a bit of practical arithmetic, and the way the accounts are kept is a miracle of book-keeping. The pigs have only just arrived. Bricklaying took longer than we thought for the sties, and we had a bit of trouble with the concrete yards, but they should bring us in a substantial profit later. The left-overs from school dinners form the major part of their diet. You must bring a party over from Fairacre School to see our farm when it's really working.'

I promised that I would, and as I drove home the sound good sense behind Mr Annett's scheme for these older rural pupils, impressed me more and more. One thing that he had said I found particularly significant.

'I started by using these out-of-door and practical activities as a means to defeat apathy. After all, for generations most country children of fourteen and over have been out in the world earning their living. It is not surprising that today some still resent being kept at school, particularly if there's nothing new or absorbing to learn offered them. But the surprising thing is this. The defeat of apathy is only a by-product. For this itself is real education for the majority of the Beech Green children. Working with these methods brings out the patience, the endurance and the innate sagacity of the countryman; and, all the time, I am working WITH and not AGAINST the grain, as I so often felt I was when I urged them along reluctantly with book-work for which they had little sympathy.'

Mr Annett is a townsman by birth and breeding, so that it is all the more remarkable that he has stumbled on this truth, after a relatively short time as a country-dweller; but there are hundreds of rural schoolteachers from Land's End to John o' Groats who will endorse his views, and who know that the education of the countryman is a matter which must be given immediate and intelligent thought. Land today in England is more precious than ever before. It is our heritage and in trust for future generations. It is only right that it should be tilled and cared for by people who are not only capable and trained for this work, but who also are happy and contented to live among the farms and fields which give them their livelihood and—even more—a deep inner satisfaction.

Rural education must be tackled realistically if the drift to the towns is to stop. In this way village life will come into its own again, not as a picturesque setting for week-end visitors to enjoy, when they come down, in some cases, to see how a most satisfactory way of income-tax evasion is getting on, but as a vital working unit.

The first rehearsal at the vicarage went splendidly. Mrs Partridge said that she felt we really ought to get used to going barefoot, so that we removed our shoes and stockings, with varying degrees of reluctance, and left them on the veranda while we hobbled painfully over the gravel to the comparative comfort of the lawn, where we sat down to discuss casting plans.

It was decided that twelve of our more comely members would constitute the invading Roman force, and that the rest would be Ancient Britons of both sexes. I watched Mrs

Partridge running an appraising eye over the legs of the assembled company, rather as the local trainers do as they watch their race-horses on the gallops above Fairacre.

Mrs Moffat, that brave volunteer to the Ancient Britons' ranks, was persuaded to be pack-leader, captain, or whatever the Roman equivalent might be for the one in charge, instead. She is tall and carries herself well, and her legs are impeccable. Mrs Partridge obviously feared that there might be an ugly rush for the other eleven places, for she spoke firmly to Mrs Pratt when she rose from her seat on the lawn.

'Now please, Mrs Pratt, I do so want you to be a rather influential Ancient Briton woman, with possibly a bundle of faggots, so will you forgo being a Roman?'

Mrs Pratt looked mildly surprised.

'I only got up because I was sitting on a thistle,' she said, in some bewilderment. Mrs Partridge said she had quite misunderstood her gesture, and were there any volunteers?

As usual in Fairacre, the word 'volunteers' struck temporary paralysis upon its hearers, and we all sat, eyes glazed and limbs frozen, like so many flies in amber. It was quite apparent that far from being an ugly rush to the Roman standard, Fairacre W.I. had elected to be Ancient Britons to a woman.

At last Mrs Partridge broke the silence.

'Miss Read, would you be a Roman?'

I said that I should be delighted to be called to the colours at my age. This seemed to break the ice a little, and two young women who cycle over from Springbourne to our meetings, offered to join the ranks too. Gradually our twelve were collected, and if some of us were a trifle long in the tooth, at least we were reasonably athletic.

There had been an awkward moment when Mrs Pringle had boomed a grudging offer of martial assistance, but Mrs

Partridge had turned temporarily deaf, and as Mrs Fowler from Tyler's Row spoke up at the same time, all was well.

'Now,' said Mrs Partridge brightly, 'if you Romans would sit over here near the rose-bed—but do mind your nylons—we shall know where we are. Perhaps we can work out how much cardboard we shall need for armour; but that must wait for another time.'

'Breastplates and backplates should be enough,' said one of the Springbourne girls.

'And helmets,' said the other.

'And greaves,' said Mrs Moffat.

'Graves?' boomed Mrs Pringle from the Ancient Britons' camp opposite. 'Graves? We having a war then? If so, I tell you straight, my leg won't stand up to it!'

'Leg-pads—like in cricket,' volunteered a nephew of Mr Rogers at the forge, who attends Caxley Grammar School and is well up in greaves, helmets and other martial garments.

Mrs Pringle snorted her disgust.

'Got quite enough on me leg with me elastic stocking,' said that lady, 'without getting meself dolled-up in wicket-keeper's rubbish.'

With brilliant dash Mrs Partridge put all to rights.

'You won't need to be bothered with leg-pads, Mrs Pringle. As an Ancient Briton, I want you to be the mother of the chief warrior—a most important person—and you will sit on a kind of throne by the camp fire—which won't try your poor leg that you're always so brave about—and generally keep an eye on the rest of the tribe.'

Mrs Pringle allowed herself to be mollified, and something very like a gratified smirk spread over her dour features. It is no wonder that Mrs Partridge is elected annually as our president. No one else can touch her for spontaneous and inspired diplomacy.

As a nasty little wind had sneaked up, and the children

were beginning to get restive, it was thought best to have a rudimentary rehearsal of the scene at once.

'You must pretend to have weapons and tools,' shouted Mrs Partridge, above the general movement. 'One of you boys fetch a stool for Mrs Pringle, and that flower urn can be the camp fire.'

Slowly the Ancient Britons began to move shamefacedly about their occupations, their children tending to stand about with broad grins on their faces and with many a giggle behind hands. Mrs Pringle squatted in an unlovely attitude on her small stool, and folded her arms regally. Other women stirred imaginary pots, washed imaginary clothes, swept imaginary floors and occasionally cuffed far-from-imaginary children who crossed their path.

Meanwhile we Roman soldiers formed a ragged column behind the laurel bushes, awaiting our entrance. We waited until one of the tribesmen had returned to his fellows, showing by gestures that we were about to descend upon them. The Ancient Britons were then supposed to point towards us dramatically, making low uncouth cries at the same time, as they bunched together in trepidation.

The low, uncouth cries they did rather well, as dramatically out-flung arms hit nearby bodies with considerable force. At a nervous command from our leader, Mrs Moffat, we marched into action from behind the laurels. The fact that some of us had started on the left, and some on the right foot, that we were all too close and tended to trip each other up, did not enhance our war-like aspect. But never can a Roman cohort have been so polite, and it was quite pretty to hear us all apologizing to each other as we stumbled along.

We approached our future captives, smiling faintly upon them. They beamed back, and we all mingled together in the happiest fraternity round the flower-urn and Mrs Pringle.

Mrs Partridge clapped her hands and we sat down thankfully.

'Very good indeed,' said she, with the greatest vigour. 'I think it's a wonderful beginning. When the soldiers have got their cardboard armour on, and their kilts,' (Mr Rogers's nephew, as a coming classics man, shuddered and turned pale) 'and the Ancient Britons are wearing their old fur and dreary hair, I think we shall all be quite——' she searched for the exact word, looked it over, found it good, and flung it at us triumphantly—'quite *irresistible*!'

Flown with such heady praise we all returned, in great good spirits, to our homes.

MAY

As usual, the holidays slipped by in a golden haze. Apart from four crowded days in London, staying with a married friend with three young children, and having the excitement of an evening at the ballet, shopping and meals out, I spent the rest of the time here at the school-house. The garden is at its best, and the fruit trees, planted by those who taught at Fairacre long ago, are a mass of pink and white blossom. Mr Willet and all the other good gardeners pull long faces and say: 'Don't like to see it so early. Bound to get some late frosts, mark my words.'

A blackbird has built a nest in the lilac bush near the gate —so idiotically low that Tibby is much interested and spends her time glowering upon the foolish bird, from the top of the gate. I have tried to screen it with hazel boughs, but with small success. At my suggestion, to Mr Willet, that I might drape it with netting from the fruit cage, he looked at me pityingly, blew out his ragged old moustache, and said: 'Why not let the poor cat have a good meal? He's waited patient enough, ain't he?'

Mrs Pringle came to give me a hand with some spring-cleaning during the holidays, which she did with much puffing and blowing. To hear her disparaging comments on the condition of the backs of the bookcases, and the loot that she extracted from the sides of the arm-chairs, one might wonder why I hadn't died of typhus.

'Mrs Hope, what lived here in my young days, though an ailing woman with a child, and a husband with a Failing,' she told me, as she hauled out the loose cover from the crack of the sofa, 'never had so much as a biscuit crumb in her folds, they being brushed out regular twice a week, as is necessary for common cleanliness.' To add point to this stricture, she jerked out the last bit of the cover and projected a light shower of crumbs—biscuit and otherwise—two pencils, a safety-pin, a knitting needle and a liquorice allsort, upon the carpet. I was unrepentant.

Term is now a week old. The children look all the better for their freedom and fresh air, and it is very pleasant to have Miss Clare back again in the infants' room, where she reigned for so many years. However it is not without certain small difficulties. The children are used to Mrs Annett's more modern methods, and have been allowed to move about the classroom, to talk a little and to make much more noise than Miss Clare will allow. They are finding Miss Clare's more formal methods rather irksome.

'Can we play shops?' I heard Joseph Coggs ask, as I was collecting Miss Clare's savings money. 'Mrs Annett lets us play shops instead of writing down sums.' His dark eyes were fixed pleadingly upon her.

'I think we'll have table practice first,' was the kind, but firm, answer; and Joseph trailed back to his desk, with a pouting underlip.

'Do use all the apparatus that is here,' I said, waving to the desk-load of sugar cartons, cocoa tins and the like, that constitute 'the shop' at the side of the room, 'and don't worry about the noise—my children don't take any notice of a little hum next door.' But my gentle hints were of no avail. I could see from Miss Clare's quizzical glance that she knew exactly what was going on inside my head, and knew too that she was too old a dog to learn new tricks—even if she felt that they were the right ones, which, in this case, she doubts.

In a week or two the children will have become accustomed to a slower and steadier regime, and will respond to Miss Clare's methods as well as earlier generations of Fairacre children have done. Meanwhile, I have offered to take her class, as well as my own, for the games and physical training lessons, for not only is this too much of a strain on her elderly and delicate heart, but the small children revel in scampering and jumping and using the wealth of individual apparatus—balls, hoops, skipping ropes and the like—which they miss sorely in the formal four lines for head, arm, leg and trunk exercises which are used for the major part of Miss Clare's lessons.

It has not been easy to persuade Miss Clare to part with any of her duties, for she is the most conscientious woman alive; but after some demurring she acquiesced, not only in this matter but also in my suggestion that she rested for twenty minutes on my sofa during the dinner hour. It took some lurid word-painting on my behalf, of my own predicament if she should have an attack in school time, to make her agree to this measure, but a lucky thought of mine that she should make a pot of tea for us both, at the end of the twenty minutes, which would also be the end of my midday playground duty, just turned the balance, and the daily rest means that she returns to her afternoon session much refreshed.

My class this term has been enriched by the addition of an eight-year-old American boy. His parents return to the United States in, what he calls, "the fall." On first hearing this expression, Patrick, more scripturally-minded than most, began asking complicated questions about the Garden of Eden, which he was obviously confusing with Erle's native land, and was considerably surprised, and slightly disappointed, on being told that it was only another name for autumn.

The Fairacre children have taken Erle very much under their wing. He is a most attractive little boy, with a crew-cut, a cheerful grin and no trace of shyness. He appeared on the second morning with two pistols slung on a formidable, studded holster, round his checked jeans. I broke it to him, as gently as I could, that I did not allow guns, knives, bows and arrows or any other weapons, on school premises, though, of course, he could do as he liked at home. I was conscious of the exchange of disgusted glances among my class, for this old sore still rankles, but Erle parted with his holster, with a grin that crinkled his eyes engagingly. He put it with a resounding clanking of pistolry on the old desk at the side of the room, among the paper bags containing elevenses, and the other, less lethal, toys, that had been brought for play-time.

There was an amusing sequel to this incident. At play-time I sat alone in the classroom, marking history test papers, when I became conscious of voices in the adjoining lobby.

'Never you mind, Erle,' said Eric earnestly, 'us'll play cowboys with you tonight down the rec. That ol' Miss Read—' he spoke witheringly, 'she treats us awful. Don't let us do nothin'. A proper ol' spoil-sport!'

'Aw well!' came Erle's good-natured drawl, 'I guess teachers is teachers everywhere!' He spoke as one who has suffered in the past, and is resigned—fairly cheerfully—to suffering in the future.

'Don't you bring them no more, though,' warned Eric. 'The ol' girl locks 'em up in the cupboard till the end of term, and kicks up horrid.' His voice, dark with foreboding, suddenly took on a more jubilant note.

'Tell you what—come and play Indians up the coke-pile!' And with joyous whoopings, this enlightening conversation came to an end.

Mr Arnold, one of Her Majesty's Inspectors, spent most of the day with us. This is his second visit to Fairacre School. His first one was brought to an abrupt close by a violent thunderstorm last summer, when we had to get the children home as best we could by various means. The vicar, I remember, stuffed a record number into his car that afternoon, and the old golfing umbrella, that lives in the corner cupboard with the maps, had bobbed its way through the downpour with the Tyler's Row contingent.

He remembered Mrs Annett—Miss Gray, as she had been when he last visited the infants' room—and said that she appeared to have done an excellent job with the younger children; but didn't I feel that the reading was being pushed a little too hard? He put this point with the utmost delicacy, suggesting that perhaps Miss Clare was the person who was taking this subject a trifle too seriously, but I told him at once that this fault—if it were indeed a fault—was of my making.

This led us to a most agreeable and stimulating argument

about children's reading. Mr Arnold sat inelegantly on the front desk, with his back to the class. Poor Patrick meekly wrote up his nature notes on the six square inches of desk lid which were not occupied by Mr Arnold's well-cut lovat tweed trousers. I sat at my desk and we argued over the massive brass and oak inkstand.

He maintained that children are not ready to read before the age of six, or even seven; and that all sorts of nervous tensions and eyestrain can be set up by too much emphasis on early reading.

I maintain that each child should go at its own rate, and that the modern tendency is to go at the rate of the slowest member of a reading group, and that this is wrong. There are, to my mind, far more bright children being bored and frustrated because they are not getting on fast enough with their reading, than there are slow ones who are being harmed by too-rapid progress. I have known several children—I was one myself—who could read enough simply-written stories to amuse themselves at the age of four and a half to five. We were not forced, but it was just one of those things we could do easily, and the advantages were enormous.

In the first place we *could* amuse ourselves, and reading also gave us a quiet and relaxed time for recovering from the violent activity which is the usual five-year-old's way of passing the time.

Secondly, the amount of general knowledge we unconsciously imbibed, stood us in good stead in later years. Today, with the eleven-plus examination to face, this is particularly pertinent. Incidentally, I have known children who have come to reading so late in the primary school, that they have found real difficulty in reading the questions, let alone knowing enough to answer them. Even more important, the early poems and rhymes, read and learnt so easily at this stage have been a constant and abiding joy.

Thirdly, the wealth of literature written and presented expressly for the four to six age-group—the Beatrix Potter books are the first that spring to mind—can be used, loved and treasured to an extent that is not possible to a late reader. The child who has never been taught to read until the age of seven or eight has missed the thrill of discovering a vast number of attractive books. He is beginning to want fairy stories, adventures, legends and so on, which may well be in language still too difficult for his retarded mechanics of reading.

The battle raged with great zest.

'I have never over-worked a child in my life,' I insisted. 'It always seems to me to be a most difficult thing to accomplish anyway, natural resistance to learning is remarkably resilient. There are some here who never will be able to read with ease—but, broadly speaking, I expect the average child to be able to read well enough to amuse and instruct himself by the time he is eight—and if he can't, then he is probably below average and will need a little extra encouragement. And if I get the odd infant who can rattle away at five—why then, good luck to him—and all the books in Fairacre School, and in Fairacre School-house, for that matter, are at his disposal.'

Mr Arnold twinkled, and said I was a renegade, but that he must admit that he had seen no cases of nervous disorders in my school. And after school, he, Miss Clare and I enjoyed a cup of tea in my garden, among the apple blossom, with the greatest goodwill, each knowing that he would never convert the other, but content to let it be so.

Erle and Eric have struck up a strong friendship and are quite inseparable. It dates, I think, from the day when I banished Erle's weapons from school premises, and, united against stern tyranny, the pair flourish. Before prayers this morning, as I was wondering if I could manage five flats in the morning hymn and dusting the yellow piano keys, I listened to their conversation. Eric was giving out hymn books, dropping them with a satisfying smack on each desk, as the rest of the class wandered in, deposited their elevenses on the side table, or waited beside my desk with bunches of flowers or messages from their mothers. Erle trailed behind him giving brief information about education in American schools.

'We don't have all this,' he said, touching a hymn book, 'we have the pledge.'

'The what?' said Eric, stopping dead. 'Like what you have in the Band of Hope?'

'Don't know nothin' about a Band of Hope,' replied Erle. 'The pledge is what we say every morning. We all look at the flag—our flag, Stars and Stripes—and promise to be real good Americans.'

Eric looked surprised and mildly disgusted.

'You tells all that to a *flag*?' he enquired.

Erle's good-natured face took on a perplexed expression.

'It's THE flag,' he explained. 'It's a real good flag, with gold fringe and all.' Eric's reply was crushing.

'We got a flag too. But we don't keep all on about it.' He resumed his hymn-book slinging as though the matter were closed. Erle was not to be side-tracked.

'Well, forget the flags,' he said doggedly, 'but we don't have hymns and prayers like you do. That's all I said. We just have this pledge—like I told you.'

Eric flicked the last hymn book on to the corner desk with a pretty turn of the wrist. Satisfied with the results, he dusted his hands down his shirt, and explained the position succinctly to this stranger from another shore.

'Well, that's all right where you come from, I don't doubt. But over here, Miss Read says we has a bit about God each morning—and rain or shine, a bit about God we has!'

* * *

Miss Clare invited me to her cottage for the evening. She refuses to let me fetch her or run her home in the car, but cycles, very slowly and as upright as ever, on her venerable old bicycle.

As usual, the best china, the snowiest cloth and the most delicious supper awaited me.

Miss Clare's cottage is a model of neatness. The roof was thatched by her father, who was the local thatcher for many years. She has an early-flowering honeysuckle over her white trellis porch, and jasmine smothers another archway down the garden path.

In the centre of the table stood a cut-glass vase of magnificent tulips, flanked by a cold brisket of beef on a willow-pattern dish garnished with sprigs of parsley from her garden, and an enormous salad. The freshly-plucked spring onions, were thoughtfully put separately in a little shallow dish.

'It's not everyone that can digest them,' said Miss Clare, crunching one with much enjoyment, 'but my mother always said they were a wonderful tonic, and cleared the blood after the winter.'

Miss Clare's silver was old and heavy and gleamed with recent cleaning. How she finds time to keep everything so immaculate I don't know. Her house puts mine to shame, and she has no one to help her at all, whereas I do have Mrs Pringle occasionally to turn a disdainful hand to my affairs.

After we had consumed an apple and blackberry pie, the fruits of Miss Clare's earlier bottling, we folded our yard-square napkins—which were stiff with starch and exquisitely darned here and there—and washed up in the long, low kitchen, while the coffee heated on the Primus stove.

Miss Clare's larder is one of the pleasantest places I know. It is a long narrow room, at the side of the kitchen and has a red brick floor and whitewashed walls. The wooden shelves have been scrubbed so often and so well that the grain stands out in fine ribs.

From the ceiling hang ropes of bronze onions, dried herbs in muslin bags, and a ham, equally well-draped, which I know her brother gave her at his last pig-killing. Bottles of fruit, cherries, plums, blackberries, greengages and gooseberries, and jars of jam and jelly, flash like jewels, as they stand in serried ranks: and on the floor stand bottles of home-made wine, dandelion, parsnip, sloe and damson, beside two large crocks containing salted runner beans. How Miss Clare ever gets through these stores I don't know, for she has little time for entertaining and has her main meal at school, more often than not; but as a true countrywoman she bottles, preserves, salts and stores all the good things that grow in her own garden and are given her by kindly neighbours, and would count it a disgrace not to have a larder well-stocked for any emergency.

That she is generous with her possessions, I do know, from personal experience and from hearsay. No one goes away empty-handed; and I suspect that many of those bottles of fruit and wine will be carried away by visitors. Typical of her largeness of heart is the shilling which always waits on the corner of the mantelpiece in the dining-room.

'I keep one there for whoever calls,' she told me. 'They are all treated the same—Salvation Army, Soldiers and Sailors, Roman Catholics, Blind Babies, Red Cross, and all the rest.' When I think of Miss Clare's tiny pension and see how ready she is to give—not only these impartial shillings, but cakes to fêtes and bazaars, knitting to raffles, gifts to sales of work and the like, and always unfailingly, her time and little store of strength—to any good work in the village, I cannot help contrasting her attitude of mind with those others among us, earning perhaps five times as much, who never give one penny, one minute or one thought to others around them, but grab all, and grumble because it isn't more.

In the end, of course, it is Miss Clare, who scores, for she, *ipso facto*, is a happy woman, while their treasure turns to dust and ashes.

Mrs Moffat has undertaken to make Amy's costume for the forthcoming county pageant. Bent, the village where Amy lives, has been lucky enough to draw 'The Visit of Charles II and Queen Catherine of Braganza to Branscombe Castle' for its part in the series. Amy is to play the queen, and is full of enthusiasm. Her handbag was crammed with patterns of silks, satins, lace and brocade, and a number of small portraits of that royal lady, culled from the postcard stands at the National Portrait Gallery to snippets from the historical features in back numbers of *Everybody's*.

She had been to discuss the costume early in the afternoon, and called at the school as we were about to go home. She smiled kindly upon Linda, and took in, with an expert's eye, the cut of the tartan pinafore frock that Miss Moffat was wearing.

'She's going to be a beauty,' was her comment, when the children had trickled out into the sunshine. 'And with a mother like that to make her clothes, she's going to be a very lucky girl'

She helped me to stack away the paintings which were draped around the room, on the piano top, the fire-guard, the side desk, window-sills—anywhere for that matter where the masterpieces could have ten minutes' peace in which to dry—and rattled on excitedly about Mrs Moffat's genius for dressmaking. Four or five other members of Bent W.I. had also enlisted her services, one of whom was an authority on costume and had worked, before her marriage, as an adviser on historical costume to a film company. Amy had high hopes that she would take an especial interest in Mrs Moffat's work and that this might lead to great things in the future, for the Moffat-Finch-Edwards partnership.

'And what might this be?' she enquired suddenly, holding up a damp painting by one corner. I said it was supposed to be Mr Lamb at the Post Office unlocking the post-box and taking out the letters.

'But it's a lilac letter-box,' objected Amy. 'There's not a spot of scarlet anywhere!'

'There's not a spot of scarlet in the whole wretched range of powder paint,' I told her. 'You can have anything from lime green to clover. We're all a bit greenery-yallery these days.'

'We had three good fat squeezes of red, blue, and yellow, when I was at school,' said Amy, looking back across the years. 'Primary colours, you know, and we made all the others from those three. Much more fun than these myriad pots of depressing paint.' She surveyed, with dislike, the large tray, laden with jam jars of paint, that stood on my desk.

I agreed heartily, and told her that in some painting lessons the children did exactly as she had done as a child, and that I believed they found the mixing of colours more absorbing than slapping on those already done for them.

'To have no really good red!' mused Amy sadly, as we locked up, and went across to the school-house. 'How you manage these days when it comes to buses and mail-vans and geraniums and poppies, I really can't think!'

I switched on the kettle, and washed my hands at the kitchen sink. I was amused to see how seriously Amy had taken this art problem. Her troubled gaze was fixed, unseeing, on the garden.

'Not to mention Chelsea pensioners and lobsters!' she added.

Mr Mawne has paid us his long-awaited visit. The children were delighted to have someone fresh to listen to, and a few of Miss Clare's older children were allowed to come in with their elders to hear his talk on our local birds.

He had some excellent coloured pictures, some of which he had drawn and coloured himself, and these he has very generously handed over to Fairacre School. He had to hurry away, as he had promised the vicar that he would help him with the church accounts after an early tea, but he met Mrs Pringle as she was stumping in from the lobby with her broom. The arch smile that I was treated to, enhanced by the loss of her upper plate, broken earlier in the week, was so infuriating in its toad-like hideousness that I could cheerfully have floored her with my weighty ink-stand, but alas!—common civility stayed my hand.

'A real gentleman that!' was her comment, as she watched his thin retreating back. 'Wouldn't stop to tea, I'll be bound. Wouldn't want people to start talking!' She bent, wincing, to pick up a milk straw from the floor. Her leg, I noticed, was dragging slightly, as she limped towards the waste-paper basket.

'Not,' she went on, 'that he'd take advantage of anyone!'

I could have wished that Mrs Pringle had used a less dubious phrase. But torn between amusement and irritation, I made my way to the house, there to order some films about birds, for the first Wednesday in June, when the mobile film van pays us its next visit, to follow up poor misjudged Mr Mawne's excellent discourse.

This morning, while I was in the playground, directing litter-collecting in an unpleasantly cold wind, Mrs Partridge drew up in the ancient Ford. It was stuffed with spring cabbages, bunches of young carrots, spring onions and lettuces, for Mrs Partridge was on her way to Caxley to put her produce on the W.I. stall in the market.

She told me that Mrs Pratt's father had had a stroke the day before, and that Dr Martin was afraid that he would be completely helpless, perhaps for many months. Mrs Pratt had been obliged to give up the secretaryship of the W.I. and would I be willing to take over if the members agreed to this proposition.

I said cautiously that I would think about it, and let her know tomorrow, but if the meetings were to be held, as they always have been, in the afternoons, it was, of course, out of the question. The vicar's wife said: 'Of course, of course! How could I have forgotten! Well, we'll see what can be done! Perhaps Mrs Moffat might consider it. Linda's at school in the afternoon.' And with that, she drove off.

I collected my class, who had now tidied the playground with such zeal that Erle was now dusting the shoe-scraper with his handkerchief, and we returned to the classroom, grateful to be out of the wind.

As the children worked at their arithmetic, my mind wandered back to the problem of running village activities. In Fairacre we manage fairly well owing to the small number of clubs and so on, and to the hard work of Mr and Mrs Partridge who are more than willing to undertake extra duties. But Beech Green, which is a much larger village and has a good bus service to Caxley, has great difficulty in finding people ready to take office in such things as their Women's Institute, the Scouts, and the Sports Club.

The vicar shakes his mild old head about dwindling numbers there and comments sadly on the flourishing men's clubs, glee clubs and the like, which had so many keen supporters twenty or more years ago. But then the buses to Caxley from Fairacre and Beech Green, were non-existent and the villagers were thrown on their own resources. Families were much larger, and there were more people to each age-group than there are now. Bands of friends would join the appropriate activity and keep the thing going. Then too, there were leisured people, who willingly gave their time and money to support village affairs, who would come to the rescue when a financial crisis arose, who would lend houses and gardens generously, and would put their ideas and inspirations at the disposal of the village. This invaluable source of village richness is now no more.

When I think of those on Fairacre's and Beech Green's various committees I am struck by the fact that they are, in the main, outsiders, and not natives of the village. Now, why is this? Does it mean that organized activities are not needed by those for whom they are intended? Or does it mean that newcomers to a village enjoy running things, harking back perhaps to their own childhood in other villages, when such affairs were in their heyday? On one thing committee members are united. They lament the fact that they get little or no support from the bulk of the populace. Are they, perhaps, an anachronism in this transition period? Will organized activity come into its own again if and when the villages flourish again, when rural education is improved, and the drift from the countryside is halted?

That there is social intercourse is undeniable. We here in Fairacre are constantly visiting each other for tea parties, morning coffee, evenings at cards, or for watching television programmes, and we are always ready to stop and have delicious friendly gossips over our garden gates.

The 'Beetle and Wedge' is crowded nightly, and this is where the men really meet to exchange news and grumbles, and to relax after work. As P. G. Wodehouse truly says of the tap-room, 'The rich smell of mixed liquors, the gay clamour of carefree men arguing about the weather, the Government, the Royal Family, greyhound racing, the tax on beer, pugilism, religion and the price of bananas—these things are medicine to the bruised soul.'

There is a natural disinclination to go out on winter evenings, and in the summer our gardens occupy a major part of our time. Perhaps church-going, the visits to the pub, the occasional whist-drive or fête, and the entertainment of neighbours is all that busy countrymen have time for at this stage of village life. With easy transport to Caxley and television in their own homes to supply entertainment, the people of our two villages certainly seem to find enough to occupy them, and whether one can expect large and flourishing clubs, admirable though they are, is a moot point.

We had a most unnerving accident here today. Eileen Burton, one of the infants, tripped over her own trailing shoe lace and fell like a log on to the metal milk crate. She hit her forehead on the sharp edge, concussing herself, and getting a horrible gash along the right eyebrow.

Joseph Coggs, who, once before, when Miss Clare was taken ill, was a harbinger of woeful tidings, was sent in to tell me of the catastrophe.

'Eileen Burton's busted 'er 'ead,' was his greeting and, as I hastened to the next room I heard him say, with relish to my round-eyed class: ' 'Er's prob'ly dead!'

You could have heard a pin drop in the infants' room. Miss Clare was mopping the child's head with a swab of damp cotton-wool. It was obvious that she would need stitches in the gash, and that we must get her to hospital.

'I'll get the car out and take her straight to Caxley, if you can manage both classes,' I said.

'Mr Roberts may not have gone to market yet,' said Miss Clare, looking up at the big wall-clock. 'Do you think he'd help?'

Mr Roberts farms next door to the school, is one of the school's managers and always a tower of strength. I sent a message over to the farm by Patrick, and returned to Eileen, still prostrate on the floor, but now with a cushion under her head and a rug over her from the school-house. My class surged ghoulishly in the partition doorway, and were dispatched to their desks with hard words and threats of no-play-for-nuisances.

Eileen began to come round as Patrick returned.

'Mr Roberts has gone, and Mrs Roberts too; so Jim's dad said.' He nodded to Jim in the back row. 'But he says if you wants a stretcher, he's got a hurdle he can send over.'

It was quite apparent that word would already have flown round the village grapevine that Eileen Burton—and probably a couple more—were lying with every limb broken and at the point of death, in Fairacre School.

'I must get a message to her mother,' I said hastily, 'before I take her into Caxley.'

'She's back at the fish-shop,' chorused the children. 'Sutton's, miss! At Caxley, miss! You'd see her there, miss! Market day, she's bound to be there, miss!' continued the helpful babble. I quelled them with that daunting glance which every teacher worth her salt keeps in her armoury, and when peace was restored helped Miss Clare to fasten the bandage round Eileen's head.

She had a drink of water and looked a little better. At last we propped her gently in the car, and I gave my children last-minute admonitions about helping Miss Clare, before setting off for the out-patients' department of Caxley hospital. I did not feel at all happy about leaving Miss Clare, for the shock had obviously upset her, and I hoped that the extra children would not be too much for her.

On the other hand, I told myself as we drove past Beech Green school, how fortunate that there was another teacher to leave in charge. If Fairacre had had a one-teacher school, as so many villages have, what would have happened in a case like this? Either the child must have been given second-best treatment, on the spot, or the services of a kindly neighbour with a car enlisted—as we had hoped to do when we appealed to Mr Roberts—with the possibility of no one being available. Otherwise the school must have been dismissed, while the patient was taken to hospital, or the children given work to do without supervision—both most unsatisfactory arrangements.

A telephone call to the hospital would have been the other alternative, but there are many schools without this service, and the time taken to send the message and to wait for the ambulance to arrive might be considerable. No, I decided, as I drew up at Sutton's fish shop to break the news to Mrs Burton—and to take her with us if possible—I was very glad that I did not have to face all these hazards alone, as so many country head teachers are obliged to do.

May has ended with a cold, gusty day, which has shivered the young elm leaves, and whipped the windows with little whirlwinds of upflung dust, twigs and straws. During afternoon play-time a vicious hail storm sent the children scurrying into school for shelter. It fell heavily, looking like slanting rods of steel, and the playground and adjoining churchyard were quickly white.

From the schoolroom window I could see Mr Willet, who had been trimming the grass paths, sheltering from the storm in the church porch. He had folded the sack, on which had had been kneeling, to make a hood to shelter his head and shoulders from the onslaught which had overtaken him, and as he stood there with his rough brown hood, and his drab trousers bound round the legs to stop them flapping, he might have been a figure from any century.

So must his forefathers have often stood, from Norman times on, dressed in sober serviceable cloth, waiting patiently for the weather to clear, gnarled old hands nursing elbows and long-sighted eyes fixed on the sky above the massive walls of their church.

JUNE

THE Whitsun and half-term holiday combined gave Fair-acre School almost a week's break, which I spent, most agreeably, at Cambridge, with an old college friend. The Backs, enchanting at any time and season, seemed lovelier than ever, and Evensong at King's College Chapel exerted the same magic as it did on my first visit, with the same friend, many years ago.

What a hauntingly lovely place Cambridge is! It has a

gentleness, an ambience, a wistful elegance that is unique. A visit to London, or Oxford, or any other great and ancient city for that matter, exhilarates and stimulates me; but Cambridge always gives something more—so deeply stirring, that I could not dismiss it simply as nostalgia for my long-lost youth. Tentative questioning of other people has confirmed my suspicions, that Cambridge has a quality, compounded of great skies, shimmering willows and water, ephemeral youth in age-old buildings and the loneliness of its setting in the desolate fens, which evokes a strangely powerful response from those who walk her ways.

The train journey back to Caxley was a tedious cross-country affair lasting over three hours. Luckily Mr and Mrs Annett were shopping near the station and gave me a lift to Fairacre, so that I did not have to wait another hour for the local bus.

The school-house was unnaturally quiet, when the sound of the Annetts' car had died away. I prowled round, savouring the joys of the newly-returned. The clock had stopped at four-twenty, the house was flowerless, and, in the kitchen, the dishcloth hung dry and stiff, arched over the edge of the sink, like a miniature canvas tunnel.

I put the kettle on for that first inspiring cup of tea, and resumed my prowling upstairs. Tibby, curled up comfortably in a patch of sunlight on my eiderdown, stretched out luxuriously, all claws extended, gave a welcoming yowl, half-yawn, half-mew, and resumed her interrupted slumbers again.

Mrs Pringle had been detailed to feed the cat, and when I returned to my singing kettle, I noticed that every morsel of food had been used. As I had left an imposing variety of delicacies, including cold meat, cold fish, dried cat-food and two tins of another variety much appreciated by Tibby, as well as half a pint of milk daily, my companion had obviously been living like a lord, and I could see that I should have the unenviable job of restoring her to a more humble way of life.

With all the windows in the house opened, I sat down with my tea tray and thought how lovely it was to be back. I feel like a sword in a scabbard, I told myself, and instantly decided that a sword was much too dashing. Perhaps a cup, hanging again on its accustomed hook on the kitchen dresser, would be a better simile. At any rate, to be a village schoolmistress, with a fine border of pinks just breaking before me, and the sound of rooks cawing overhead, seemed a very right and proper thing to be, and I envied no man.

The second half of the term has started in a blaze of sunshine. Yesterday the temperature was up in the eighties, and we had the schoolroom door propped open with the biggest upturned flower-pot that Mr Willet could find. The green paint on the doors and windows of Fairacre School has long since faded to a soft silvery green, like a cabbage leaf with a fine bloom on it. It is a most beautiful colour, and I regret that we are due to be repainted in the summer holidays. The managers have not decided on the new colour, I hear, but Mr Willet tells me that Mr Roberts, the farmer, favours a deep beetroot, Colonel Wesley 'a sensible chocolate,' and the vicar is pressing for green once again. I am doing a little subtle propaganda each time I see the vicar, and supporting his claim, as the least objectionable of the three colours.

The children spend their play-time and dinner hour in the shade of the elm trees, at the corner of the playground. The heat thrown up from our poorly-asphalted playground is unbelievable, and the two buckets of drinking water, which Mr Willet carries over from my kitchen daily, have been increased to three.

The distant clatter and hum of Mr Roberts' grass cutter

at work, is a real high summer sound, and while the children loll in their desks, fidgeting as the backs of their knees stick uncomfortably to the edge of their wooden seats, they can hear the swallows screaming as they flash by St Patrick's spire next door, and the drone of a captive bee who has blundered through the Gothic window.

The flowers have burst into bloom in this heat, and the cottage gardens blaze with irises, lilies, cornflowers and peonies. Miss Clare brought a bunch of her white jasmine to the infants' room and Jimmy Waites brought me a bouquet of roses, but it is a pity to pick these lovely things while the weather is so phenomenally hot, for they dropped in a day.

I have never seen the elder bushes so covered in flowers, and, until this year, had never realized what beautiful trees they are with their hundreds of floating white faces, all tilted at the same angle, each composed of a myriad tiny flowers, each flower having five petals star-wise, with five golden stamens projecting above and looking like a *tremblant* piece of jewellery. The bushes in this summer heat are dazzling. Their luminous quality, compounded of their massed moons against young green leaves, which Sir Alfred Munnings has caught so brilliantly in paint, has never struck me so forcibly as during this vivid spell of weather.

The road through Fairacre, which the rural district council saw fit to tar and gravel a few weeks ago much to the joy of the schoolchildren—who arrived late because 'we was helping the steam-roller man'—is now a sticky black mess, which is ruinous to shoes, and is driving all the dogs in the neighbourhood mad, as the tar squelches between their paws.

Last night, as I returned from taking Miss Clare some gooseberries, I rounded the sharp corner into the village and nearly ran down Joseph Coggs and his two little sisters, who were squatting in the middle of the road, popping tar bubbles with leisurely forefingers.

The car screeched to an abrupt stop, while I lashed the amazed trio with my tongue. Joseph was as shaken as I was, and inclined to be tearful.

'We wasn't doing no harm,' he faltered, underlip quivering.

'You wasn't doing no good either,' I retorted wrathfully, letting the hand brake go—and it wasn't until I had changed into third gear, and was cooling down slightly, that my ungrammatical echo burst fully upon me.

Amy spent Saturday afternoon and evening with me, as James had been called away on a mysterious errand connected with the firm's business, which necessitated absence from home for the whole of the week-end.

As we sat in the shade of the apple trees, topping and tailing gooseberries for bottling, Amy surprised me by asking:

'Tell me, what do you do with your time when you're not in school?'

'Why, this sort of thing!' I replied, holding up a whiskery giant, 'I have to do all the things that other women do, I suppose. I wash my clothes, and iron them, and bake cakes, and mend things, and fetch in coal and clean the windows——' I could have continued the list indefinitely, but I could see that that was not really what Amy wanted to know. How did I use my leisure, and more particularly, was I happy here, living alone—a solitary woman, exposed to the interested gaze of my village neighbours and with virtually no private life of my own? Did I ever crave for city pleasures, for crowds, for shops, for excitement? Would I like to change my way of life? Wasn't I in danger of becoming a vegetable?

I don't know whether Amy believed me when I answered truthfully, that I was completely happy; for single women living alone like me—and there are thousands of us up and down the country—are often the object of pity and speculation. Amy had voiced the unspoken queries of many married people that I knew.

Amy said sternly that with the world in the state it was, and the misery that surrounded us on every side, she was surprised to hear me say that I was happy. To which jeremiad I replied sturdily that I knew just as much about the world's miseries as she did, but still remained incorrigibly content, and that nobody would find me apologetic for being so.

'But don't you feel you ought to be more ambitious?' persisted Amy, slightly nettled. 'Do you want to do nothing better than be schoolmistress at Fairacre School?'

'It suits me,' I said equably. Amy said: 'Tchah!' which I'd always hoped to hear somebody say one day, and flicked tops and tails off with a vicious snapping of scissors. I was mildly sorry that I had riled her, but I thought over our conversation when she had departed in the glorious car, and came to the conclusion that we should never see things in the same light. For Amy is the victim of today's common malaise—too much self analysis; while I, finding myself remarkably uninteresting, am only too pleased to observe others and the natural objects around me. Thus I am spared the pangs of self-reproach, and, as my lot is cast in pleasant places, find endless cause for happiness and amusement.

One of Mr Roberts' calves strayed into the garden last night. The only damage it did was to lean heavily against a wooden post which supports a rose tree, while it scratched its back, leaving the post at a sad angle.

Mr Willet and I put it straight during play-time. I held it

nervously, while Mr Willet, perched on a kitchen chair, smote it mightily on the top with a mallet. At every massive shudder I expected either to have my hand mangled or for Mr Willet to crash through the chair seat, but luck was with us.

'There!' he said at length, surveying his handiwork from aloft. He suddenly caught sight of someone in the lane, invisible to me on my lower plane.

'Now who might that be?' he pondered, eyes screwed up against the sun.

'The vicar?' I hazarded, picking a few pinks. Mr Willet was applying all the fierce concentration of a villager confronted with a stranger.

'No. This chap's got a new panama hat on.'

'Mr Roberts?'

'No, no. I knows 'ee,' Mr Willet said testily. Silence fell. I picked a few more pinks, while Mr Willet remained rooted to the kitchen chair.

'Must be a gen'leman,' observed Mr Willet. 'Blows 'is nose on a 'andkerchief.' I found this social nicety very interesting, but did not like to pursue it further.

'He's coming this way,' continued my look-out. 'Why——' his voice fell an octave with disappointment. 'It's only that chap Mawne.' He checked suddenly, and added hastily: 'But there, I expect you'll be pleased to see him. You run along, miss. I'll put the chair back. You don't want to keep him waiting.'

Mr Mawne had called to see if I would go with him to the Caxley Orchestral Society's concert next week. He has tickets for Wednesday evening's performance, and I have offered to drive him in. The Annetts and other friends will be playing, and it should be a very pleasant evening.

Exactly twenty minutes after accepting Mr Mawne's invitation, Mrs Pringle arrived with a basket full of cleaning rags to store in her special cupboard in the lobby. She gave me an alarmingly coy smirk.

'Enjoy yourself on Wednesday,' said Mrs Pringle.

So much for Fairacre's efficient bush telegraph.

Miss Clare, Mr Willet and I were gossipping in the empty classroom after school today. Mr Willet was sitting on the old desk against the side wall.

'See this?' he said to Miss Clare. She went over and peered down at the desk, where his horny forefinger was pressed. There, carved in the ribby top were the letters A.G.W.

'Alfred George Willet,' said the owner, with pride. 'Done 'em in poetry once. Chipped away careful under my book. We was supposed to be learning some bit about Westminster Bridge with a dull soul passing by. Old Hope was a great one for poetry, wasn't he?'

Miss Clare, who is a few years older than Mr Willet, agreed. She was a pupil teacher in the same infants' room, when Mr Hope was headmaster at Fairacre. I have heard many tales of this interesting man, who used to live in the house I now occupy.

He was village schoolmaster for several years. His life was tragic, for his only child, Harriet, died at the age of twelve; his wife fell ill and he became addicted to drink. Soon after the first World War he left Fairacre and took a post in the north. He wrote verse himself, and his pupils were set inordinate amounts of poetry to learn weekly. I have often heard the older people in Fairacre tell of his powers of story-telling, and his pupils produced a play by Shakespeare annually, in the vicarage garden, no mean accomplishment in a small, unbookish village.

I should like to have known Mr Hope, that sad gifted man, whose small nervous handwriting fills so many pages in an earlier school log-book in my desk drawer. He was thought much of, but he was not beloved. As far as I can gather from latter-day comments, he was feared by many of his pupils, and looked upon as 'a crank' by their parents. One rarely hears of pity for him, which seems strange to me. I was interested to hear Miss Clare and Mr Willet exchanging memories as they surveyed the youthful Willet's handiwork of many years ago.

'Fine old temper he had,' observed Mr Willet. ' "Out in the lobby, boy," he shouted at me, when he saw this. And out I went, touched my toes and got six. You wants to try a bit more of that, miss,' he added, in a half jocular way that did not cloak his inner belief in the adequacy of Mr Hope's methods. Miss Clare shook her white head slowly.

'There was too much of it, Alfred,' she said gravely. 'You bigger boys treated that far-too-frequent caning as a huge joke. You had to—otherwise you were afraid that your companions would think you cowardly. In fact it had two bad effects. Its frequency undermined Mr Hope's authority in the end—I'm sure that was one of the reasons that took him so often to "The Beetle." And secondly, the little ones in my room were terrified of him. They heard the shoutings and the canings, and I know for a fact that they dreaded him coming into the infants' room.'

'I don't think they minded that much,' said Mr Willet. 'We was all used to a tight rein then—big and little. Remember how we used to sit on these forms, with no backs to rest against? Got spoke to pretty sharp too if we sagged a bit.'

'It was quite wrong,' said Miss Clare firmly, 'to expect children to sit as they did then; and as for folding their arms across their backs—well, I told Mr Hope flatly, that I would not train the babies to sit so. It was one of the few things I did have words about. Mostly, he was very reasonable and helped me a great deal with the preparation of lessons.'

'Never made no friends, did 'ee?' mused Mr Willet, fingering his stained moustache. 'Looked down on us working class, and tried to keep in with the gentry too much.'

'Oh come,' protested Miss Clare, 'I'm sure he didn't look down on anyone! He found his home and family, and the school-house garden and his books and poetry, filled his free time. As for the gentry, don't forget that those that he had dealings with were his school managers, and it was necessary to see quite a bit of them, as a matter of school routine. No, you're not quite fair to Mr Hope.'

Mr Willet lumbered off the desk lid that had set so many far-off things stirring, and unconsciously summed up the enigma of Mr Hope.

'Fact is, I never understood the chap. He was a fish out of water in Fairacre, and to us folk—well, he smelt a bit odd.'

Mrs Pringle collects our metal milk-tops 'for blind dogs,' as she herself asserts. Despite careful explanation on my part to the children, I am quite sure that they imagine that Mrs Pringle purchases spectacles in various sizes to fit myopic pekes or bloodhounds, as this phrase is in general use. It was while she was stuffing these tops into her shiny black bag, that she told me a little more about education in Fairacre over forty years ago.

'Not all this playing about when I was in the infants' room,' she said flatly, 'we was kept down to pot-hooks and hangers, on our slates, and then on paper, until we could do 'em absolutely perfect. Time I was six I could write a good copper-plate hand better than your top ones can these days.' Even allowing for Mrs Pringle's self-esteem, and the rosy veil which covers distant years, I could well believe this assertion. I have come across old exercise books, and 'fair copies' which have won prizes in their time, and certainly the standard of penmanship was far ahead of anything that I can get my own pupils to produce.

In arithmetic and reading too Mrs Pringle's generation, as a whole, reached a high standard, rather earlier than the present Fairacre pupils. Of course, there were the ineducable and, I suspect, several rather backward children who were dumped with the ineducables, and might have done better with more individual help which they would have had these days. Discipline was rigid, and almost all the hours of the timetable were devoted to the three R's in some form. I do not regret the somewhat lower standard of early attainment in the three R's—except for the modern *laissez faire* attitude to reading which is a personal hobby-horse of mine and on which I entered the lists against Mr Arnold recently—for there is no doubt that today's children have a much wider and better balanced grounding. Physical training, personal hygiene, school milk and meals, the medical services and better school conditions have all contributed to the wonderful improvement in their physique. The timetable embraces handwork of every description, music—both to listen to and of their own making with the percussion band and singing—educational visits and much valuable material put out by the schools broadcasting service and the mobile film units, which range the countryside.

There is no doubt that the children today are much more responsible, friendly and alert, and though their ability and dexterity in the basic three R's may not compare favourably with their parents' at, say, the age of eight years, yet I am positive that they become as proficient in the end, and have a multitude of other interests in addition.

What I do feel that the modern child lacks, when compared with the earlier generation, is concentration, and the sheer dogged grit to carry a long job through. Teaching through playing is right. It is, in fact, the only way to teach young children. But as they get older they find that any attainment needs application, and fun alone will not bring completion to a project. This is the danger-point. The older generation, resigned to hum-drum methods and a whacking here and there if there were any marked falling-off from hard work, got almost all their satisfaction from seeing the job completed and perhaps a word or two of approval as a titbit. They were geared, as it were, to low returns for much effort.

The child today, used as he is to much praise and encouragement, finds it much more difficult to keep going as his task gets progressively long. Helping children to face up to a certain amount of drudgery, cheerfully and energetically, is one of the biggest problems that teachers, in these days of ubiquitous entertainment, have to face in our schools; and the negative attitude, in so many homes, of 'How-much-money-can-I-get-for-how-little-work?' does nothing to help them in their daily battle.

I have been forced to have a day off from school—the first since I have taught here—as I have been the prey of rending toothache.

It began last night, soon after I had got to bed, and recurred every twenty minutes with awful intensity. I spent the night roaming the house, completely demoralized with pain, and quite powerless to overcome it with aspirin, oil of cloves, hot bottles or any other comforts.

It made me realize how much one's mind is at the mercy of one's physical well-being, as at times I felt quite demented. My admiration for people who withhold information under torture has increased ten-fold since this ghastly night, for I am quite certain that even the threat of such pain would be enough to make me blab out any secret, and even to make up further disclosures if I felt that these might mitigate the pain at all. Truly, a most shattering revelation.

My kind dentist in Caxley sees emergency cases at nine-thirty each morning, and having explained the position to Miss Clare, who was all sympathy and understanding, I left her in charge, drove to Caxley and presented my woebegone visage for inspection. Mr Chubb, that angel of mercy, decreed 'a little snooze, and they'll never hurt again.' Never was a patient so eager to breathe in gas, and within an hour I was back in Fairacre, minus two back teeth, and brimming with thankfulness.

Miss Clare insisted on my going to bed, brought me hot milk, and tucked me in. I am ashamed to admit that I slept like a top from eleven o'clock till four. I awoke to hear the children whooping and laughing as they ran out of school, and to hear the clock on St Patrick's spire striking. A most unusual day for a headmistress. Most assuredly, the blessing of good health, which I blithely take for granted, will be more esteemed by me in the future.

The vicar called in to bring me news of the Scripture examination which is to take place next week. This is an annual affair, under the auspices of the diocese, and usually a clergyman from a nearby village examines the children orally in the morning, and the afternoon is given as a holiday. The children usually enjoy this departure from school routine, and we have had some very interesting talks and sound teaching from most of our visiting examiners. This year, an old friend of Mr Partridge's, recently returned from Africa, and newly settled in the neighbourhood, has been selected by the board to visit Fairacre and to donate the Bishop's Bibles to the most worthy pupils here.

He also brought an invitation to tea from Mrs Partridge, so that after school, I put on one of my new frocks made by Mrs Moffat, and made my way to the vicarage.

The Gloire de Dijon rose which scrambles over the front

of the vicarage was a mass of bloom, and bumbling with bees. I remembered how much Mrs Bradley had admired it at the fête last year, and enquired after the old lady's health.

'Excellent, excellent!' said the vicar plummily, through a mouthful of rich fruit cake. 'Told me to burn my gloves! Just think of that!' He beamed delightedly at the idea. Privately, I was in complete agreement with the irascible Mrs Bradley's direction, for the vicar's aged leopard-skin gloves moult far too often on my own desk for my liking.

'I laughed,' said the vicar, repeating the process heartily, 'I just laughed! "They'll do many a winter yet," I told the dear old lady. She will have her little joke, you know.'

'She has her likes and dislikes, as we all have,' commented Mrs Partridge, filling tea-cups placidly.

'Loves and hates, I should have said, in Mrs Bradley's case,' I added. 'She is a person of strong feelings.'

'Who isn't?' said Mrs Partridge, stirring her cup lazily. 'Even the mildest person has some particular private hatreds locked up like tigers inside him.'

'Oh come, my dear,' protested the vicar, and rushing in where angels feared to tread, 'I'm quite positive that you, for instance, have no such violent passions.'

'On the contrary,' replied Mrs Partridge, with the greatest composure, 'I have two great ramping, roaring hatreds, of which, happily, you are unaware, Gerald.'

The vicar's gentle countenance clouded over, and his mouth fell slightly open. His wife surveyed him blandly.

'They are—cruelty to animals and spitting,' she announced with decision, passing the sugar basin to her astounded husband.

'My dear! Really, my dear——' stammered the poor fellow. And so flustered was he, at his wife's shocking revelation, that he put a large lump of sugar into his mouth instead of his cup, and crunched unhappily while our conversation turned to the happier subject of the pageant.

Mrs Pringle, it appears, has taken umbrage because some malicious busybody saw fit to report Arthur Coggs's comments on Mrs Pringle's probable appearance in armour. A much bowdlerized version of Arthur Coggs's remarks was to the effect that Mrs P. would resemble a so-and-so bullet-proof tank and that she would be enough to make a cat laugh. This insult Mrs Pringle retailed to Mrs Partridge, and declared herself not only a deserter from the Roman army but hinted at a possible removal from the low company of Fairacre altogether, drawing a gloomy picture of the village's future without her indispensable support.

Mrs Partridge had not batted an eyelid evidently, and had soothed the savage breast with honeyed words. Mrs Pringle had allowed herself to be persuaded against such a dire decision and returned to her cottage with honour avenged and an armful of flowers.

'I've asked her to count heads for us at the outing,' went on Mrs Partridge. 'She loves to be in charge of something, and Gerald finds counting two busloads of fidgety people almost impossible.'

'Where is it to be this year?' I asked. We have an annual church outing comprising the school children and their mothers, the choir, bellringers, and anyone else remotely connected with St Patrick's.

'Barrisford again,' said Mrs Partridge. 'It takes a lot of beating, and Bunce's always do such a good tea. Gerald says almost everyone has put Barrisford on the list in the church porch. Oh yes—and another piece of good news! Mr Mawne has asked if he can come with us! Now, isn't that nice?'

She smiled at me with a mixture of triumph and gratification which I found almost insupportable.

'Poor man!' she continued happily, 'he leads such a lonely life. So sad that he has lost his wife.'

'When did she die?' I asked. Mrs Partridge looked momentarily disconcerted.

'Well, do you know, I've never quite found out. I gathered from John Parr that Mr Mawne had been alone for several years.'

'He has a portrait of her in his rooms,' vouchsafed the vicar. 'A handsome gel.'

'Of course he never mentions her,' went on Mrs Partridge, 'but naturally he wouldn't, would he?'

' "Thoughts that do often lie too deep for tears," ' quoted the vicar sadly, and was about to add a gusty sigh, which luckily, took a wrong turning, and was transformed into a mighty sneeze, which considerably relieved the melancholy of the moment.

'Well, we must all do what we can to cheer him up,' said Mrs Partridge briskly, in her president-of-the-W.I. manner. 'I have promised him a seat by you, so that you can both enjoy a really long chat on the way to Barrisford. You do him a lot of good, you know.'

I felt quite unequal to responding to this alarming speech except in strong terms which I knew I should later regret; so I made my farewells as civilly as I could under such provocation, and returned through the golden evening to my own quiet house, debating meanwhile which was harder to bear—Mrs Pringle's roguish innuendos or Mrs Partridge's business-like and unwelcome forwarding of my affairs.

The Moffats are taking their summer holiday early this year which means that Linda has to miss a fortnight at school. The little kitten has grown into a bigger cat than my Tibby, and I offered to feed him while they were away. Mrs

Moffat was delighted, and refused to take her proper payment for a skirt she had altered for me.

'Shall I give you the key? Or shall I put it in the usual hiding place?' she asked. 'We always put it behind the oil-can in the shed.'

I decided to take the key with me, and walked home thinking of all the hiding places in Fairacre that I knew for our village keys.

Mrs Willet puts hers under the outside doormat. Mrs Pringle, who has a weighty monster which looks as though it belongs to Canterbury Cathedral, lodges hers on a beam under her front thatch. Miss Clare hangs hers by a loop of string inside her coal shed. Mrs Waites, in Tyler's Row, hides hers under a large white shell beside her front door; while slatternly Mrs Coggs next door puts hers under the old bucket that serves for a dustbin. Mrs Partridge drops hers inside the left gumboot of a pair that stand in her porch as a challenge to the weather, and my own is lodged on a jutting brick by the back door.

We all know each other's key places and it says much for Fairacre's honesty that there is remarkably little pilfering. If anyone's house were to be broken into the first cry would be: 'A stranger must've done it!'

The day of the Scripture examination dawned hot and cloudless. The children arrived looking fresh and expectant. Their mothers always take especial pains to dress them well for 'the Bishop's exam,' which they remember as an important event from their own schooldays. In many a Fairacre home the 'Bishop's Bible,' presented so many years ago, has pride of place on the front parlour table.

The boys had smoothed down their locks with wet brushes, and even Erle's crew-cut shone with some strange unguent. His normally vivid shirt had been exchanged for one of dazzling whiteness, and he presented a sober and sedate picture of American childhood. Even the Coggs family appeared to have met soap and water in a rather less perfunctory manner than was usual, and I felt sure that our visitor, even if he found our godliness a little deficient, could not find fault with our cleanliness.

At ten o'clock footsteps were heard and men's voices. Mr Partridge ushered in his friend, the Reverend James Enderby, the children leapt to their feet, and introductions were made.

Our examiner was in exact contrast to Mr Partridge, who is tall, thin and very gentle. Mr Enderby was a stocky man, short necked and red faced, and walked about the room, with impatient strides. The children watched, fascinated.

Mr Partridge made his farewells, regretting that he could not persuade his friend to stay to lunch, and assuring him that the eleven-thirty bus to Caxley would connect comfortably with the twelve-fifteen bus, which was to carry him to a ruri-decanal conference at the other end of the county.

'Now,' said Mr Enderby briskly, as the door closed behind the vicar's linen summer jacket, 'we'll put this where we can see it.' He pulled a large silver watch, with a fussy tick, from his pocket, and propped it up against the inkstand.

After a short prayer, during which I noticed many a half-shut eye peeping at this unusually business-like visitor, the children were settled in their seats, I retreated to a chair in the corner, and the Scripture examination began.

Our syllabus had included the story of Joseph in the Old Testament and John the Baptist in the New, and it was these two particular stories that Mr Enderby concentrated on.

He gave an admirably lucid and terse résumé of Joseph's history to refresh his hearers' memories, and then began more detailed questioning. It was doubtful to me if many of the children had followed his swift account clearly, for they are used to a much slower tempo, and in any case were somewhat over-awed by the visitor and becoming drowsy with the growing heat. Ernest and Eric, however, struggled nobly with the questions, and I wished that Linda Moffat had been present to answer with her quick intelligence, instead of being far away on the sunny beach at Bournemouth. Several of the younger ones slid lower in their seats and allowed the fire of questioning to go over their heads.

The door, propped open with Mr Willet's flower-pot, gave a glimpse of the summer world outside. The distant downs shimmered in a blue haze, and the air was murmurous with a myriad insects' wings. From my garden came the scent of pinks, and on the desk, hard by Mr Enderby's watch, a rose dropped fleshy petals now and again, with a little pattering. I watched Tibby swing indolently across the playground and collapse in the cool grass beneath the elm trees. A blackbird, motionless nearby, with beak half agape, watched him too, with no fear—confident that such heat killed all enmity.

Meanwhile the rapid questioning continued.

'And who was it ruled in Egypt at this time?'

There was a sluggish silence.

'Come now!' Mr Enderby glanced at his watch. 'Come along. Who ruled in Egypt?'

Patrick, in the front row, stirred uneasily.

'God?' he hazarded.

'No, no, not God,' said Mr Enderby with firm kindness. Silence fell again, and with a second glance at his timepiece, Mr Enderby was obliged to answer his question himself.

'Pharaoh. The ruler of Egypt was called Pharaoh. Who remembers that?'

As one man, Fairacre School raised sticky, and untruthful, hands.

'Good, good! Well, who remembers the name of the Egyptian man that Joseph worked for?'

Silence fell again. In the far distance a cuckoo called, and another rose-petal fluttered to join the pink shells on the desk.

'It begins with the same letter as "Pharaoh,"' urged Mr Enderby. Joseph Coggs let out a mighty yawn.

Ernest, who really was trying, said in a perplexed voice:

'Farouk, sir?' He was, very properly, ignored.

Mr Enderby's questing finger roamed around the class like a searchlight, but no one ventured any further revelation. He pounced again on poor Patrick.

'God?' said Patrick once more, with doubt, this time.

'*Potiphar*,' said Mr Enderby loudly. 'Joseph worked for *Potiphar*.' He cast me a look, more in sorrow than in anger, and started afresh with the New Testament.

The clock crept on to eleven-fifteen.

The questions were as brisk as ever, but the answers came with increasing languor. Joseph Coggs had given up all attempts at listening, and with his head pillowed on his arms, and his eyes half-shut, hummed a tuneless lullaby to himself.

Ernest was our only mainstay, supported at times by Erle who was treating the occasion with unaccustomed solemnity, like some chance sightseer who, thrusting cheerfully at a cathedral door, finds himself in the midst of choral eucharist.

'And what sort of man was John the Baptist?' enquired Mr Enderby, of this freckle-faced listener.

'I guess he kinda reckoned the people needed noos, and he was the one who brought 'em the noos,' said Erle sagely. Mr Enderby smiled his approval.

'And who was he bringing news of?' persisted Mr Enderby.

Ernest opened his mouth to speak and shut it again. Erle was now grovelling under his desk for a dropped pencil. The rest of Fairacre School would have been better off in their beds for all the interest they were taking. Poor Patrick again fell prey to that probing finger. Jerked back from some private daydream, he gave his only answer.

'God?' he repeated.

Mr Enderby curbed his exasperation laudably and said: 'In a way. Yes, in a way.' Ernest, emboldened, gave the right answer, and all was well. I felt rather sorry for Patrick. His stock answer, so safe and so often right, had not stood him in good stead this morning.

At two minutes before the half-hour Mr Enderby congratulated the children and me on a good year's work, on their alert answering and their courteous behaviour. He promised to send the Bishop's Bible to Ernest, who was pink with delight, and stammered polite thanks. Mr Enderby then hurried away to catch his bus.

'Please, miss, can I have a drink of water?' pleaded Joseph Coggs, as the footsteps died away.

His cry was taken up by a thirsty chorus. The long-awaited Scripture examination was over for another year and Fairacre School looked forward after all its exertions, to a glorious half-holiday, amidst all the country delights of a June afternoon.

JULY

Arthur Coggs has been in trouble again, and the village is having a great deal of secret enjoyment at his expense. Mr Willet was my informant, punctuating his account with so many guffaws that I found myself roaring with laughter, long before the point of the story had been told me.

It appears that Jim Waites had been missing chicken food from his store at the end of the garden at Tyler's Row, on several occasions, and he strongly suspected that Arthur Coggs helped himself, under cover of darkness, to a few handfuls of corn and bran for his own bedraggled hens, that led a miserably-confined existence in a ramshackle run next door.

Jim Waites kept the chicken food in an old air-raid shelter. In the musty darkness bicycles jostled garden tools, ropes of onions swung overhead, firewood was stacked in one corner, and other awkward objects, too cumbersome to find a home in the little cottage, here found a resting place.

The shelter had been erected at the beginning of the war by a don from Cambridge who had taken over the cottage for his wife and young family. Two things keep his memory fresh in Fairacre—the incredible speed with which he had completed this air-raid shelter, and the looks of his progeny.

'Never seed a chap rush at a job so,' Mr Rogers, at the forge, told me once. 'Skinny little bit he was too, all teeth and glasses, but his arms was like flails waving round. One minute there was an ol' 'edge there—next minute this 'ere contraption. Cor! 'E fair flung 'isself at work, that chap!'

Mrs Pringle supplied details of his family.

'Four of them under six, all as thin as scarecrows, with braces on their teeth—those as 'ad 'em—and their clothes! Them open sandals, all weathers, and skirts and jerseys you'd have thought twice about sending to the jumble. Fed on health foods they was—and no advertisement for them neither. And she was a funny lot too. Said she'd been to an Economical School up in London somewhere, and she didn't have no objection to her kids playing with the village ones.' Mrs Pringle bristled at the memory, her three chins wobbling aggressively.

'I sorted her out proper. "Perhaps our village women," I says to her haughty, "has some objection to *our* kids playing with *yours*." She didn't like that, I could see! Why, if she washed once a month it was a miracle, and then the whites was as black as a crow—and I know for a fact she never done no boiling! Shameful, she were!'

One night recently, Jim Waites had been on the look-out for his shady neighbour. He had settled himself comfortably on an upturned wheelbarrow, behind the ivy-covered privy at the end of his garden, and patiently surveyed the stars above, as he listened for any suspicious sounds. In his pocket, the heavy key of the shelter door, which he had looked out, lay against his thigh.

The regulars, including Arthur Coggs, had returned from 'The Beetle,' when, about half an hour later, Jim Waites heard some furtive rustlings among the elder bushes which now overhung the building, and the soft clanking of a pail, which, presumably, was to carry home the stolen goods. Jim heard the scrape of the door on the stone floor, and cautiously peered round the corner of the privy. A flickering torchlight hovered about inside the shelter.

Swiftly, Jim Waites ran down the three rickety steps, drew the door to, and locked it securely. The torch had been switched off hastily, and there was no sound from the dark interior. Whistling jauntily, swinging the key round and round on his finger, Jim Waites made his way to bed.

He said nothing to his pretty wife about the matter until three o'clock in the morning. She had woken him saying: 'Jim, Jim! There's someone trying to get in! Listen!'

From a distance came the sound of heavy thumping, an occasional crash and outburst of invective. Arthur Coggs was getting belligerent and having thought up a story—thin enough, but he hoped plausible—was ready to bluff his way back to everyday life.

'Go to sleep,' counselled Jim Waites. 'It's only that fool Arthur Coggs. I've left him to cool his heels in the shelter.' He told his wife the story, and although she was worried about the poor wife next door, she recognized the rough justice of her husband's action, and even began to enjoy the distant rumblings from the end of the garden.

'Serves him right,' said Mrs Waites, plumping up her pillow, 'Cathy and me took a week to glean that corn. That'll teach him a lesson.' She slept again.

Mrs Coggs next door had also heard the rumpus, and knew instantly that her husband was the cause. She had known of these illicit excursions, although no words had passed, and she wondered now what she should do. The idea that Jim Waites had purposely trapped Arthur did not occur to her. She imagined that the door had blown to, imprisoning the malefactor, and she trembled at the thought of the Waites next door being awakened, and investigating the disturbance.

Should she creep down and release him before the Waites discovered him? A proper wife wouldn't think twice about it. A distant roar, as of a caged tiger, prompted a more prudent course. Many a bruise on poor Mrs Coggs' unlovely and neglected person had been bestowed there by her husband's heavy fist, when in just such a temper as he was now. Best let him cool off, thought Mrs Coggs, with seven years of married wisdom behind her. He put himself in there, didn't he? Well then, he could get himself out! Meanwhile, she stretched herself luxuriously amidst the frowsy blankets, enjoying the unwonted pleasure of plenty of room in the bed. Time enough to face the trouble when it came, she told her uneasy conscience grimly. There would always be plenty of that as long as she was Arthur Coggs' wife. She fell into a troubled sleep.

At half-past six she rose. All was quiet, and the summer sun warmed the dilapidated thatch of the cottages in Tyler's Row. She crept down the creaking stairs, lit the primus stove to heat the kettle for tea, put a packet of cereal on the table for the children's breakfast, and was about to set off for the shelter, when she heard the kitchen door of the Waites' house slam, and Jim Waites' cheerful voice.

'I'll feed the hens for you. Got to go down!'

Mrs Coggs was torn between fear and curiosity. The latter won. Snatching up a bowl of kitchen scraps, she too hurried down the garden to feed her own chickens. Unseen by Jim Waites, who was descending the steps to the shelter, she prudently hid behind her own hen-house, where she could hear what transpired.

Jim Waites pushed back the door, and stood, key in hand, smiling at his sullen prisoner.

'Had a good night, Arthur?' he asked. A torrent of abuse greeted this mild opening. Arthur Coggs had had ample time to think up his story, and he presented it with all the righteous indignation of the born liar.

'I'll 'ave the law on you!' he blustered. 'I come round 'ere last night to see if my Leghorn had strayed in. Didn't want her eating up your corn.'

'Did you find her?' queried the unruffled Jim.

'No, I never!' said Arthur shortly, 'but her's missing. Only Leghorn I got too. Bet that ol' dog fox that's bin around has 'ad 'er.' He warmed again to his original theme, all the more annoyed because of this side issue which had distracted him.

'But you've no call to lock folks up all night—innocent folks too. What about me poor wife?'

'Glad to see the back of you for a bit, I daresay,' rejoined the other equably. The listener behind the neighbouring hen-house concurred silently. 'What did you bring that pail for? To carry your hen in?'

'If you must know,' said Arthur with cold dignity, 'I brought a bit of corn round to try and tempt her home!'

Jim Waites burst into loud laughter.

'You're the biggest liar I've ever met! Why didn't you tell me this yarn last night, when I turned the key? You was mighty quiet then! Hoping you could sneak out when I'd hopped it, eh? Found you couldn't, and worked up this rigmarole. There's not a soul in Fairacre will believe that lot of nonsense, Arthur Coggs, and you know it. Clear off home, will 'ee, and don't come in here pinching again, or *I'll* have the law on *you* next time!'

Still muttering dark threats, his tousled neighbour emerged into the sunlight, and pushed through the ragged dividing hedge, to his own cinder path.

'And take your rubbish with you,' shouted Jim Waites, who had just glimpsed his wife at the back door, and decided he must put on a more masterful display. The bucket sailed over the hedge, landing with a clatter among the squawking hens. Jim Waites saw the flutter of Mrs Coggs' crumpled skirt among the flying wings.

'Got your Leghorn there safely, Mrs Coggs?' he bellowed mischievously.

'Yes, thank you,' said Mrs Coggs timidly.

'You keep your trap shut!' growled her husband furiously, and stumped towards the kitchen door.

The Coggs entered together. The kettle had boiled over. The primus poured forth a hissing cloud of noxious paraffin vapour. Joseph Coggs stood by the table, his fist inside the cereal packet. He watched his father stamp blackly up the stairs.

'Where's dad bin?' he asked his grim-faced mother.

'Making a fool of himself,' said she, giving herself the satisfaction of raising her voice so that it could be clearly heard above. It was one of her rare moments of triumph.

The first Saturday in July was set aside for Fairacre's combined Sunday School and Choir Outing, as usual. Miss Clare was unable to come with us this year as she had promised to go with her sister to visit an old friend, who had come from Scotland to spend a few days in the neighbourhood.

The vicar fluttered round the two coaches, which were drawn up in front of the church, like a mother-hen with straying chicks. Mrs Pringle, swollen with majesty as head-counter-for-the-day, had taken up her stance at the top of the steps inside the coach, and seriously impeded the entrances and exits of the party.

'If,' she boomed heavily, the cherries on her straw hat trembling, 'you was to sit quiet and steady in your own seats, it would be an insistence to me counting.' This reproof was ignored, as squeaking children changed places, excited parents bobbed up and down to put things on the rack, and relatives and well-wishers from the other coach constantly appeared, vanished, reappeared, and generally made themselves as ubiquitous as possible. As Mrs Partridge had foreseen, when bestowing this office on Mrs Pringle, it was going to keep that lady very busy.

Mr Mawne, looking vaguely about him, was the last to appear, and Mrs Partridge led him triumphantly along our crowded coach to the empty seat beside me. The hum of noisy chattering stopped suddenly, a pregnant silence taking its place, while knowing looks and nudges were exchanged.

'There we are!' said Mrs Partridge in the comforting tone of one returning a lost baby to its mother. It says much for civilization that Mr Mawne and I were capable of greeting each other with smiles, under such provocation.

'Thirty-two!' bellowed Mrs Pringle from the front. 'Thirty-two! Right?' she poked her head out of the door to shout this to the vicar, who stood on the steps of the coach in front.

'It should be thirty-three, dear Mrs Pringle!' the vicar's pulpit-voice fluted back.

A hubbub of counting began in our coach, half the travellers standing up, and the other half begging them to sit down. The din was appalling.

'I makes it thirty-one now! said Mr Willet in a desperate tone. He looked uncomfortably spruce in his Sunday dark-blue serge, and his face shone red above a tight white collar.

'I was on the floor,' said a husky voice, and Joseph Coggs emerged from beneath a seat, wiping his filthy hands on the front of his best jersey.

'Thirty-two!' boomed Mrs Pringle again, with awful finality. I wondered if it would be engraved on her heart when she died, and if so, would it be in letters or figures? This idle fancy was interrupted by Mr Mawne saying firmly: 'You have forgotten yourself, Mrs Pringle. Thirty-two—and you make thirty-three!'

Sourly Mrs Pringle intimated that this was, in fact, the case, waved approval to the vicar, and then puffed her way down the aisle to the seat behind Mr Mawne and me. To rousing cheers the party set off to Barrisford.

Mr Mawne had an ill-assorted collection of luggage with him, for a day's outing. Three books, in an insecure strap, he put up on the rack, together with a small fishing net, and a rather messy packet, in greaseproof paper, which presumably held his lunch, and a very large green apple, obviously intended by the Almighty for baking, served with plenty of brown sugar and cream.

His magnificent camera, housed in a leather case which gleamed like a horse chestnut, he held carefully on his thin knees, occasionally whizzing the strap round and round, in an absent-minded fashion, perilously near my face.

For the first part of the journey he seemed content to gaze about him silently, but after we had stopped for coffee at a roadside café and resumed our seats, he became quite talkative. Mrs Pringle leant forward behind us, the better to hear the conversation.

'Do you go out much in the evenings?' asked Mr Mawne

politely. 'Or do you have school work—marking, and so on—to occupy you?'

I told him that I usually spent a little time on school affairs, chiefly correspondence with the local education office, ordering new stock, checking school accounts and so on, but that otherwise household matters and the garden filled up most of my time.

'And I read a lot,' I added.

'Excellent, excellent!' said he, 'but surely you find your life a little lonely at times?'

I was conscious of Mrs Pringle's heightened interest behind me. I was obliged to tell Mr Mawne, quite truthfully, that I had never felt lonely in my life.

'It seems, if I may say so, a very—er—*restricted* life, for a woman. Particularly an attractive woman.' He essayed a small bow, but was somewhat impeded by the camera. Mrs Pringle's breathing became more marked by my left ear.

'I can assure you,' I said, acknowledging the compliment with a polite smile, 'that it's a very full life. Too full at times. The days don't seem long enough.'

Mr Mawne dropped his eyes to his lap, and spoke sadly.

'I find them too long, I'm afraid. Particularly cold, long summer evenings.'

By this time Mrs Pringle's face was almost between our heads, and I could see the agitated cherries from the corner of my eye. Ignoring the pathos of poor Mr Mawne's tone, I hurled myself into an over-bright description of making jam on just such a cold, long summer evening as Mr Mawne disliked, steering erratically, and perhaps a trifle hysterically from the particular to the general, while Mrs Pringle's breathing stirred the hair on my neck.

When at last I paused for breath, Mr Mawne gave me a gentle, sad smile.

'You are very lucky,' he said slowly. 'I think, perhaps, a

man needs companionship more than a woman does.' He relapsed into dreamy silence, and we both watched the outskirts of Barrisford rushing past the windows.

Mrs Pringle released the iron grip she had held on the back of our seat, and, well content with her eavesdropping, settled her bulk back on her own cushions, and gave a gusty sigh.

To my relief and, no doubt, to Mrs Pringle's disappointment, Mr Mawne bade me a kindly farewell at Barrisford and set off, with brisk, purposeful strides, along the beach, to some far distant rocks which were awash with a lazy tide. The children rushed seawards whilst we older Fairacre folk settled ourselves on the warm sand, and screwing up our eyes against the dazzle, watched the sea-gulls swooping and crying in the vivid blue sky.

Mrs Moffat watched Linda setting off to the water, clad in a dashing yellow sun-suit of her making, then sat herself down beside me. She obviously had something of importance to say.

'Do you mind?' she began. 'I wanted to speak to you on the coach, but I didn't like to interrupt your conversation with Mr Mawne. He looked so happy.' This was all very hard to bear, I thought, and could only hope that the recording angel was ready, with pencil, to note with what fortitude and long-suffering I was enduring these mortifications.

'I wanted to thank you for sending your friend to me. She's introduced several more people from Bent, and Hilda and I are making nearly a dozen costumes for the pageant.'

I said that that was wonderful, and did Hilda—Mrs Finch-Edwards—find she could manage this work with the baby?

'She's marvellous!' said Mrs Moffat with fervour. 'She's

borrowed dozens of books about costume from the County Library, and Mrs Bond who is in charge of the organizing of the pageant is coming over to see us both next week to see how we're getting on. The costumes must be historically correct, of course. It's fascinating work.'

I asked her if Amy had been able yet to introduce them both to the film producer.

'Not yet,' she replied, 'but I believe Mrs Bond knows him well. She may tell us more when we see her.'

She rose in answer to a distant shout from her daughter, who was gazing, fascinated, at something in the surf that swirled about her ankles.

I leant back against a sunny breakwater, and dozed off.

'Our Mr Edward' at Bunce's, the famous tea shop, was elegant in a light fawn worsted suit, exquisitely cut. He bowed us to our tables in an upper room, and personally supervised the serving of delicious ham and salad, swooping round with plates ranged up his arm. Mr Mawne did not appear at tea, but we found him when we returned to the coach, busily making notes in the margin of one of his three books. It was, I saw, a book about birds. His face was bright pink with the sunshine and salt air, and he greeted me almost boisterously. I was glad to see that his spirits had revived.

Mrs Pringle bared her teeth at us in a ghastly, sickly leer as she sidled by to her place.

'Now you two will be all right,' she said, as though bestowing a blessing on a bridal pair. Mr Mawne appeared not to hear, and continued with his animated account of the purple sandpiper.

'I knew it!' he said emphatically, slapping his book gaily. 'When I heard that Barrisford was the place, I thought, "Now's my chance!" '

Mrs Pringle, catching the last few words, inclined the cherries a little nearer.

'I saw quite a dozen sandpipers—the *purple* sandpiper——' he added, peering anxiously into my face. 'There are a number of sandpipers, you know.'

I went into a pleasant trance while he rattled on. 'The purple sandpiper,' I said silently to myself, 'and the *lesser* sandpiper, and the *crested* sandpiper, and the *continental* sandpiper, and, of course, the *English speaking* sandpiper . . .'

The coach roared on, and we must have been half-way to Fairacre before he finished, triumphantly.

'And I've taken twenty-three photographs, both wading and on the wing, so I've really accomplished more than I set out to do today! I shall set this fellow Huggett to rights!' Here he slapped the book again.

'A pompous ass! We were at school together, and what he knows about the purple sandpiper could be written on a pin head!'

And with this charitable remark he settled back with the evening paper, and read, with the closest attention, a very sordid account of a young girl drug-addict who had been found murdered on one of the ugliest divans ever to find its way into the photographs of the evening press.

The Monday following an outing often brings some absentees from school, and today was no exception. The twins, Helen and Diana, were reported to have nettlerash and colds—which sound suspiciously like chicken-pox to Miss Clare and me. Several others look decidedly mopey, and Ernest, in my room, has spent most of his school day rubbing his back against the desk behind him, in order to gain relief from 'an itching sunburn, miss, done Saturday.'

Miss Clare confessed over her morning tea that it was a relief not to have the twins in her classroom.

'There they sit,' said she sadly, 'breathing away through their mouths, eyes glazed, and nothing in their heads after five terms! They still choose a penny instead of sixpence, because it's bigger—although I've put out six pennies for sixpence, and explained it time and time again.'

I sympathized with her.

'And, mark my words,' continued their far-seeing teacher, 'they'll both have anything up to six children apiece, and as dull as they are themselves! Just you wait and see!'

In the evening I drove Mrs Annett to Springbourne to see if Minnie Pringle would come daily to Beech Green school-house when Mrs Annett is confined.

'There just seems to be no one else to ask,' she said as we wound along the narrow lane from Fairacre. 'There are no nice spare women these days—no kind single aunts to step into the breach, and I've no sisters who might spare a few days.'

She looked rosy and cheerful despite it all, and trotted very nimbly up the brick path to the thatched cottage which housed Minnie, her three illegitimate children and her virago of a mother. I drove up the cart track, just off the narrow road, to wait till the business was over.

It was an oppressive evening, with a stillness that held the threat of thunder. The trees were beginning to look over-heavy and shabby, and, in the field beside the car, there spread into the hazy distance, the sullen khaki shade of July wheat.

It was so quiet that small sounds, usually unheard, were quite clear. A dead bramble leaf, swinging brown and brittle on a thread nearby, cracked dryly as it touched a twig. A pigeon rocketed over the hedge, and clapped its wings shut, with the hollow, bony snap of a closing fan.

I felt as though I had been worlds away by the time Mrs Annett returned to the car, all her arrangements as satisfactorily made as would ever be possible with such a scatter-brained creature as Minnie Pringle. We drove home together under the lowering sky, and were safely indoors before the storm broke.

A spell of fine weather, following the storm, has kept us all happy and indolent in the village. Apart from the growing frenzy of pageant preparations—the great day is only a few weeks distant—everyone agrees that it is too hot to do any gardening, or to go shopping in Caxley, or to wash the blankets, or to do the outside painting, or, in fact, to cope with any of the jobs which we have been postponing for weeks 'until we get a fine spell.'

My garden is looking lovely, and the new potatoes and peas are at their best. There is nothing I enjoy more than turning up a root of pale golden potatoes, in the warm crumbly earth, secure in the knowledge that treasure so freshly dug will mean easy skinning.

The peas have done well, and I sit on the lawn shelling them for my supper, and enjoying the scent of a freshly popped pod, packed with fat moist peas, as much as the delicious eating later.

The new teacher, who has been appointed straight from college to take up her post in the infants' room here next term, called to see us yesterday. Her name is Hilary Jackson, and she is nearly twenty-one. She seemed a conscientious, rather earnest young woman, squarish in build, with a shaggy hair-cut and horn-rimmed glasses. She was dressed in a crumpled blouse and a gathered skirt of glazed chintz, and she wore aggressively tough sandals.

I hope she settles down with us, but at the moment she is well above all our heads.

'Have you read *A Little Child's Approach to Relativity?*' she asked me. I admitted that, so far, I had not met this work.

'But you should!' she insisted, looking rather shocked. 'It's the text of the Heslop-Erchsteiner-Cod lectures, which he gave last autumn.'

'Who?' I asked, with genuine interest.

'Why, Professor Emil Gascoigne,' she replied, eyes wide behind the glasses. 'He gave the Heslop-Erchsteiner-Cod series at Minnesota—no, I'm wrong!' She stopped, appalled at her own mistake, and stared fiercely at Ernest and Patrick in the front desk, who were supposed to be pasting a geometrical pattern, but had done very little, I noticed, preferring to read one of Mrs Waites' magazines which had been spread on their desk lid to catch the paste drops.

'Could it be Minneapolis?' she asked, turning a distraught face to me.

'Or Minnehaha perhaps,' I returned, beginning to get a little tired of it all, in this heat.

'Oh no!' she assured me earnestly, 'not Minnehaha. I think you're confusing it with Longfellow.'

Suitably and deservedly crushed, I bore her off to Miss Clare's room, where her new class surveyed her, round-eyed.

Miss Clare greeted her very kindly and took her to the large cupboard in the corner to show her the number apparatus.

'But surely,' I heard Miss Jackson remark, in ringing tones, as I returned to my own class, 'those out-of-date old bead frames aren't *still* in use. Child psychologists *everywhere* have agreed for *years*, that the inch-cube is the only possible medium for basic number . . .'

I left them to it, closed the dividing door gently behind me and walked round my own desks, where the children snipped and pasted with unusual industry now that my eye was upon them.

The reason for Ernest and Patrick s paucity of work was readily apparent when I saw the page at which Mrs Waites' favourite weekly was opened. Scissors held idly in their laps, mouths open and eyes bursting from their heads, they sat engrossed—Ernest in an article headed 'How To Wean Baby,' from which no intimate details were spared, and Patrick in an outspoken dissertation on family-planning, on the opposite page.

The vicar called in, as is his custom on a Friday afternoon, and after his talk with the children, asked me if I thought that Mrs Moffat would be able to give Miss Jackson accommodation next term, as she had once done for Mrs Annett, then Miss Gray.

I knew that she was now so busy with her needlework that the chances were slight. The spare room, which had been Miss Gray's, was an enchanting mass of rich costumes, at the moment, in preparation for the pageant, but after that great day, it was doubtful if Mrs Moffat would be any less busy, for her name, as an excellent and imaginative dressmaker, was getting widely known, thanks to Amy's recommendation.

We discussed again the difficulties of obtaining suitable lodgings for young women in a village. The cottages are crowded, and often have no bathroom. The people with large houses, like the vicar, seem strangely averse to letting a room, and as most of them are elderly, it would not be easy for them or for their lodger. On the other hand, I sometimes think that perhaps this possibility never enters their heads. I have been present when the managers have met together, cudgelling their brains for somewhere to put an innocuous and respectable young woman—who would be delighted to do for herself, and quite probably be away every week-end—and have been amused to hear them suggesting that Mrs So-and-So (who has a husband, four children and no help whatsoever), might be delighted to let that little slip room of hers that looks out on to the wall of the village bakehouse; whilst large empty rooms in their own houses, inhabited by a moth or two and a stray mouse, cry out for a bit of fire and an airing.

There was no other hope but Mrs Moffat, as we both well knew, and as the vicar's kind old face began to pucker into ever-growing anxiety, I rose to the occasion and said that Miss Jackson could stay in my spare room for the time being, until she found somewhere that she really liked. It is not an ideal arrangement, but it is the only way out of the difficulty; and the vicar, breathing relief and thanks, departed a much happier man.

As we suspected, it was chicken-pox which reared its ugly head just after the outing, and nearly half the school is down with it. Dr Martin, whom I met at the school gate, said that the attack was very mild.

'As I hope it is!' I rejoined, waving a hand to a bunch of my spotty pupils, playing near the church gates. 'What's the point of excluding them from school, if their mothers let them mix with all and sundry?'

'Won't hurt them,' responded Dr Martin, with that fine careless rapture with which so many present-day doctors dismiss children's infectious diseases. He drove off hastily, before the tart remarks that trembled on my tongue had time to fall.

It was the day after this encounter that Miss Clare and Arthur Coggs crossed swords. I had driven into Caxley during the dinner hour, to drop in some forms at the Education Office. Unfortunately I had forgotten that it was market day, and the town was jammed with traffic. Cattle vans jostled farmers' cars, while my battered little Austin tried to nose along in their wake. Country ladies, indistinguishable in their market-day uniforms of grey flannel suit, white blouse, marcasite clip, dark glasses and classic grey felt hat (jay's feather at side), gave tongue to each other across the traffic, and exchanged news of their families in tones which would have filled the Albert Hall comfortably.

The children were already in school when I returned. My pox-free few were busy with a spelling game, the infants with bricks and jig-saw puzzles. Miss Clare told me of her adventure as they worked.

We had sent Joseph Coggs home again, on his arrival at school that morning, for he was obviously suffering from chicken-pox. Arthur Coggs, who had elected to have the day off work, was furious about this, and had marched him up again for afternoon school, breathing fire and threats. School was compulsory, wasn't it? he had blustered at Miss Clare, the children, half-frightened, half-thrilled gazing on. Soon complained if the kid was kept away, that there office, and now here young Joe was packed off home. There was much more to the same effect, while poor Joe drooped beside him, shaken with fever and fear.

'Have you called in Dr Martin?' asked Miss Clare.

'No, nor shall I!' retorted Arthur. 'That kid's got nothing wrong with him, but a few gnat bites.'

He also said that Joe 'ate too rich,' added Miss Clare to me.

'Ha-ha!' I commented mirthlessly.

Miss Clare had then watched the tears pour hotly down Joe's flushed cheeks, and had taken decisive action.

'The child is ill and must have medical attention,' she said firmly. 'If you refuse to call in Dr Martin, I shall do so!' And grasping Joe's hand she walked swiftly to the school-house, followed by Arthur Coggs, bellowing and gesticulating. She adjured the child to lie on the sofa, ignored Arthur's vociferous shoutings about a father's rights and what happened to kidnappers, and rang Dr Martin's house.

Luckily, he answered the telephone himself, heard the rumpus in the background, and came to the rescue within a few minutes. He had diagnosed chicken-pox, taken poor Joe's temperature, which now stood at 103°, and had told Arthur Coggs, in good round terms which had delighted and shocked Miss Clare, his opinion of him. He had now taken Arthur back to his cottage, keeping up a rapid fire of advice and threat of 'taking-it-to-the-police' under which the craven Arthur soon wilted, and was there now, seeing that a decent bed was prepared for his patient and that the parents knew what to do for him.

'Well done!' I said heartily to Miss Clare. 'I'll go over and see Joe. And then I think you'd better have a rest yourself after all that bother!'

'Nonsense!' said my assistant rebelliously. 'Stuff and nonsense! It's done me a world of good to have a battle with that wretched Arthur Coggs. And as for Dr Martin's language——!' Her old eyes sparkled at the recollection. 'It was quite wonderful! So fluent and so *really dreadful!*' Her voice was full of admiration and awe.

Within an hour Dr Martin returned, carried the now sleeping Joe wrapped in a rug, to his car, and settled him on the back seat. I had picked the finest roses I could find in my garden for Dr Martin, for I knew that roses were his first love.

'And the best one's for your button-hole,' I told him, fixing it through the car window. 'We can't thank you enough!'

'You're a good girl—despite your crotchety-old-maid ways,' retorted Dr Martin, blowing me a kiss as he drove slowly away.

'*Well!*' said an outraged boom behind me, and I turned to confront Mrs Pringle, purple with stupefaction. 'Such goings-on——!'

I concealed my mirth as best I could, and shook my head regretfully.

'I'm afraid Dr Martin is hopelessly susceptible!' I said. And assuming the air of a *femme fatale* I returned, in great good spirits, to the children.

Miss Clare's bouquet, on the last day of term, was even larger than Dr Martin's, for all the children had contributed from their gardens, and southernwood and lavender added their aromatic, spicy scent to that of the roses and carnations which formed the largest part of the massive bunch.

Joseph Coggs was not there, as he was still in the throes of chicken-pox, but Mrs Coggs had sent some madonna lilies to swell the bunch, and we recognized them as a silent tribute to her son's champion.

The schoolroom was very quiet when they had all gone. Bereft of pictures, piles of books, and flowers, it looked bare and forlorn. The floorboards sounded hollowly as I made my way to the door.

Mrs Pringle had told me that she would start 'that back-breaking scrubbing' the next day, so I locked the school door, admiring the soft, old green paint, so soon to be burnt off and replaced.

The sun scorched my back as I bent to the lock. Swinging the massive key round and round on my finger, I went to hang it up in its allotted place on the nail in the coal cellar.

Dazzled with sunshine I hummed my way back to the school-house. The swallows screamed excitedly round St Patrick's spire and seven glorious, golden weeks stretched ahead.

AUGUST

THE first few days of the holiday were gloriously hot, but the weather broke during the first week in August and steady relentless rain has covered the country. I spent ten days with an old friend at the sea—luckily during the fine spell—and returned to Fairacre to find the garden sodden, and farmers beginning to look gloomily at their corn.

'It can't keep on at this rate,' I said to Mr Roberts, when I encountered him in the lane. 'It's much too heavy to last.'

'You'd be surprised!' he rejoined grimly, surveying his farmyard, which looked more like a lake. Rain drummed steadily on the corrugated-iron roof of the barn, and pattered on my umbrella. Little rivulets, carrying twigs and leaves, coursed down each side of the lane, and the heavy sky looked as though it held plenty of rain in reserve.

'Don't suppose it'll be fit for the pageant,' said Mrs Pringle, with gloomy relish. 'Muck things up a treat, this will. 'Twouldn't be safe to have the children running about the grounds at Branscombe Castle, in this lot—the river's fair rushing through, I'm told, and there's many a life been lost by that weir there.'

The pageant overshadows everything. Nothing is safe from the marauding hands of pageant-producers and actors. We are all busy sticking gummed labels on the undersides of old pieces of furniture, which have been requisitioned for the day, and our wardrobes have been ransacked—not only for fur for our own simple Ancient Britons' costumes—but for hats, cloaks, velvet jackets, feathers, jewels, buckles and belts for the rest of the county. I quite dread Amy's visits at the moment, as I see her predatory eye ranging round my house, and even over my person, for any little titbit that might further Bent's glory on the day of the pageant.

'You can't need that great pearl ring,' she insisted, on her last foray, eyes agleam. In vain to protest that it was a bridesmaid's present years ago, and that I was much attached to it. After five minutes of Amy's browbeating, I found myself taking it off and handing it over, having to content myself with awful threats if any ill befell it.

So it goes on all over the county, and many an old friendship is cracking under the strain, I surmise.

* * *

I drove through squelching lanes to Beech Green schoolhouse yesterday to have tea with the Annetts. They are not going away this summer, as the baby is due to arrive next week.

Mr. Annett was in the throes of revising his time-table. His farming project is going well, but the difficulties in arranging other school activities are great.

'I shall have a hundred and forty next term,' he said, 'from five to fifteen—and only four teachers for the lot.'

I knew that Miss Young took the infants' class and that it involved teaching thirty-odd infants aged from five to eight. Miss Hodge had the juniors, from eight to eleven, which meant that they took the eleven-plus examination from her room. Mr Hopgood and Mr Annett took the older boys and girls, having about forty in each class. Several neighbouring schools—mine included—send their children on to Beech Green School, at the age of eleven, so that the top two classes are usually large and the children do not know each other as well as do those in the lower two classes.

'It's arranging games that is giving me a headache,' confessed Mr Annett, running his fingers through his hair. 'Miss Young can take netball with the girls on Wednesday afternoon, while I take football with the boys from the top two classes, but that means we have about forty apiece to cope with, and it's too much. It means that Miss Young has three netball games to supervise, and I have two football teams. It also means that Hopgood has to go into the junior room to free Miss Hodge who takes the infants while Miss Young's out, and frankly, Hopgood's no earthly good with young children.'

'Can't he take the football?' I suggested.

'Got a gammy leg,' said Mr Annett, running an ink-stained finger round the inside of a nice white collar. 'Can you wonder,' he went on, 'that I've had two visits from parents who are trying to get their children accepted at that new secondary modern school this side of Caxley? In theory we're offering their children the same education—but are we? Here I have forty children, from thirteen to fifteen in my class, ranging from complete duffers to bright ones. True the girls have a day at the cookery and housewifery centre once a week, and the boys have a day at carpentry. But what facilities have I got here at Beech Green to offer them, compared with the schools in Caxley?

'The parents know as well as I do that there are two, if not three, streams there, and the bright ones will get the chance to get along at their own pace, instead of being held back by the dim-wits. They will have a gymnasium, a metal-work room, a woodwork room, decent sanitation—and what's more, properly-trained specialist teachers to take them in different subjects—not a poor old hack like me who has to teach everything, in between filling in the forms and interviewing the hundred and one callers who come during the day.'

I protested that he was doing a difficult job very well.

'But that's not enough,' said he vehemently, making the tea-cups jump as he banged a bony fist on the table. 'I often think the children would be better off staying in their own small schools. Take Springbourne, that closed recently. Miss Davis's fifteen children come here now; the school-house has been sold to somebody "up-the-atomic," and I see that the school itself is for sale, advertised in this week's *Caxley Chronicle* as "a commodious building suitable for conversion."'

'But it would have cost an enormous amount to repair properly—and for fifteen children——' I began.

'But *why* for fifteen children?' argued Mr Annett. 'I know as well as you do that a one-teacher school is uneconomic, but there were two good classrooms there, and a school-house. Why not let dear old Miss Davis stay on, give her an assistant for the infants, and take some of the children who now burst our walls apart, over there to make up a worth-while little two-class school? As it is, I have ten children from Badger's End, only a stone's throw from Springbourne School, and there are a dozen council houses just finished on the other side—I expect all the children there will come driving gaily past empty little Springbourne School and squash in here with all the rest.'

Mr Annett sounded so bitter that I felt quite guilty when I remembered that three of my old pupils would be adding to the congestion at Beech Green next term. Mrs Annett tactfully changed the subject by asking me if I would like to see the baby's layette, and thankfully we climbed the stairs to happier things, leaving Mr Annett to tear himself to shreds over the injustices of present-day rural education.

Tibby has become a renowned mouse and rat catcher, doubtless an admirable trait in a country cat, but one which gives me many a pang, for rats and mice I just cannot endure, and Tibby insists on dragging home her dead trophies to display proudly before me.

There is something about rodents—possibly their long, ghastly, naked tails—which fills me with the deepest revulsion, and I am quite unable to cope with these dreadful offerings which Tibby lays at my door. Imagine, then, my horror when, on reaching down for a saucepan from the cupboard under the sink, a *live* rat bolted across the kitchen. Obviously the cat had let it escape and being unable to get it out from its retreat, had sauntered off in search of further prey. I gave a yelp and fled upstairs.

After a few minutes' shuddering I tried to decide how on earth I could get rid of the wretched thing. To touch it at all—let alone kill it—was beyond me, and I was just working out a plan whereby I would go out of the front door, open the kitchen one, and pray that it made its own way out, when I heard the oil van stop outside.

Leonard, who drives it, was one of my pupils when I first came to Fairacre. A weakly, adenoidal boy, and not over-bright, he appeared, on this occasion, to have the attributes of Apollo himself.

'Leonard!' I called in quavering tones, from the bedroom window. He looked dimly about him, at ground floor level, until I was forced to call:

'I'm upstairs, Leonard!' His gaze slowly travelled upward.

'Never saw you, miss!' he responded. 'Want anything?'

'The usual gallon,' I answered, 'and a dozen matches—not those dreadful things I had last time, but Bryant and May's.' He began to open the van doors at the back, as I screwed up my courage to ask for help.

'And Leonard——' I pleaded, 'could you possibly see to a rat that's in my kitchen? Get rid of it for me somehow?' I very nearly added, so low was my morale, that I was sorry that I had kept him in so often as a child, but a teacher's blood, even though at its lowest ebb, still trickled in my veins, and I forbore.

Leonard became positively brisk. His eye lit up and his manner became energetic.

'Got a stick?' he asked, advancing swiftly up the path.

'In the hall——' I faltered, and sat on the bed with my fingers in my ears as the first blood-curdling whacks began.

Five minutes later Leonard appeared underneath my bedroom window.

' 'E's finished!' he said with great zest, 'I've chucked him out the back—over the far ditch. Made a bit of a mess, but I've mopped up with a bit of old clorth!'

Trying not to let my horror at these words show in my face, I thanked him deeply.

'That's all right, miss. I likes a bash at a rat!' said my bloodthirsty ex-pupil. I thought wryly of the numberless talks I had given the children on kindness to animals—but who was I to criticize? He waved good-bye, climbed into the rickety van, and roared off.

Shaking, I crept down to the scene of carnage. It was all very quiet. A new tea-cloth, gruesomely stained, was draped along the sink. Shuddering, I picked it off with the fire-tongs and dropped it in the dust-bin. It seemed a small price to pay for Leonard's services.

Throughout the rest of the day I found I had a marked aversion to opening cupboards and even drawers, and I made a mental note to be less severe with the children, in future, when they fussed about wasps, gnats and so on in school.

I decided that an early bath and bed would be a good idea, having sampled a radio play, so obscure and so full of people with dreadful allegorical names like Mr Striving and Lady Haughtyblood as to drive one mad.

The kitchen is also the bathroom at the school-house. The rain-water is tipped, bucket by bucket, into an electric copper and while it heats, I spread a bath-mat, fetch the zinc bath that hangs in the back porch and pour in two buckets of cold rain-water in readiness. There are quite a few preparations to make for a rain-water bath—including skimming out a few leaves—but the result is well worth it, and the soft scented water really gets one clean.

The telephone rang as I was soaking, but I ignored it. At ten o'clock I was in bed, and at half-past ten, asleep. To my alarm, the telephone rang shrilly again, in the middle of the night—or so it seemed to my befuddled brain, as I crossly grabbed my dressing-gown, and groped downstairs.

I managed to get one arm in a sleeve on the way. The rest trailed behind.

'Hello, hello!' said an exuberant voice, 'George Annett here. Thought you'd like to know that Isobel's had a boy. Five pounds!'

I said that that was wonderful and how were they both? There was a cruel draught under the door and my feet were frozen. I attempted to put my other arm in the second sleeve behind my back, found the sleeve was inside out, and gently put the receiver down, in order to arrange myself.

'Hi!' said an alarmed voice. 'Have you rung off? What's that click? You there?'

I put my mouth down to the table and spoke with what patience I could muster with both arms behind me, and my nightclothes twisted all round, and no shoes on, at a quarter to twelve at night.

'Yes, I'm here!'

'We're so pleased about it being a boy. Isn't it amazing? We wanted a boy, you see. And five pounds! Pretty good for a first attempt, isn't it? It's got a lot of black hair—doesn't seem to grow any particular way. Can't think how we'll part it!' Mr Annett sounded concerned. With a superhuman effort I wrenched my second sleeve out, to a nasty snapping of stitches, and inserted my second arm.

'What are you going to call him?' I asked.

'Well, my father's name was Oswald——' began Mr Annett, and rattled gaily on, as I hitched my frozen feet on the chair rail out of the draught, and made fruitless efforts to wrap them in the bottom of my dressing-gown.

At last the voice slowed down. The clock stood at midnight, and pleased though I was to hear such very good news, my bed called me seductively.

'Now you must go to bed,' I said to Mr Annett. 'You must be very tired after all this excitement.'

'Funnily enough,' said the tireless fellow, 'I feel fine. I'm just going to ring one or two more friends—I've done the relatives!'

Feeling that I should drop asleep at the table if I stayed there one minute more, I promised to come and see Isobel and the baby in a day or two's time, rang off firmly, and took my icy feet to bed.

'I hope to goodness they think of something better than Oswald,' I thought to myself, as I crept into bed. 'Such a pursed-lips-and-Adam's-appley sort of name.' I racked my brain to think why I disliked it so. The only Oswald I could think of was an old friend, of whom I have always been very fond, a man of great charm and vivacity, but even this fact could not reconcile me to the name.

I heard St Patrick's clock strike two before I finally fell asleep.

On the day of the pageant, I woke to hear the rain gurgling merrily down the pipe from the gutter to the rain-water butt, by the back door. Large puddles lay in the hollows of our uneven playground, and Tibby, rushing into the kitchen, shook drops disdainfully from her paws, and mewed her complaints.

We were due to start off for Branscombe Castle at eleven sharp. The coach was to appear outside the church well before that time, and Mrs Partridge had impressed upon us the great need for punctuality.

'And bring packed lunch,' she had said at the end of our last rehearsal, 'and don't let the children have anything too rich, *please*!'

Our costumes had been packed the night before in two enormous wicker hampers, one labelled A. BRITONS and the other ROMANS. Mrs Moffat kept guard over these. Mrs Finch-Edwards was coming over later when she had settled her young daughter after lunch.

By ten o'clock the rain was getting lighter, though an unpleasantly chilly wind still blew. I could see from my bedroom window, as I was dressing, little knots of women and children converging upon the church. The coach arrived soon after.

By the time the excited mothers and children had sorted themselves out, there seemed to be remarkably little space left for the properties. The two hampers were piled, one on top of the other, at the front of the coach, but we had a collection of ungainly 'props,' including a squat pouffe, which, covered with grey crayon paper (from the school cupboard), represented a boulder on which Mrs Pringle was tc be seated by the fire. Worse still was a stuffed deer, which was to be slung on a pole and brought in by the Ancient Briton hunters. No one who has not attempted to travel in a modern coach with a stuffed deer can have any idea how much room the animal needs. We found that it was too long to be propped up on end. It was too fat to go on the rack. Its rigid legs were an insuperable obstacle, and it was only by lodging the poor thing athwart the back of one seat, with its front legs down one side and its rear ones down the other, that we got it in at all.

The younger children were scared of it—as well they might be, for its glass eyes had not been set in quite straight and it had the most horrific and malignant squint.

A strong smell of raw fish pervaded the coach as we drove the ten miles to Branscombe Castle. This came from a brown-paper bag, of which I had unhappy charge, and was given off by a pound of sprats, due to be cooked at the Ancient Britons' camp-fire. There had been a certain amount of argument as to the menu and cooking facilities of Ancient Britons.

'A big black cauldron, surely,' someone had suggested. 'Fixed on a tripod.'

Mrs Willet had offered her coal scuttle, which, she assured us, was just like a cauldron, and Caxley had had it when the Methodist witches did *Macbeth* last autumn.

Mrs Partridge said that she was positive that tripods and hanging cooking-pots came much later, and that she thought that something baked, on its own as it were, in the embers, would be the thing.

'Potatoes?' suggested Mrs Pringle.

Mrs Partridge said surely potatoes hadn't been introduced as early as that?

Mrs Pringle, taking umbrage, said she hadn't had the schooling that some had had—mentioning no names—as she had been sent out to service to bring in an honest penny to as hard-working a pair of parents as ever a girl had. She then added that her potatoes were excellent bakers and no one had ever sniffed at them before.

Mrs Partridge, who can cope with this sort of thing with one hand tied behind her, said she had no doubt that Mrs Pringle's potatoes were fine specimens, as everyone who attended Harvest Festival could testify, but that that was quite beside the point.

Rushing in where angels fear to tread, I said I thought that Raleigh had something to do with bringing potatoes back from America.

Mrs Partridge said: 'Of course, of course! And his servant thought he was on fire, when he was smoking. Or am I confusing that with Drake and singeing the King of Spain's beard?'

(Which only goes to show how competently Messrs. Sellar and Yeatman have summed up the common man's grasp of his country's island story.)

After much discussion, equally hazy and misinformed, it had been decided to settle for fish.

'*Small* fish!' said Mrs Partridge, as though someone had

been pressing for whale steaks. I had offered to be in charge of the fish-buying, and only hoped that they would smell better cooked than they did now in their raw state.

It was nearly twelve o'clock when the coach drove through the gates of Branscombe Castle, and up the long avenue of limes which leads to the castle itself. The rain had stopped, and everyone was feeling much more cheerful.

We turned out of the coach, hampers, stuffed deer, and all, and made our way to a large barn at a little distance from the house, which had been prepared for use as a dressing-room.

Long trestle-tables were placed at intervals down its length and the place was already humming with activity. Large notices had been stencilled in green and white, and these showed which part of the barn we could claim as our particular niche. Fairacre W.I. was at one end, next door to a marquee which had been erected to give extra room. In here were two pier-glasses, hand-mirrors, and two wash-stands, for final adjustments to make-up and costume.

As is usual, in affairs run by Women's Institutes the world over, everything had been methodically and painstakingly organized. Six large dustbins, bearing the stencilled word LITTER, were ranged along the length of the barn. Hooks had been screwed to beams, and coat-hangers, in generous bunches, awaited the costumes. I wandered about, still clutching the sprats, admiring these detailed preparations.

In the marquee I was taken aback by a peremptory notice over the door which said: 'PLEASE LEAVE THIS PLACE.' But whilst I was still pondering this inhospitable request, a tall woman came in, bearing another long strip of cardboard, which she pinned securely below the first.

'AS YOU WOULD WISH TO FIND IT' it read triumphantly. My faith restored, I went back to the Fairacre contingent, who were now swarming round the two wicker hampers, and greeting their costumes of old sack and moulting fur with as much affection as they would have bestowed on new hats.

Enormous tiers of seats had been erected in a semi-circle in front of the castle itself, which was to form a most impressive setting for the pageant's scenes. By midday, people were beginning to fill up the rows, prudently spreading newspapers and mackintoshes along the wet benches, before settling themselves. The car park at the rear of the castle filled rapidly and it was apparent that despite the damp weather our county pageant would be presented to a full house.

The castle is now open to the public, but the present owner, Lady Emily Burnett, lives in its sunniest corner. Now in her seventies she still takes an active part in W.I. work, and bustled about among us in great good spirits—a little rosy bundle of a woman, with very bright eyes and short, curly, white hair. She was particularly interested in Fairacre's costumes, admiring the ingenuity which had turned rabbit skins, old muffs and even hearthrugs into passable garments.

She caught Joseph Coggs by the chin, turned his face up to hers and looked silently at his dark, amazed eyes.

'Pure Murillo!' said she decisively, releasing him gently; then bustled on to the next point of interest.

The members from Bent were further down the barn and took much longer to dress in all their finery than we did. Amy and I took chairs outside to have our lunch, for by this time a watery sun had emerged, and, out of the wind, it was almost warm.

She looked magnificent in deep-blue satin and cream lace and I noticed that my pearl ring was being worn.

Amy's lunch was put up in a very dashing tartan case.

Her chicken sandwiches had the crusts trimmed off and were cut into neat triangles. There was a small blue plate and a mug to match. A tube of mustard and a small cut-glass salt-shaker were tucked into corners, and a snowy napkin lay folded over it all. Her flask was a magnificent affair of leather with a silver top, and I admired this well-appointed meal openly.

My own consisted of some Ryvita, two wrapped cheeses, a hard-boiled egg, a hearty-looking apple and a squashed piece of fruit cake, and my napkin had served to tie it all up and now acted as my plate. The salt was in a serviceable but homely screw of greaseproof paper—and I could not help feeling that the serving of my meal lacked Amy's polish.

'You might just as well have put a hunk of cheese and a raw onion in a red-spotted handkerchief,' said Amy severely. 'You're much too inclined to Let Yourself Go.' Meekly I agreed, and Amy, relenting, offered me some of her very good coffee, which I accepted with proper humility. Once I had safely downed it, I pointed out that she had a dab of mustard perilously near my pearl ring, and that Gone As I Had I still fed myself cleanly.

At this childish retort Amy and I both broke down into uncontrollable laughter, which took us back twenty years and made us feel very much better.

After lunch the fun began. As Fairacre's scene was the first on the programme, we crowded into the marquee to put on our make-up and collect our properties. The children milled about under our feet, patting the stuffed deer—now in an advanced state of moult—pulling each others' rabbit skins, jeering at each others' appearances and generally making nuisances of themselves.

Mrs Pringle, matriarchal in a piece of grey blanket and an inconsequent strip of fur which she wore as a tippet, was sitting on a chair in front of one of the mirrors, thus successfully blocking the way for anyone else who might wish to use it.

Mrs Partridge was energetically shaking talcum powder into Mrs Pringle's scanty hair, rather as a cook dredges flour over a joint.

'Just enough to give it a touch of grey,' shouted Mrs Partridge above the growing din. Mrs Pringle nodded grimly from her scented cloud.

'And have you all taken off your shoes?' shouted Mrs Partridge to the Ancient Britons, who were now twittering around the marquee in a fine state of nerves. Mrs Moffat had dragooned her self-conscious Roman cohort into a column near the tent-flap. We stood wriggling our gold-painted dishcloths into more comfortable positions and easing our cardboard bootees from our sore ankle-bones. The Roman standard had taken a beating on the way, and the eagle was apt to collapse forwards, displaying the cereal carton of which it was made, with horrid clarity. Mrs Moffat had effected hasty repairs with tape and gummed paper, but we trembled to think of the effect of a strong wind on our proud emblem.

'Nobody gets these boots off my feet until I'm settled,' announced Mrs Pringle with awful deliberation. She rose from under Mrs Partridge's ministrations and stumped heavily towards her tribe. One of the twins darted across her path as she ploughed inexorably onward. There was a squeal of pain, the child hopped round in a frenzy, and Mrs Pringle, majestic in grey blanket and tousled locks—like some fore-shortened Lear,—checked in her advance.

'Should of looked where you was going,' she said sourly. 'Good thing I'd kept me boots on, or me corns would have been done in proper.'

* * *

By two-fifteen, when the pageant was due to open, the excitement was feverish. All the stands were packed and ground sheets had been spread in front to take the overflow. A number of schools had brought coach-loads of children. They chattered like starlings and were only silenced when, with a fine rolling of drums and a fanfare of trumpets, two heralds strode on to the stage to deliver the prologue.

Fairacre W.I. was now divided into two parties. The Ancient Britons were on one side awaiting their entry, complete with paraffin-drenched sticks for the camp-fire, a few noisome sprats, and the stuffed deer, which had now split across the neck and lost one glass eye.

Nerves already strained to breaking-point had almost snapped when Mrs Willet had said idly whilst they waited: 'Wonder where that eye's got to?' and was answered by Eileen Burton who said smugly that 'one of the kids had swallowed it!'

'*Which*?' screamed a dozen frenzied mothers, converging upon their informant menacingly.

'Don't remember,' confessed the child, and was spared further recriminations by the trumpets' brazen cry which announced that Fairacre's greatest hour was upon it.

We Romans, huddled behind a hurdle on the other side of the lawn, watched our fellow-members at their primitive tasks. Mrs Pringle was an awe-inspiring sight, as, boots removed, she settled her great bulk on the groaning pouffe. Regally she made signs to Mrs Willet, unrecognizable in a moth-eaten tiger-skin from the vicarage landing, to light the fire.

This Mrs Willet knelt to do, braving the dampness to her bare knees. She vigorously rubbed two sticks and then artfully dropped a lighted match into the paraffin-soaked twigs. A blazing yellow flame shot into the air, amidst great applause, and shouts of 'What-ho! The atom bomb!' from a hilarious party of preparatory school boys sitting on the ground-sheets.

The sprats were put to sizzle, Ancient Briton mothers tended their grinning children, the stuffed deer luckily hung together long enough to be borne in by Mrs Pratt and one of the members from Springbourne, and at last came the moment when tidings were brought of the Romans' approach.

Near-panic broke out behind our hurdle, as one of our number was suddenly stricken with stage-fright. Surprisingly enough, it was staid Mrs Fowler from Tyler's Row.

'I just can't go on,' she fluttered, 'my stomach's turned right over. I'm all ashake!'

We all did our best to encourage our weaker brother, though our own knees were knocking.

'You'll be all right as soon as you're on,' one insisted.

'Put your head between your knees,' said another.

'No don't,' advised a third, 'you'll have your helmet off!'

Mrs Moffat proved herself a born leader. Advancing with our wobbly eagle, she said fiercely: 'Mrs Andrews has been waving at the other Ancient Britons for a full two minutes. We MUST go on. Come on Mrs Fowler, follow me!'

And with standard upraised she marched valiantly from behind the hurdle, while, with hearts aflutter beneath our gilded cardboard armour, we stumbled in her wake.

We Romans got through the scene very well once we had overcome our initial stage-fright, and we even jostled, in a lady-like way, for the best places near the camp-fire, which was roaring away merrily. The sprats were done to a turn by the time we arrived, and I wished I could secrete a few about my Roman garments, for Tibby's supper.

The children, who were supposed to flee with their parents at our coming, had become very interested in the schoolboys, and had to be poked sharply in the back to recall them to their actors' duties, but otherwise there was no hitch. Mrs Pringle, shuffling crab-wise and picking her barefoot way carefully over damp patches, was a sight I shall long remember.

Storms of applause greeted our bows, and we hastened off full of relief. Behind the hurdles waited a motley set of Saxons, hiding behind large cotton-wool beards and adjusting their cross-garters. They, poor dears, were as frightened as we had been ten minutes before.

'It's nothing!' we told them airily, as we swept by to the changing-room. We could afford to be blasée now.

During the interval Mrs Bond, who had organized the pageant, collected Mrs Moffat and Mrs Finch-Edwards and took them along to meet Andrew Beverley, a very famous film-producer indeed. He was a small, diffident individual, and from a distance looked far too fragile for the hurly-burly of the film world. It was only when one caught sight of his grey and glittering eyes, as compelling as those of the Ancient Mariner himself, that one realized the latent power that lay in his diminutive frame.

When he had returned to his seat the two friends, much awed, showed me the card that he had given them.

'And he's written the name of his wardrobe mistress on the back,' breathed Mrs Moffat.

'With his own pencil!' echoed Mrs Finch-Edwards, her eyes like stars. 'And we can call at his studios any time while he's shooting his new film, to see the costumes.'

'Isn't it wonderful!' whispered Mrs Moffat, sitting down heavily on the pouffe. Mrs Finch-Edwards sat beside her. Together they gazed before them at that rosy world which lay ahead. There was nothing more to say, and they sat there together in blissful silence.

I tiptoed quietly away, leaving them to their dreams.

The sun was setting behind St Patrick's spire when we arrived at Fairacre. We were all tired, but proud of our efforts. There, in the wicker hampers, lay the battered remains of our past splendour. The eagle had fallen long ago, and had been left behind in one of the litter bins at Branscombe Castle. The stuffed deer, much the worse for wear, had been used as a pillow by three children asleep on the back seat, throughout the journey.

Stiffly we clambered down from the coach, tired and dirty. Only the dabs of gilt about our persons gave any hint of the brief Roman glory that had been ours. We could scarcely believe that, at last, the pageant was behind us.

SEPTEMBER

Erle arrived on the doorstep at nine-thirty this morning, armed with a box of chocolates, a bouquet of pink carnations and a note of thanks and farewell from his parents. It was a typically American gesture of generosity and courtesy, and I was much touched.

'We're off to Southampton right now,' said Erle, when I asked him in, 'so I mustn't.' He offered me his hand solemnly.

'Well, I guess it's good-bye,' he said, pumping mine energetically up and down. He nodded his crew-cut across at the little school.

'That's the best school I've ever been teached at!' he said warmly.

I watched him run up the lane, somewhat comforted by this compliment. I shall not forget Erle. He and his classmates at Fairacre School have been living proof of Anglo-American friendship.

Mr Roberts brought me over a basket of plums this evening—the first, I suspect, of many which will find their way from generous neighbours to the school-house.

He told me that Abbot, his cowman, is leaving him at Michaelmas.

'He's got a job at the research station evidently,' said Mr Roberts. 'His brother's there already, and he's found them a house nearby. Another good man leaving the village—I don't like to see it.'

I asked him why he was going.

'Well, the hours are shorter, for one thing. Cows have to be milked, Sundays and all, and there's no knowing when a cowman may not have to spend a night up with a sick cow. It's heavy work too. I think the women have a lot to do with their menfolk leaving the land. They look upon farmwork as something inferior. If they can say: "My husband works at Garfield" instead of "at Roberts' old farm," they feel it's a step up the social ladder.'

'Will he get more money?' I asked.

'Yes, he will. But his rent will be three times what it is now—and though I says it as shouldn't—he will be lucky to find as easy a landlord.' I knew this to be true, for Mr Roberts's farm cottages are kept in good repair.

'Oh yes, his pay will go up,' said Mr Roberts somewhat

bitterly, 'but what a waste of knowledge! It's taken forty years to make that good cowman; I'd trust him with a champion, that chap—and all that's to be wasted on some soulless routine job that any ass could do. And where am I to get another? The days have gone when I could go to Caxley Michaelmas Fair and give my shilling to one of a row of good cowmen waiting to be hired—as my father did!'

I felt very sorry for Mr Roberts, as he stood, kicking morosely with his enormous boots at my doorstep, pondering this sad problem. This is only one case, among many, of old village families leaving their ancient home and going to bigger centres to find new jobs. There must be some positive answer to this drift from the country to the town. It cannot be only the promise of high wages that draws the countryman, though naturally that is the major attraction, offering as it does an easier mode of living for his wife and family.

'I picks up five pound a week for doing nothing,' boasted one elderly villager recently. Sad comment indeed, if this is true, on the outlay of public money and of his own starved mental outlook.

Perhaps, for a family man, the advantages of bigger and more modern schools for his children are an added incentive; and I thought again of Mr Annett's outburst about his own all-standard country school, which, he is clear-sighted enough to see, runs a poor second to the new secondary modern school which can offer so much more to his older children.

The new school year started today, and we have forty-three children in Fairacre School.

Miss Jackson is esconced in the infants' room with twenty children, aged from five to seven; and I have the rest, up to eleven years of age, in my class.

Among the new entrants is Robin Pratt, who created such

a dramatic stir one year, when we went on our outing to Barrisford, by suffering an accident to his eye. His sister Peggy has been promoted to my class this term, and as Robin was rather tearful on his first morning, he was allowed to sit with her until he felt capable of facing life in the infants' room, without any family support. His eye has suffered no permanent damage, and he is going to be a most attractive addition to the infants' class.

Miss Jackson has been unable to get lodgings in the village, and is with me at the moment. She is rather heavy going, and inclined to 'tell me what' in a way which I find mildly offensive. However, I put it down to youth and, perhaps, a little shyness, though the latter is not apparent in any other form. Getting her up in the morning is going to be a formidable task, I foresee, if she sleeps as heavily as she did last night. It was eight o'clock before I finally roused her, and my fifth assault upon the spare-room door.

The wet weather, which persisted through the major part of the holidays, has now—naturally enough—taken a turn for the better. The farmers look much more hopeful as they set about getting in a very damp harvest, and Mr Roberts' corn-drier hums a cheerful background drone to our schoolday.

To my middle-aged eye, the new entrants appear more babylike than ever, and my top group more juvenile than ever before; but this I find is a perennial phenomenon, and I can only put it down to advancing age on my part. For I notice too, these days, how irresponsibly young all the policemen look, and on my rare visits to Oxford or Cambridge I find myself looking anxiously about to see who is in charge of the undergraduate innocents, dodging at large among the traffic.

Yesterday evening Mr Mawne called at the school-house,

bearing yet another basket of plums. This makes the seventh plum-offering to date, and really they are becoming an embarrassment.

Miss Jackson and I were about to start our supper of ham and salad, and we invited him to join us. This he seemed delighted to do, making a substantial meal and finishing up all the cheese and bread in the house, so that we were obliged to have our breakfast eggs this morning without toast, but with Ryvita.

He told us, in some detail, about his correspondence with his friend Huggett on the subject of the purple sandpiper, and it was eleven o'clock before he made a move to return to his own home. Miss Jackson bore up very well, taking a markedly intelligent interest in all Mr Mawne's exhaustive (and to my mind, exhausting) data on birds; but I was in pretty poor shape by ten o'clock, answering mechanically 'Oh!' and 'Really?' between badly-stifled yawns. Although I am not averse to Mr Mawne, and realize that his life is—as he himself has frequently told me—a trifle lonely, yet I must confess that, to put it plainly, I find him a bore.

'What an interesting man!' enthused Miss Jackson, as I closed the front door thankfully upon him. 'He's just what you need—a really stimulating companion!'

More dead than alive, I crawled to bed.

This morning Mrs Pringle said that she hoped I'd enjoyed my evening with Mr Mawne, and it was shameful the way his underclothes wanted mending.

'I'm doing for him while his housekeeper's having her fortnight's break,' she told me. 'If ever a man needed a woman to look after him, that poor Mr Mawne does. He sits about, moping in an armchair, with me dusting round him, as you might say. And not a rag has he got to his back that doesn't need a stitch somewhere!'

I said, with some asperity, that that was no concern of

mine, and had she removed my red marking pen from the ink stand.

Ignoring this retreat to safer ground, Mrs Pringle sidled nearer, dropping her usual bellow to an even more offensive lugubrious whine.

'Ah! But there's plenty thinks as you should make it your concern. He's fair eating his heart out—and the whole village knows it, but you!'

This was the last straw. I had suffered enough, heavens knows, from hints and knowing glances lately, but now that Mrs Pringle had the temerity and impertinence to bring this into the open, I had the chance to put my side plainly.

I pointed out, with considerable hauteur, that she was doing a grave injustice to Mr Mawne and to me, that to repeat idle gossip was not only foolish, but could be scandalous, in which case I should have no hesitation in asking for my solicitor's advice and recommending Mr Mawne to do the same.

At the dread name of 'solicitor' even Mrs Pringle's complacency buckled, and seeing her unwonted abjection, I hastened to press home my attack.

'Understand this,' I said in the voice I keep for those about to be caned, 'I will have no more behind-hand tittle-tattle about this poor man and me. I count upon you to give the lie to such utter rubbish that is flying about Fairacre. Meanwhile I shall write for legal advice this evening.'

Purple-faced, but silent, Mrs Pringle positively slunk back to her copper in the lobby; whilst I, full of righteous wrath, looked out our morning hymn. *Fight the good fight* seemed as proper a choice as any, and my militant rendering so shook the ancient piano that quite a large shred of red silk fell from behind its fretwork front and landed among the viciously-pounded keys.

*   *   *

Throughout the day Mrs Pringle maintained a sullen silence and, as I expected, arrived at the school-house after tea to give in her notice. This is the eighth or ninth time she has done this and, as usual, I accepted it with the greatest enthusiasm.

'I am delighted to hear that you are giving up,' I told her truthfully. 'After this morning's disclosures, it's the best possible thing for you to do!'

Mrs Pringle bridled.

'Never been spoke to so in my life,' she boomed. 'Threatened me—that's what you done. I said to Pringle: "I've had plenty thrown in my face—but when it comes to solicitors—Well!" So you must make do without me in the future.'

I said that we should doubtless manage very well, wished her good night and returned to the sitting-room. Miss Jackson looked up with a scared expression.

'I say! What an awful row! What will you do without her?'

'Enjoy myself,' I said stoutly. 'Not that I shall get the chance. She'll turn up again in a day or two, and as there's really no one else to take the job on, we'll shake down together again I expect. It'll do her good to lose a few days' pay and to turn things over in her mind for a bit. Offensive old woman!'

Much exhilarated by this encounter I propped up on the mantelpiece the grubby scrap of paper—torn from the rent book I suspected—on which Mrs Pringle had announced her retirement, and suggested that we celebrated in a bottle of cider.

'Lovely!' said Miss Jackson, catching my high spirits and beaming through her unlovely spectacles, 'and if you like I'll make tomato omelettes for supper!'

And very good they were.

I have paid my promised visit to the Annetts to see

Malcolm (not Oswald, I am relieved to know). He is a neat, compact, little baby, who eats and sleeps well, and is giving his mother as little trouble as can be expected from someone who needs attention for twenty-two hours out of the twenty-four.

I felt greatly honoured when I was asked to be godmother and accepted this high office with much pleasure, for although I have two delightful goddaughters, this will be my only godson. The christening is fixed for the first Sunday in October and I am looking forward to a trip into Caxley to find a really attractive silver rattle and coral, worthy of such a fine boy.

'My brother Ted is to be one of the godfathers,' said Mr Annett, 'and Isobel's cousin, who is in the Merchant Navy, is the other. With any luck he may have shore leave just then. If not, I'll stand proxy.'

He rubbed his hands gleefully.

'I must say I enjoy a party,' he went on. 'We'll have a real good one for every baby we have. Will you take it as a standing invitation?'

I said indeed I would, and that I looked forward to many happy occasions. But Mrs Annett, I noticed, was not so enthusiastic.

As is customary in Fairacre at harvest time, the children at the school helped to decorate the church for Harvest Festival.

Mr Roberts sent over a generous sheaf of corn and the children had a blissful morning tying it into small bundles to decorate the ends of the pews. The floor was littered with straw and grain, and I was glad that Mrs Pringle had given in her notice and that we could make as much mess as we liked without hearing many sour comments when that lady passed through the classroom.

Miss Jackson was inclined to be scathing about our efforts

and also about the use to which we should apply the fruits of our labours.

'Straw,' she announced, 'is a most difficult medium for children to work in. Why, even the Ukrainians, who are acknowledged to be the most inspired straw-workers, reckon to serve an apprenticeship—or so our psychology teacher told us.'

One of the Coggs twins held up a fistful of ragged ears for my inspection at this point.

'Lovely!' I said, tying it securely with a piece of raffia, 'that will look very nice at the end of a pew.'

Flattered, she swaggered back to her place on the floor, collecting her second bunch with renewed zest. Miss Jackson looked scornful.

'And I don't know that it's not absolutely primitive—all this corn and fruit and stuff! Makes one think of fertility rites. I did a thesis on them for Miss Crabbe at college.'

'Harvest Festival,' I said firmly, 'is a good old Christian custom, and we here in Fairacre put our hearts into it. If you object to such practices, I don't quite know why you have accepted an appointment in a church school.' She had the grace to look abashed, and the preparations went forward without further comment, except for one dark mutter about it being a good thing that Miss Crabbe—the psychology lecturer, who seems to have exerted a disproportionate influence on my assistant—doesn't live in Fairacre; with which statement I silently concurred.

In the afternoon we all trooped over to the church, bearing our corn bundles, about two bushels of plums, six bulbous marrows and some rather dashing cape gooseberries.

The children love decorating the church and do their part very well. The boys lashed the corn to the pew ends while the girls threaded cape gooseberries through the altar rails, and put a neat little row of plums—with a marrow at regular intervals—along the foot. It all looked very formal and childlike—and none the less effective for that.

The tranquil atmosphere of the church did much to soothe our nerves, after the excitement of the morning, and we returned much refreshed in spirit, to practise *We plough the fields and scatter* ready for the great day. And so busy were Miss Jackson and I trying to wean our charges from singing: *But it is fed and wor-hor-tered* that it was time to send them home before we knew where we were.

I usually do my washing on Saturday morning and iron, if I've been lucky with the weather, just after tea. With the kitchen door propped open I have a very pleasant view of the garden. I find ironing one of the less objectionable forms of housework, for it is quiet, clean and warm, three attributes which rarely come together in other household activities.

Miss Jackson manages to get home most week-ends, which gives me time to catch up with all the little jobs which a schoolmistress has to leave until then, without bothering over much about Saturday's meals.

This week-end she relieved me of two large vegetable marrows, which, she said, her mother would welcome for jam. The spate of plums has begun to slacken, but marrows —alas!—are arriving in a steady stream at the back door. As Miss Jackson and I can only cope with about half a marrow between us in a week, I can see that I shall have to start digging, under cover of darkness, and inter the unwieldy monsters. To give them away again, in Fairacre itself, might cause the greatest offence, and in any case, every garden seems to boast a fertile heap swarming with flourishing marrows. Oddly enough, the majority of people who grow them in Fairacre say, as they hand them over: 'Funny thing! I don't care for them myself. In fact, none of the family likes them!' But still they plant them. It must be the fascination of seeing such a wonderful return for one small seed, that keeps marrow-growers at their dubious task.

As I ironed, I amused myself by watching a starling at the edge of the garden bed. He was busy detaching the petals from an anemone, conscious that I was watching, and half-afraid, but persisting in his destruction. His iridescent feathers, as smooth and sleek as if oil had been stroked over them, gleamed like chain-mail in the level rays of the sinking sun. Having finished with the anemone, he began to run, squawking, about the lawn, his feet thrown rather high and forward, which gave him a droll, clown-like air. In time, others joined him, and I realized that they had found the remains of Tibby's cornflakes which I had thrown out. Chattering, quarrelling and complaining, they threw themselves energetically into this job of self-nourishment. As suddenly as they had arrived, they checked, and then whirred away over the house.

This short scene, I thought as I pressed handkerchiefs, is typical of the richness that surrounds the country dweller and which contributes to his well-being. As he works, he sees about him other ways of life being pursued at their own tempo—not only animal life, but that of crops and trees, of flowers and insects—all set within the greater cycle of the four seasons. It has a therapeutic value, this awareness of the myriad forms and varied pace of other lives. Man, particularly the town dweller, scurrying to catch up with what he considers the important jobs, which none but he can do, presses himself onward at a crueller pace daily. He scuttles from stone and steel office to arid tube-station. If he sees a blade of grass, prising its way between the paving stones, it only registers itself to his overwrought brain as something which should be reported to the corporation. Small wonder that sleeping pills lie within reach of so many tousled beds, when man has lost sight of the elementary fact that he must go at his own pace, or face the consequences.

Two other benisons are more generously bestowed in the country—solitude and handling earth. Not to be alone—ever—is one of my ideas of hell, and a day when I have had no solitude at all in which 'to catch up with myself' I find mentally, physically and spiritually exhausting.

When one is alone one is receptive—a ready vessel for the sights, the scents and sounds which pour in through relaxed and animated senses to refresh the inner man.

As for the healing that lies in the garden, let Mr Willet's wise words be heard. 'Proper twizzled up, I was after that row at the Parish Council. I went and earthed up my celery, on my own. That sorted me out a treat!'

While Mrs Pringle has been preserving a dignified silence at her cottage for the past week, Minnie Pringle has called in after school, 'to give us a lick-round,' as she so truly says.

It is convenient for her at the moment, as she spends most of the day at Mrs Annett's, leaves there at half-past three, and arrives here at about ten to four ready for her labours. She then cycles on to Springbourne.

We finish our last lesson of the day, and sing our grace, to the accompaniment of Minnie's clatterings in the lobby as she washes up the dinner things. In theory, Miss Jackson, whose room leads into the kitchen-lobby, switches on the copper at three fifteen, but for three days it slipped her mind and Minnie arrived to find a copper full of cold rain-water, in which swam half a dozen hardy earwigs.

'Good thing you never switched on,' was her comment. 'Think of they poor little dears being boiled alive like lobsters!'

Miss Jackson, when I reminded her about the copper, said that her mind was so engaged with the Harvest project in her classroom and in making out a case-history for each child (which she was amazed to find had never been done in Fairacre—despite the strong recommendations of the Perth-Pullinger investigating committee as long ago as 1952), that she very much doubted if she could wrench it from the sort of work for which she imagined she had been trained, in order to deal with a domestic trifle of such a lowly nature.

I said that in that case I would give Ernest the job of walking through her room at three-fifteen each afternoon, and she must put up with the interruption. Various biting retorts, which rose to my lips, I forbore to utter, which made me feel unwontedly virtuous.

We have dusted our own classrooms each morning, and things have gone very smoothly, but with the colder weather coming I can see that we shall have to accept Mrs Pringle's return. Minnie finishes at Mrs Annett's in a week's time, and the tortoise stoves, which have so far remained unlit, will soon be roaring away.

Meanwhile, fired by the accounts from Miss Jackson of the excellent preserve which her mother concocted from the two marrows and at my wits' end to know just what to do with yet another monster which had appeared on the back doorstep, I decided to turn it into marrow jam.

I collected a most delectable mass of ingredients on the kitchen table; lemons, ground ginger, sugar and a small screw of greaseproof paper, which Minnie Pringle had brought from the chemist in Caxley, containing knobbly pale lumps of root ginger.

'It says: "Bruise the ginger," ' I remarked to Miss Jackson, who was busy filling up the copper for her bath. We pored over the recipe together. 'How did your mother do that?'

'Just banged it, I think,' said she vaguely, 'with a rolling-pin, or something.'

I carried my screw of greaseproof paper out on to the

back step. There was a cold wind blowing, and I anchored the ginger with a large flint while I found a hammer.

I was busily pounding at my little parcel when Mr Willet arrived, bearing a brown-paper carrier-bag.

'Don't like the way the wind's turned east,' he said, blowing on his fingers. 'Fair shrammed I am, I can tell 'ee. Vicar said would I tell you he won't be able to get over this Friday after all. Got a funeral over at Springbourne.'

I said was it anyone we knew?

'Oh no, no one what matters,' said Mr Willet airily. 'Some old boy from London what only lived there two or three months. Just come to die, so to speak.' He peered down at my little parcel and the large hammer.

'And what are you up to?'

'I'm bruising ginger,' I replied. Busily I unwrapped the folds of greaseproof paper and displayed the flattened contents. I looked at them anxiously.

'Would you say I'd bruised that?' I enquired. Mr Willet broke into a guffaw.

'Bruised it? You've dam' well pulverized it!' He laughed until he had to lean against the wall for support, while I collected the squashed remains carefully together, out of the wind's harm.

'Ah well!' he said, recovering at last. 'I'll get back to my supper. Steak and kidney pudden my old woman's had on the hob all day—with a dozen button mushrooms inside it. Proper sharp-set I be—I'll do justice to that!'

I wished him good-bye and accompanied him to the corner of the house.

'Oh!' I said, looking back. 'You've left your carrier-bag.'

'That's all right,' replied Mr Willet cheerfully. 'It is for you. A marrow!'

This morning, with the wind still in the east, I decided

that the school stoves ought to be lit. In theory, they are supposed to wait until October 1, but with the vagaries of the British climate we could often do with them in June. Mr Willet has chopped a neat stack of kindling wood, ready for the cold weather, and the coke pile in the playground looms over all.

'I'll light these 'ere for you each morning,' volunteered Mr Willet, 'until her ladyship turns up again. Fancy it won't be long now. Heard her telling my old woman yesterday that it was hard times for the unemployed and she wouldn't be going to the Whist Drive this week. It's a Fur and Feather too—so she must be hard pressed to miss that!'

Sure enough, in the evening, I found Mrs Pringle at my front door, her face set in a series of down-turned arcs, which made her look like a disgruntled tortoise.

'Come in,' I said politely, and settled her in the armchair by the fire. She looked at the flames with disgust.

'Fancy having a fire as early as this!' was her comment. 'Some has money to burn, seemingly!' I let this charitable remark go by, and asked if there was anything I could do for her.

'I've made up my mind to come back,' announced Mrs Pringle majestically. I was on the point of answering that no one wanted her back, but prudence restrained me. After all, Minnie would be leaving on Friday, and the school must have a cleaner. And funnily enough, though the wicked old woman before me drove me quite mad at times with her sulks and her downright rudeness—yet somehow, I had a soft spot for her. It had cost her something, I could see, to pocket her pride this evening and offer to come again—even if it were to suit herself in the long run. For never before had our 'little upsets,' as the Vicar calls them, had quite such personal point as this one, and never before had I been quite so fierce with her.

'Minnie will be here until Friday,' I pointed out. 'She came to help us over a difficult patch, so I can't turn her away immediately.'

'Suits me,' said she, rising with some difficulty from the depths of the chair. 'I'll be along Monday.' I noticed, with some amusement, that there was no word of apology. What was past was now past, I supposed.

She hung her black shiny shopping bag, from which she is never parted, over her arm, and stumped towards the door.

On the doorstep she turned. Her face was grimmer than ever.

'I see them chimneys smoking today,' she said, jerking her head towards the school. 'I don't let no one else meddle with my stoves—even if they has been lit days before the Office gives the word. We'll be needing a new tin of black-lead, and a new blacklead brush. Mine's worn right down to the board. I'll bring 'em with me Monday—and the bill.'

She fished inside the black bag, withdrew a paper one and pressed it upon me. Before I could find words, she had trudged off to the gate.

'See you Monday!' she boomed threateningly, and vanished round the bend of the lane.

When I opened the paper bag I found six brown eggs, double-yokers to a man, and with the bloom of that day's laying on them.

It was Mrs Pringle's peace-offering and silent apology.

Michaelmas Fair at Caxley, is an enormous affair, held in the market-place, where it causes the greatest disturbance possible and utter confusion to normal traffic conditions. The inhabitants of Caxley and the surrounding countryside curse roundly about the noise and the congestion, but look forward to its advent as soon as the dahlias are out, and would be the first to fight, with jealous pride, if anything were done to stop its coming.

'Livens things up a bit!' remarked the girl in Budd's knitwear department to me, as I chose a twin-set. She stood by the window gazing bright-eyed at the swarthy men who were erecting helter-skelters and swing-boats. Customers reckon to take second place in the shops overlooking the fair-ground, and no one would be so pernickety as to complain about inattention from the staff. We all face the simple fact that if you want whole-hearted and devoted service in the choice of purchases, then to choose to shop in Fair Week is asking for trouble.

The children have talked of nothing else, and the infants' room which is the scene of Miss Jackson's fair-ground project is a jumble of stalls with trays of plasticine toffee-apples, candy-floss made of dyed cotton-wool, and a table laid out with a model fair with roundabouts, switch-backs and all, contrived from cardboard and paper. It is the joy of the whole school; and my class have to be routed out from there at playtimes, as they stand entranced—and full of suggestions for further delights—forgetting to drink their milk, eat their elevenses, call at the lavatory, find their handkerchiefs and generally do all the things that very properly should be done at play-time.

It was their delight in this project that first gave me the idea of taking a party of children to the Michaelmas Fair this year.

'Most of them will go with their parents or with "Caxley aunties," ' I told Miss Jackson, as we sipped our tea in the school-house, 'and I don't think we can take the real babies—those who have just entered—it's too big a responsibility. But would you be willing to help me with those that are left? Probably eight or ten of them?'

Miss Jackson was most enthusiastic. We decided that we would discreetly make a list of all those definitely going, and then see how many were left. If the parents in the village knew of our scheme we guessed that they would cheerfully let us take the lot, and that was rather more than we could face.

'Miss Clare will give us a hand I know,' I said, 'and perhaps Mrs Partridge. It seems a pity for the children to miss it, especially as you've fired them so with your project. It's been most successful.'

Miss Jackson said that she felt it had eased many nervous tensions in the less well-co-ordinated members of her class, and she welcomed the idea of the visit to Caxley. She would take a note-book, she said, so that she could make up the case-histories after the event, as it would give her an excellent opportunity of observing the children's individual emotional reaction to the stimulus of strong colour, noise and movement.

'I can tell you that,' I said. 'They just shout. Or are sick.'

About six o'clock on the great day, almost the whole of Fairacre School stood outside St Patrick's. Although only twelve were coming with Mrs Partridge, Miss Jackson and me, the rest had come along to see us safely on the 6.10 bus. The din was terrific.

Our charges included Linda Moffat whose mother had a heavy cold and was unable to take her, and Joseph Coggs. They were all unbelievably clean and neat, with faces as shiny as apples.

Joseph had on his best jersey, and Linda was most suitably dressed for the fair in a chic ensemble of dark-green tartan dungarees and a thick red sweater.

'I don't usually wear trousers to an evening outing,' she

assured me, 'but mum thought they'd be better than a skirt on the roundabouts.' Her ideas on the sartorial fitness of things is already strongly advanced.

We waved good-bye to our well-wishers from the bus, and then settled down to a rousing journey to Caxley. Miss Clare was waiting outside her gate, just before the road bends to Beech Green. She looked very neat and trim in her navy-blue coat and sensible felt hat. Not one of her white hairs was out of place, and I knew that, however tousled the rest of us would look after an hour or two at the Michaelmas Fair, Miss Clare would be as tidy as when she boarded the bus.

She was greeted with the greatest affection by the children, who all besought her to let them sit by her, and she made the journey into Caxley with one on her lap and two other lucky ones squeezed beside her on the seat.

The evening was a great success. The Fairacre party wandered enchanted among the blaze of electric lights, the pounding engines and the coils of oily cable that snaked across the market square.

Pink and white candy floss vanished like magic. One minute a child would be waving a billowing cloud of it on a stick, and the next he would be licking the stick itself with fervour.

Joseph Coggs spent most of his time at the helter-skelter plodding patiently up the narrow stairs with his mat to reappear again, feet first, at the bottom of the corkscrew chute. His hair was on end, his hands black and his face transformed with bliss.

The other children seemed to prefer the games of chance, rolling pennies down grooved slopes and trying to manoeuvre horses into loose boxes, ducks into ponds and the like. The prizes, in many cases, were goldfish, and Eileen

Burton was the envy of all when she walked away with two, thrashing madly, in a jam jar.

Mrs Partridge and I enjoyed the roundabouts and switchbacks, and had quite a job to get the children to join us.

Mrs Partridge showed herself a most intrepid rider, electing to sit on the outside of the fastest roundabout, and at one stage sitting side-saddle in the most dashing and insouciant style.

Miss Clare preferred the swing-boats. From my perch on a mad-looking horse with enraged nostrils, I could see her blissfully floating up and down pulling gently on her furry caterpillar of a rope, whilst Linda Moffat hauled more energetically on the other. They were both, I noticed, as immaculate as when they started out, which could not be said about the rest of the party. My own skirt was inelegantly twisted round the ribs of my uncomfortable steed, my shoes had been stood on, and I could feel a ladder, of alarming magnitude, creeping steadily down one leg.

We caught the last bus back to Fairacre, arriving at half-past nine, gloriously dirty and tired. Even Miss Jackson looked young and happy, and had a prodigious mass of notes which she looked forward to incorporating into the case-histories.

The next morning the usual mob of admirers stood round the fair-ground model in her room, discussing the excitement of the night before.

'And that candy-floss,' said one with rapture, 'Coo! Didn't half taste good!'

'But this 'ere,' said another indicating the dyed and dusty cotton-wool substitute before him, '*looks* more like it!'

Could loyalty go further?

OCTOBER

'ADJER!'

'Adjerback!' came floating through the window from the playground this morning. These cryptic sounds, suggesting some exotic mid-European dialect, are readily construed by the initiated into 'Had you!' and 'Had you back!' and are a sure indication that autumn is really upon us and that the weather is cold enough for a brisk game of 'He' before school begins.

Mrs Pringle, austerely reserved in her conversation at the moment, is back in full force. The stoves gleam like black satin, the kitchen copper steams cheerfully and such dirge-like hymns as *Oft in danger, oft in woe*, mooed in Mrs Pringle's lugubrious contralto, once again sound among the pitch-pine rafters.

Mr Mawne's name has not passed her lips, but the vicar told me that he is in Ireland with friends, for a short holiday.

'Do you know that he is thinking of buying a small house, somewhere in the neighbourhood?' added the vicar. He has resurrected the leopard-skin gloves now that the weather is cooler, and he beat them gently together, filling the air with floating pieces of fur which Patrick and Ernest caught surreptitiously as they fluttered near the front desk.

I said that I had not heard the news.

'A good sign, I think,' went on the vicar. 'It looks as though he intends to settle here. That place of Parr's is all very well in its way, but really only suitable for a bachelor.' He looked at me speculatively.

I was about to ask if Mr Mawne proposed to change his status, but thought better of it.

'Not that I can see him as a family man,' mused the vicar, half to himself. 'Not a *large* family man, anyway!' He pondered for a moment, and then shook himself together.

'But a wonderful head for the church accounts,' he finished triumphantly. 'I do so hope he stays!'

Amy spent the evening with me and was unusually preoccupied.

It was a cold, blustery evening. The rose outside the window scrabbled at the pane. Every now and again a particularly fierce gust shuddered the door in its frame; and the roaring in the elm trees at the corner of the playground compelled us to raise our voices as we talked.

Amy surprised me by saying that she hoped I realized how lucky I was in being a single woman. As Amy's usual cry is: 'How much better you would be if only you were married,' I was a little taken aback by this *volte-face*. Before I could get my breath, she said that she had been thinking a lot about the married state recently, as a friend of hers was having some trouble.

It appeared, said Amy, that her husband was much attracted to a young woman in his office, that his wife knew of it, but could not make up her mind if it would be wiser to ignore the whole thing—despite her great unhappiness—or if it would be better to tax the man with it.

At this point Amy put her knitting in her lap, with such a despairing gesture, that I was glad the twilight veiled both our faces. There was nothing that I could say to help, and after a few minutes' silence, Amy continued.

It wasn't as if her friend were a young woman, she pointed out. Twenty years ago she would have been able to snap her fingers in the man's face, go out and earn her living, and have thought herself glad to be shot of such a wastrel. But now it wasn't so simple. She was older, was not so keen on, or so capable of making a good living on her own. And in any case, he was *her* husband, after all, and she was fond of him, they were accustomed to each other, and her friend could easily forgive, if not forget, these little peccadilloes.

Amy's voice faltered slightly towards the end of this narrative, and she rummaged in her sleeve for her handkerchief. For what it was worth I gave my spinsterish advice.

'If I were your friend,' I began cautiously, 'I should say nothing. It's bound to blow over, and there's no point in breaking up twenty years of comfortable married life for a week or two's nonsense. "Least said soonest mended" I should think.'

'My feelings entirely,' said Amy, blowing her nose briskly. She stuffed her handkerchief away, and talked of some new rose bushes that she had just ordered, and her plans for their arrangement.

So we passed the evening, and I was careful not to put the light on until Amy had completely regained her composure.

At half-past nine she rose to go and I accompanied her to the gorgeous car, by the hedge. The wind still roared, and the trees groaned, as they were wrenched this way and that. Round our feet the dead leaves scurried in whispering eddies.

To my surprise Amy gave me a sudden and most unexpected kiss, then entered her car.

'Lucky old maid!' she said, but I was relieved to hear the laughter in her voice. And with a final toot, she drove away.

The storm raged for hours, and to sleep right through the night was, even for me, quite impossible.

A terrific crack woke me soon after two o'clock and I lay wondering if I could be bothered to get up and investigate. By the time I had persuaded myself that it might only be the chest of drawers giving one of its occasional gun-like reports, it was almost three o'clock, and by that time I was ravenous.

I wished I were as provident as Miss Clare, who kept by her bedside a tin of biscuits, and a smaller one of peppermints, for just such an occasion as this. Downstairs I knew were such delicacies as fruit cake, apples, cream cheese, eggs and a hundred and one delights—but that would mean getting out of my warm bed. I had fought for an hour, I told myself, I could fight again. Doubling my fist, I lay on it and wooed slumber, trying to ignore the clamours of my hunger.

By a quarter to four I had mentally cooked myself scrambled eggs on toast, bacon and tomato, grilled chop and Welsh rarebit. I had also opened a tin of peaches, mandarin oranges, Bartlett pears and some particularly luscious pineapple rings, all of which floated round my bed in the most tantalizing fashion.

At ten to four I rose, cursing, thrust my feet into slippers, descended to the kitchen, frightening poor Tibby out of her wits, collected a most unladylike hunk of fruit cake and took it back to bed—furious with myself for not doing the whole thing hours before. I was asleep in ten minutes.

This morning I discovered the source of the crack which woke me. A branch of one of the elms had split from the trunk, and lay, amidst a mass of twigs, leaves and part of the roof of the boys' lavatory, across the playground. Two tiles had slipped from my own roof, and lay askew in the guttering.

The garden was wrecked. Michaelmas daisies lay flattened, and the rose had been torn from the wall. It waved long skinny arms across the doorway.

Mrs Pringle surveyed the untidy playground sourly, as if such confusion were a personal affront.

'And only swep' up two days ago!' was her comment, 'Mr Willet'll have something to say to that!'

Her reactions to the soot which had been blown down the flues and covered the stoves and the surrounding floor, were even more violent.

'As if ash wasn't bad enough, and bits of coke scattered all round by them as should know better—mentioning no names—without this filth!' Her leg, presumably, burst into flame at this point, for she hobbled, with many a sharply-indrawn breath, to fetch the dustpan and brush.

The children were joyously garrulous about the gale's damage when they arrived.

'A great old 'ole up Mr Roberts' rick!' reported one gleefully.

'My dad says there's a tree right across the Caxley road, and half the Beech Green kids can't get to school,' said another, with the greatest satisfaction.

'My auntie's next-door neighbour's baby had a slate fall on its pram!' announced a third, 'and if it hadn't been sitting up, and a bit too far from the porch, and the wind had been stronger, it might have been in hospital!'

Altogether we had a pleasurably dramatic morning, for there is nothing like the sharing of common danger, with the added spice of others' misfortunes, to give one a sense of cosiness, and, in a village, these excitements provided by nature, give us the same stimulus as 'This Week's Sensational Programme' for our town cousins at their local cinemas.

Furthermore they stir old memories, for the countryman's recollections go back a long way. Reading little, they remember the tales passed down from father to son, tales which lose little in the telling. Mr Willet had a wonderful story to add to the general excitement today.

'It happened in the seventies,' said Mr Willet, who had come in to the classroom to borrow a boy to steady the ladder while he effected repairs to the lavatory roof. The children quietly put their pens in the grooves of their desks. I turned my history book face downward, and we all prepared to listen. Mr Willet, when wound up, goes on for a long, long time—and anyway still, in the country, thank God, there is always tomorrow.

'My old dad remembers it well. He was doing a job for old Sir Edmund up the Hall, and Mrs Pringle's old dad was up there too, doing a bit of carpentering in the back parts.' He stopped suddenly and looked round, puffing out his stained moustache.

'Here! You say if I'm interrupting. Don't want to stop the work, you know!'

I assured him that we were all keen to know the rest of

the story. The children, seeing that their eavesdropping had been legalized, relaxed somewhat and flopped forward comfortably on to their desks. Mr Willet resumed.

'Well, it was about this time of year—soon after Michaelmas Fair, because Sir Edmund had got several new hands just come to work for him, and this 'ere old gale blew up. Did it blow?' Mr Willet swivelled his eyes quite awfully, and we all shivered.

'The gals—the maids that was—fair screeched, and run about like a lot of chickens with their necks half-wrung. The cook got burnt with some sparks what blew out of the fire and give up doing the dinner, and there was a proper panic. Some of the chaps, with my dad, was sheltering in a bit of an old outhouse where they kept the firing and that, when all of a sudden——!' Here Mr Willet, with a proper sense of drama, paused and lifted his gnarled fingers. The children's eyes grew rounder, and the suspense was almost unbearable.

'All of a sudden——' repeated Mr Willet, with relish, 'there was a groanin' and tearin' and crashin' you could 'ear as far away as Springbourne. A 'orrible roarin' sort of commotion, and then the biggest crash of all! One of Sir Edmund's big old lime trees fell across the glass house! Coo—that were a crash! And after the crash my dad said you could 'ear the tinkle-tinkle of bits of glass as they fell on the tiles in the greenhouse floor. Poor old Jeff Rudge what looked after the stuff in there, he was crying, my dad said; and when they could fight their way through the wind to go and see the damage, he said there was tomatoes and cucumbers all hanging up with splinters of glass sticking out of 'em like a lot of hedgehogs!'

'And this Jeff,' he finished triumphantly, 'he put his hands up over his face, and swayed about and cried 'orrid!' Here Mr Willet did the same, much to the consternation of the children.

'And he kep' on saying, "I can't bear no more! I can't bear no more!" Poor chap——' commented Mr Willet compassionately, lowering his hands and speaking in his normal voice again. 'And old Sir Edmund had him in the kitchen and give him some of his own brandy to get him round again! Ah! That was a gale and no mistake!'

He stood silent for a few moments, his old eyes looking out across the heads of the children, as though he could see those cucumbers and tomatoes bristling with glinting glass, and the sorrow of the man who had tended them. The children watched him solemnly.

'Ah well!' he said, returning to this century with a jerk. 'I'd best choose a good stout boy for the ladder!'

At once, the children pulled themselves upright, and with chests outflung and breath held to bursting point, tried to look as stout and trustworthy as they knew Mr Willet would expect them to be, if they wanted to escape from the dull classroom to the joys of the playground and remain in his august company.

Eric was chosen and, grinning joyfully, followed Mr Willet through the door. Deflated, the rest sighed sadly and returned to their books.

Since the gale the weather has turned soft and warm. Mr Willet tells me it is Saint Luke's little summer, and very welcome it is.

Miss Jackson and I decided to take the whole school out for a nature walk, to enjoy it all. We made for the little lane that turns off by the 'Beetle and Wedge' and rises steadily until it peters out high up on the windy Downs.

The children dallied in the lane, scrambling up the high banks to collect the hazel nuts which flourish there.

'Gi'e us a bunk up!' rang the cry, and one would obligingly put his shoulder down and hoist his friend higher in the hedge. We meandered along eating nuts and blackberries and even sloes and damsons which grow thickly, powdered with a blue bloom, among their spikes.

We found a patch of dry grass half-way up the slope, sheltered by a clump of stunted thorn bushes, and here we sat to rest. The view of Fairacre below us was clear in the limpid October air. There is a unique atmosphere about a fine October day. The sky is a burning blue, which combined with the golden and auburn glow of the trees creates a sparkle and glory unseen at other more-vaunted periods of the year.

From this distance the yellow elm trees by the school looked like the chubby pieces of cauliflower that one spears from piccalilli; and in the field beyond we could see Samson, Mr Roberts' house cow, placidly grazing.

Blue smoke plumes waved from cottage chimneys, and Joseph Coggs was delighted to see his mother pegging washing on her line, far below. Some of the fields were still bright with stubble, but most of them had already been ploughed, and lay, clean and brown, awaiting next year's crops.

We spent a long time there, gazing and speculating, drinking in great draughts of the scented air. I was brought to earth by a vicious blow across the back.

Startled, I turned to see Ernest grinding something fiercely into the grass.

'A dummle wasp!' he explained. 'Crawling up you, miss. They always stings worse if they're sleepy. Ah well! He've had it now!'

I thanked him, and called to the children that we must return. They came reluctantly, bearing all sorts of treasures with them. Rose hips, feathers and toadstools were among their souvenirs, but Eric was struggling along with a colossal knobbly flint, whose weight threatened to age him considerably.

When I remonstrated with him he turned an accusing eye upon me.

'It's a meatright!' he told me. 'Saw one just like it on the telly!' And shouldering his burden he bore it painfully back to Fairacre School.

Malcolm Annett's christening party was a great occasion. The sun shone through St Patrick's windows, catching the gleaming brass on the altar and the tawny chrysanthemums which Mrs Partridge had arranged.

Mrs Moffat had made the christening gown—a miracle of tiny stroked gathers and finely-pleated tucks, with a froth of old lace at the hem. Apart from making a few popping sounds as he withdrew a wet thumb from his mouth, the baby behaved with the greatest decorum, even suffering his pink forehead to be doused with water, from a silver scallop, in quite large quantities.

Ted, Mr Annett's brother, was resplendent in his best grey suit and the other godfather was in uniform. They spoke their responses in manly tones, undertaking to renounce the works of the devil on behalf of the infant I held, as I as godmother did too. It was hard to believe that the angelic bundle was 'conceived and born in sin,' I thought privately, watching a Red Admiral butterfly hovering in the church porch, as the vicar's beautiful voice fluted benignly on.

Mrs Pringle had come to the service with her cherry-decorated hat on, and a very dashing white organdie blouse which had once been Mrs Partridge's and had been the *piéce de résistance* at a recent jumble sale. Outside, whilst brother Ted fussed with his camera and we squeezed obediently together in order to make a compact group, she came up to admire the baby.

'It's a wonder either of you are here to tell the tale,' she told Mrs Annett, 'that front room of yours is nothing better than a morgue—facing north and dripping damp. You mind you has all the rest in your back bedroom where the hot tank is!'

Mrs Annett assurred her that she would give the matter her attention, and invited her to join in the historic group, which she did with the greatest pride.

The christening party at Beech Green school-house was a hilarious affair. Miss Clare had come over from her cottage and we found a corner together.

'I didn't come to the service,' she explained, 'as Doctor Martin insists that I have a little rest in the afternoon.'

I thought that this sounded ominous and enquired if she had had any more attacks. For a moment she was silent, and then confided:

'Well, yes, my dear, I have. Doctor says I shall be quite all right if I rest more, so I'm being sensible and lying down every afternoon.'

There was not time to say much, for the cake was being cut and toasts drunk to the future felicity of young Malcolm Annett, but for me, at least, a shadow had fallen over the festivities.

Mr Annett implored me to come over to talk to brother Ted who is a mathematics professor, and who had just been honoured by an invitation to lecture at Cambridge, and was very pleased about it all.

With becoming modesty Ted admitted that his subject was to be 'The Triangulate Isotopic Hebdominal and its Associated Quotients,' (or something very like it) and would I care to be present?

Though decidedly flattered by his kindness, I was secretly glad that I was already engaged to go with Amy to the theatre on the same day, so that with polite sounds of regret we passed to other and more intelligible topics.

As six o'clock approached and young Malcolm, after

patiently waiting for us to finish our refreshments, was now vociferously demanding his own, we made our farewells. I looked around for Miss Clare, hoping to take her back with me, but she had slipped away unobserved, and I determined to call on her before many days went by.

On Monday morning Miss Jackson did not arrive until nearly eleven o'clock. She had been away for the week-end and had missed the evening train.

I was inclined to be sympathetic at first, despite the difficulty I had had in collecting dinner money and savings money, reading parents' notes and marking two registers during the first part of the morning. However, it gradually came out, through chance remarks, that Miss Jackson had had no intention of catching the Sunday evening train, as she had had the opportunity to visit Miss Crabbe who happened to be staying in her neighbourhood.

So engrossed had they become in educational and psychological affairs that they had stayed talking until past eleven o'clock. On hearing this, my own flabbergasted rage gave way to the deepest sympathy for Miss Crabbe's long-suffering hosts, who could never have bargained for such verbosity when they invited Miss Jackson to tea to renew their guest's acquaintance.

I said nothing during school hours about this behaviour, thinking it better to cool down; but after supper I pointed out, as mildly as I could, that the school must come first and that it was essential that she appeared at the correct time after a week-end.

To my astonishment I was given to understand that I was old fashioned, narrow-minded and petty. Furthermore, the inestimable advantage of listening to Miss Crabbe's wisdom far outweighed such mundane affairs as collecting dinner money and the like—all of which could be performed by those with inferior minds, (like mine, I supposed!) thus giving the more visionary educationalists (presumably Miss Jackson!) a chance of using their talents for the good of the community.

When I had regained my breath I said that I had never heard such utter nonsense, that I would have preferred a straightforward apology, that an early night might be a good thing, after her late session, that she appeared overheated and if she cared for a dose of milk of magnesia there was a bottle in the medicine cabinet.

At this, she flounced towards the door, saying that no one had ever understood her except Miss Crabbe, that it was no wonder that English education was in the state it was when prosy old women with antediluvian ideas still ruled the roost, and that she didn't want any supper.

With that she slammed the door, pounded up to her bedroom, slammed that door too and was seen no more by me. I was amused to find, later, that the top of a loaf and a hunk of cheese had vanished from the larder—and that the milk of magnesia had been used.

In all fairness to Miss Jackson I must record that she appeared very humbly at the breakfast table, apologized handsomely and brought me back a melon from Caxley, on her next visit, as a peace-offering. Moreover she went out to do her playground duty much more promptly and even got up a little earlier in the mornings, so that the outburst had good results.

A day or two after this, I was busy putting in some pink tulip bulbs, under the front windows, when I heard a hoot and saw Doctor Martin driving by. I waved and he drew up.

'What are you putting in?' he asked, seeing my trowel. I told him that I had treated myself to two dozen pink tulips and that he must look out for them in the spring.

At this moment Mrs Pringle appeared, on her way to sweep the school out. Doctor Martin hailed her.

'How's that leg?'

Mrs Pringle's gait, which had been normal, took on a shuffle-and-hop action, rather like a wooden-legged person essaying the polka. She drew a great shuddering sigh.

'Oh, doctor! If you only knew what I went through! Mighty little sympathy I gets, or asks for, for that matter, but if you was to realize the way it sometimes burns—then sometimes prickles—then sometimes jumps—then sometimes twitches—you'd wonder I didn't go down on my bended knee—always supposing I *could* go down on my bended knee, which is well nigh impossible, as the vicar can vouch for, me having to lean forward in the choir stalls, prayer-time—and beg of you to cut it off for me!'

Doctor Martin said: 'Oh rats to all that! Got your elastic stocking on?'

Mrs Pringle nodded haughtily.

'Then get a bit of weight off,' said her unsympathetic medical adviser. 'You must be three stone too heavy. No starch, no fat and no sugar! That'll do it!'

'*Some people*,' began Mrs Pringle with awful deliberation, 'has a hard day's work to do, every day that God sends. Scrubbing, sweeping, carrying buckets, and cleaning up after others—who shall be nameless! And hard work can't be tackled on an empty stummick, as my mother could have told you any day. I don't suppose I eats more than a butterfly —but a woman with my job needs a trifle of cold bacon or bread puddin' to keep her going, if she's to do all she's asked!'

'Try skipping then,' suggested the doctor, as she paused for breath. Mrs Pringle ignored this facetious interruption, and boomed inexorably on.

'Them as does their work—so-called—a-setting in a chair,

writing rubbish what no one understands in a hand what no one can read; or at best getting ailing folks to strip out when the wind's in the east, so's they can poke 'em about sharper with their cold fingers—them, I says, has no need for half the food that finds its way down their gullets. Gentry food at that too! Pheasants, partridges and other dainties I sees hanging up in the back porch as I passes.'

Dr Martin here let out a delighted guffaw, but Mrs Pringle finished her tirade unperturbed.

'And if them that *sits* to work needs that lot, stands to reason that them that *stands* and *bends* and *kneels* to labour, needs a fat lot more!'

'You're a wicked old tartar,' said Dr Martin affectionately, 'and I'll come to your funeral when you pop off with a fatty heart. Get along with you, you fascinating hussy!'

Bridling, Mrs Pringle limped ostentatiously towards the school, her stout back registering extreme disapproval. Dr Martin watched her go.

'How I do love that old termagant!' he said.

Just then my kettle let off a shrill whistle.

'Going to make one?' asked the doctor hopefully, getting smartly out of his car, and opening the front door for me, before I could answer.

Meekly I took off my gardening gloves, and we went into the kitchen.

Over the tea-tray I broached the subject of Miss Clare.

'I didn't think she looked at all well last week,' I said. 'Is there anything else wrong besides her heart?'

Doctor Martin looked steadily across the table at me.

'Do you really want to know?'

'Of course I do.'

'Well,' said the doctor, replacing his cup very carefully. 'To be blunt, she doesn't get enough to eat.'

'Good God!' I cried, appalled. My own cup crashed on to the saucer. 'You don't mean that?'

I thought of Miss Clare's larder, with the gleaming rows of jam and chutney of her own making. I thought of the onions hanging up, the carrots and parsnips in an old well-scrubbed wooden rack. I thought of my last supper party there—of the cold brisket, the tart, the salad, the glinting silver and snowy cloth.

As if he could read my mind Dr Martin spoke again.

'Yes, I know she keeps a good store cupboard. There's not a morsel of waste there. She uses every bit of produce from her garden that she can. But she can't afford to use it all. She was giving baskets of windfall apples to the neighbours last week. Before, she would have turned them into jelly—but three pounds of preserving sugar costs half a crown or so, and that wants finding.'

'This is awful——' I began. Dr Martin went on ruthlessly.

'She gets next to no butcher's meat, and things that she should have, like liver and cream and a drop of Burgundy, are beyond her these days. It stands to reason. She's got the old age pension and a minute teaching one; and though she owns that little cottage she still has to keep it in repair. She told me last week that the repairs to her well came to over five pounds. Her shoes cost between ten and fifteen shillings to mend. God knows how long she wears her clothes. Her house linen was her mother's, and when it goes she can't afford to replace it. Her father thatched the roof just before he died—what, twenty years ago now—and it'll need doing again before long. How's Miss Clare ever to get two hundred pounds together for that?'

'Fool that I am!' I said passionately. 'I should have thought of all that. But somehow—she's always so neat, and the house is so beautiful, and she's always given me such good meals——' I couldn't go on.

'Oh she'd give her guests a good meal!' agreed the doctor brutally. 'You'd have butter too. But I noticed there was only margarine in the larder when I went there last week for a teaspoon.' Indeed, I thought, there's mighty little that this wise old man misses about his patients' background. 'Mind you, she's got a kind of instinctive knowledge of nutrition, handed down from peasant forbears. She sprinkles parsley around pretty heavily. She makes herself rough oatmeal porridge—but she doesn't have all the sugar and milk with that, that she should have. She bakes a bit of bread now and again, when the oven's on; but naturally she's sparing with the firing these days.'

'You don't mean she's going cold, as well?' I said piteously.

'Hardly surprising,' rejoined the old man. 'And she can't work as she did in her garden. Peter Lamb, poor fellow, used to dig it for nothing. That idle neighbour of hers will condescend to turn it over for three bob an hour—which she can't afford anyway. I noticed that last year's potato patch is left rough this year. Less food again.'

He pushed his chair back from the table as if the matter were closed. I leant across and caught his wrist.

'Now sit down. You're not going till we've thought something out. We must help her. Besides,' I admitted, 'I can't stick this out alone, until I can see some way round it.'

The doctor smiled, hitched his chair up again and passed his cup across to be refilled.

'For a tough old schoolmarm with a good caning arm, you've got a remarkably soft heart,' he commented. 'Good Lord, girl, Miss Clare's only one of hundreds! They're the new poor; fighting a rear-guard action and keeping the standard flying. I'll bet Miss Clare puts a shilling in the collecting tin next Poppy Day, and that chap next door who's picking up twelve pounds a week, won't be able to put his hand on a bit of change!'

'I know all that,' I said, 'but come on now. Let's be practical. How can we help?'

'She won't let you. She's too proud.'

'Don't be such a *maddening* man!' I almost shouted. 'You come in here torturing me, and making me give you cups of tea—oh sorry, I forgot to fill it up——' I pushed it across hastily. 'And you put me into an absolute fantod and fever——'

'You wanted to know,' he pointed out.

'And now I do know, we must do something, or I shall go clean out of my mind, and the children will find me sitting with straws in my hair, drooling, when they come tomorrow—and you'll have another patient on your hands.'

This outburst appeared to sober him, I was glad to see; for no doctor, however zealous or impoverished, cares to hear of another patient being added to his burdens these days.

'The answer, I think,' he said slowly, 'is a nice easy-going lodger. Like your Miss Jackson.'

'I'd be delighted for Miss Clare to have her,' I said, 'but I don't know that she's exactly easy-going.'

'Well, someone like that,' pursued the doctor. 'She's got a spare bedroom and that front parlour too, that's hardly ever used. Then she'd eat more. She'd be most conscientious about giving a lodger a nourishing meal and she'd have some as well.'

'It's sounds a good idea,' I agreed. 'But could she stand the extra work?'

'Speaking from a medical point of view, I think any extra work involved—and there needn't be much, I'd have a word with the prospective lodger and tell her to pull her weight with bed-making and lifting and so on—would be offset by the advantages. She wouldn't be anxious about making ends meet—and there's nothing more fraying than that, week after week—she'd have someone else to think about, which would take her mind off her own ills a bit; solitary people can't help dwelling on 'em a bit too much, and she'd have more money to spend on food. And that's the main thing!'

He drained his cup, and then rose.

'Now I must be off. Think it over, and think about Miss Jackson going there. I'll tackle Miss Clare. I shall tell her I'd feel happier if she had someone in the house with her. I'll suggest her sister. That'll properly put her back up—and she'll consider a lodger much more readily!'

'Honestly,' I said, flabbergasted, 'I'd no idea you were such a Machiavelli! But I will suggest to Miss Jackson that she might like to make a change. But somehow—I don't know if she's quite right for Miss Clare.'

'She'll be better off with Miss Clare than with you,' said the doctor shrewdly. 'Cooped up together all day—why, you don't want to hear her news when she gets back here to tea—you know it all! Give her Miss Clare to pour her troubles out to, and she'll blossom like a rose; and so will her landlady! She'll look forward to her coming in to hear all the school gossip. Do all three of you good, I know that.'

We proceeded to the front door and I surveyed my tulip bed, still unfinished.

'And what does Miss Jackson give you for board and lodging?' he asked. I told him three pounds, which seemed to suit us both. He threw up his hands in mock horror.

'You bloated profiteer!' he exclaimed. 'On top of your fat salary too! You pass her over to Miss Clare, my girl, and put that three pounds into her pocket.' This bit of by-play I recognized for what it was—a subtle way of relieving the tension of the past hour, and of bringing us back to a more normal plane. He pointed to my tulip bulbs.

'Bought with your ill-gotten gains, I suppose.' He could not resist one final stab. 'Miss Clare makes her garden pretty with slips that friends give her. She might be able to afford bulbs if she had a lodger!'

At this moment, Mrs Pringle, her work completed, came limping back, bucket in hand.

'You are the most cruel, heartless creature I've ever met,' I told him, and hailed Mrs Pringle. 'Don't you agree?' I asked her, above the noise of the car's engine.

'Ah!' said Mrs Pringle with much satisfaction, 'that he is. He's a walking monument of vice!' We stood, side by side, waving good-bye to him. For once, Mrs Pringle and I were united.

Having given the children an earnest little homily on thrift, and the wisdom of putting some part of their money away, however small, for a rainy day, I was shocked to find that I have one and sevenpence only in my own purse.

When I think of what I earn, and my 'profiteering' three pounds a week in addition, I am ashamed of myself, for nearly every month I seem to spend the last few days of it counting out pennies and shamelessly embezzling needlework money or dinner money, until Jim Bryant brings the cheque.

This is another painful reminder of Miss Clare's plight, which is constantly in my mind. Since the doctor's visit, I have approached Miss Jackson, who seemed unflatteringly delighted to quit my portals if she could find another resting-place, so that that is one step forward.

I have no doubt that before half term is here, in another week's time, Dr Martin will have his well-laid plans in working trim.

NOVEMBER

It is wonderful to be solvent again, if only for the first week of the month. Shaken by my former extravagance, and determined to organize my expenditure, I have started an account book, and I intend to put down my daily spendings. How long this good resolution will last I can't tell.

Today's entries make disagreeable reading:

	£	s.	d.
Electricity bill	3	6	0
Coal Bill	3	18	0

Garage's bill	..	2	4	0
Weekly grocery bill	..	1	12	6

I comfort myself with the thought that the first three will not appear again for a little while, and I certainly hope that the entry which follows these four will never appear again—though I have serious doubts about that. It says: 'Repayment to needlework money tin, and dinner money tin . . . 8s. 9d.

I am going to put an elastic band round each of those Oxo tins and remove them only when the exigencies of rightful duty make it necessary.

'Always put a little by!' as I told my children firmly last week, when the savings' money had fallen below average. Sometimes I wonder that a bolt from heaven doesn't strike me.

We have had our first fog of the winter. Here, in open country, we are spared the sulphurous, choking fog that makes everything filthy, but the thick, white mist that rolls down from the hills, or that creeps up from the valley where Caxley lies, can be equally disconcerting.

It was very, very still. Drops of moisture hung in the hedges and cobwebs. From the school playground it was impossible to see the church, my house and the great elm trees. Only the occasional spattering of heavy drops from the elms showed where they were. In the distance Samson, Mr Roberts's cow, lowed in bewilderment.

Tibby dislikes these damp mornings, and has taken to accompanying me over to the classroom. Here, his doting admirers have placed a chair from the infants' room, near the stove, furnished it with an old woollen jacket from the dressing-up box, and Tibby deigns to ensconce himself there for most of the day. At play-time he accepts offers of milk, cake, and occasionally chocolate from the children.

'Don't 'e purr nice?' and

'Pretty little dear, ennit?' they say fondly to each other, as they pet him, and this adulation is, of course, exactly what his lordship likes best.

It grew so thick by midday, that I wondered if Mrs Crossley would be able to find her way along with the dinner-van. But all was well, and our canisters of stew, mashed potato, apples and custard arrived safely, only ten minutes later than usual.

'It's even worse in Caxley!' she told us. 'It seems to be general everywhere.'

The children elected to play indoors during the dinner hour, and as the weather was so appalling, it seemed the best thing to do. Jigsaw puzzles, beads, picture books, crayons and paper, and plasticine modelling kept them all engrossed, and they begged to be allowed to hear 'Listen with Mother' at a quarter to two. As a special treat I switched it on. It is, as everyone knows, a programme intended for children under school age, but most of the Fairacre children listen with attention to it. This does not surprise me with the infants, for our children are remarkably unsophisticated and appreciate stories, games, songs and so on intended for much younger people; but I am astonished that some children of eight or nine, in my own class, should still get satisfaction from this excellent programme. I should be interested to know if other teachers find that their children are equally responsive, for I should have thought that the natural reaction of the older child to 'Listen with Mother' would have been impatience. In any case, it is a compliment to the planners of this programme, which I am happy to pass on.

Joseph Coggs has brought his tortoise to school. This animal has been lost dozens of times during the summer, but has been found in various parts of the parish and returned to Joe. Now, it is comatose and ready to hibernate, and Joseph's mother has asked if we can find it accommodation in school. Today, the children put it in a box of dry earth and leaves, and it is back in the corner of the lobby. With any luck, it should survive, and will certainly be less disturbed there, despite forty-odd children's attention, than it would be in the Coggs' crowded and ramshackle cottage.

We sent the children home ten minutes earlier this afternoon, much to their jubilation. The classroom was already too dark to see properly, and the four inadequate bulbs, which hang naked from the ceiling, did little to help. The children ran off into the mist, squealing like piglets, and shouting joyfully to each other.

Miss Jackson and I stoked up a roaring fire, drew the curtains to shut out the first dismal, dispiriting day of November, and made anchovy toast for tea. I only hoped that all our pupils were as happily and snugly sheltered.

I am appalled at the amount of litter lying about in Fairacre's once tidy lane. I suppose it is more noticeable since poor old Bannister, the road man, died a few weeks ago, for no one can be found to take the job on.

At this time of year, too, the leaves are thick in the sides of the roads and any rain carries them along to the drains which soon get blocked. Then again, far more things are wrapped in paper these days; but litter baskets stand outside the grocer's shop, the butcher's and the 'Beetle and Wedge' and one would have thought that three would have been ample in a little place like Fairacre. I can't help feeling that this nuisance shows complete callousness towards the look of the place, and also an unpleasant trait in the public's attitude to the welfare state. As Mrs Pringle horrified me by saying, when commenting on the rubbish blowing about near the church: 'We pays to have it done, don't we? In rates and that?' Presumably, that should be enough!

I have been having an extraordinary anti-litter campaign at school, but with only partial success. Linda Moffat, of all people, peeled a mint sweet free from its wrappings in the playground, and let each wisp flutter delicately to the ground. When the last had fallen, I pounced upon her, and drove her into picking each minute piece up.

She obeyed, with a mixture of one-humouring-an-idiot and genuine bewilderment, which made me give yet another blistering lecture to Fairacre School, which the children listened to with great resentment, as it should have been a percussion band period, and they felt themselves most hardly used.

Mrs Willet commented on this problem too when I went down to her cottage to leave a message for Mr Willet.

'Not much good ticking off the children,' she remarked, 'when the parents are behaving like that!' She nodded through the window towards Mrs Coggs who was passing. The latest baby was blissfully clawing a newspaper and dropping the pieces over the side, while its mother gazed at it with fond pride.

Mrs Willet was busy making sloe gin when I called. She sat at her kitchen table, pricking the sloes diligently with a stout darning needle, and dropping them into a bottle half-full of gin.

'Ready at Christmas!' she said proudly. 'I do a bottle every year, and sometimes wine as well!'

She opened her larder door and displayed the riches inside. It was as well-stocked with jars and bottles as Miss Clare's, and I was struck—not for the first time—with the versatility and energy of the average countrywoman.

Mrs Willet can tackle a hundred jobs, without having been specifically *taught* any of them. She can salt pork or beef, make jams, jellies, wines, chutneys and pickles; she can bake pies—with all manner of pastries—cakes, tarts and her own bread, which is particularly delicious. She makes rugs, curtains, and her own clothes. She can help a neighbour in childbirth and—at the other end of life's span—compose a corpse's limbs for decent burial. She is as good a gardener as her husband, can distemper a room, mend a fuse, and sings in the choir.

She is, in fact, typical of most countrywomen, and with them she shares that self-reliance which is the heritage of those who have had to face tackling daily jobs of varied kinds.

Mrs Willet is small and pale and yet she is 'always on the go,' as she herself will tell you. The fact that she can do so many things, and takes enormous pride in doing them well, is, I think, the secret of this apparently inexhaustible energy. There are so many different activities to engage her, that when she tires of one, there is another to which she can turn and get refreshment. From turning her heavy old mangle in the wash-house, she will come in and sit down to stitch a new skirt. She will prepare a stew, and while it simmers on the hob, filling the little house with its fragrance, she will practise her part in Mr Annett's new anthem, ready for the next church festival. And—this perhaps is the most important thing—she sees a satisfying result from her labours. The clothes blow on the line, the skirt is folded and put away in the drawer ready for next Sunday; Mr Willet will come in 'sharp-set' and praise her bubbling stew; and, with any luck, Mr Annett will congratulate her on her grasp of that difficult passage just before the basses come in.

It is a creative life. There is something worth while to show for energy expended which engenders the desire to accomplish more. Small wonder that the Mrs Willets of this world are happy, and deserve to be so.

Mr Willet, as the school's shipshape condition testifies, is equally resourceful. There are very few jobs that are beyond Mr Willet's powers. He replaces hinges, panes of glass, roof tiles, fence palings, and other casualties of school life. I have seen him giving a hand with thatching, cleaning out a well, felling a tree, and catching a frightened horse. He can build a shed or a garage, laying bricks and smoothing cement with the best of them, fashion a pair of wooden gates, or erect a bird bath or sundial. He knows how to prune any shrub that grows, how to graft, how to lay a hedge, where to get the best manure, pea-sticks, bean-poles and everything else necessary to maintain a flourishing garden. To me and to the managers of Fairacre school he is beyond price, saving many a repair bill and foreseeing any possible trouble and forestalling it with his capable old hands.

And yet, when his modest cheque arrives at the end of the month, he receives it with a bashfulness which puts my own eagerness to shame.

Two days before half term I received a note from Miss Clare inviting me there for the next evening.

Dr Martin had hailed me from his car, soon after his visit, and told me that 'he'd had a word with Miss Clare about having someone in the house.' With that he had driven off —so that I wondered how much Miss Clare knew, when I approached her door.

She greeted me as warmly as ever, and before long, introduced the subject of lodgers herself.

'Dr Martin suggested that I joined forces with my sister Ada, but of course that's out of the question. He insists that someone should be with me—foolishly, I think—but I feel that I must do as he says. Do you think my spare bedroom and the little front parlour would be suitable?'

I said that any lodger would be lucky to get them. Then

I took a deep breath, and said that I believed Miss Jackson would be prepared to make a change.

'But I must warn you,' I said, 'that she's not awfully easy in some ways. Getting her up is a dreadful job each morning. She sleeps like the dead—and you shouldn't have to run up and down stairs after her, with your wonky heart.'

'I shouldn't dream of doing so,' answered Miss Clare, 'and in any case Dr Martin said that she would have to understand, from the first, that I could not do all I should wish to do for her——' She broke off and began to laugh. 'There! Now the cat's out of the bag! Yes, my dear, I'm afraid the doctor and I have been discussing this business. Quite unforgiveable of us, behind your back!'

'Don't worry,' I said. 'I can guess who started the conversation, and, frankly, I should be glad to be relieved of my lodger. We see too much of each other for the thing to work properly—and I'm probably a bit irritable after school, and let things rile me unnecessarily.'

'As we're being honest, I'd better tell you that Doctor Martin said as much. His words were: "If you want to see Miss Read staying sane, you'll take pity on her and remove her assistant. That poor girl gets a pretty thin time of it, living with her headmistress"!'

'Well!' I exclaimed, flabbergasted at Doctor Martin's duplicity. He'd certainly seen the best way to get Miss Clare to fall in with his machinations! I wouldn't mind betting, I thought to myself, that the harrowing tale he had pitched me was all part of his low cunning! However, I could not help feeling amused at the skilful way in which he had worked on us both, and could do nothing of course to let Miss Clare know of his conversation with me, which had led up to the present situation.

'I'm sure he's right,' I said, swallowing my bitter pill. 'She'll be much happier with you, if you feel up to coping with the extra work. Why not write to her? I'll take a note back, if you like.'

She fetched her old red leather writing-case, which the Partridges had given her one Christmas, and sat down at the table. The room was very quiet as she wrote. A coal clinked into the hearth and the tabby cat stretched itself on the rug. I leant back and closed my eyes and thought wryly of the lengths to which conscientious doctors will go for their favourite patients.

At last the letter was finished, and Miss Clare handed it over for my perusal. It said:

Dear Miss Jackson,

I understand from Miss Read that you are still looking for permanent lodgings. Would you care to come here? I can offer you a bedroom and a separate sitting-room, and should be very glad to welcome you.

If this interests you perhaps you could come to tea one day soon, to see if the accommodation is suitable and to discuss other arrangements.

Yours sincerely,
Dorothy Clare

It was written in her beautiful, flowing, copper-plate hand, which has been Fairacre's model for forty years, and, with its even spacing and equal margins was a work of art, most pleasing to the eye.

'I'm sure she'll jump at the chance,' I told her, handing it back to be put in its envelope, 'and I shall be able to revert to my pleasant solitary state, and talk nonsense to the cat without being afraid that I'm overheard.'

And so Miss Jackson's future was settled, to the great comfort of Miss Clare, Dr Martin, Fairacre's headmistress—and, most important, to the happiness of Miss Jackson herself.

* * *

'Heard about that chap Mawne?' asked Mr Willet, the next morning. 'They were saying after choir practice that there's two places he's trying for. That pair of old cottages on the road to Springbourne, where Mr Roberts' old shepherd lived some while ago, afore he moved up to the council houses; and Captain Whatsisname's—you knows, up the back there.' He waved a massive thumb in the direction of the 'Beetle and Wedge.'

'Bit big, aren't they?' I said, and then wished I hadn't.

'They says as he's settling down here,' said Mr Willet stolidly. I was grateful for his sober face. 'Maybe he's having relations, and that, to live there too.'

'Quite likely,' I said.

'It do seem wrong to me,' went on Mr Willet thoughtfully, 'the way that folks with a bit of money, buys up these old cottages us village chaps have always lived in. Don't leave nothing for us.'

'But everyone's bursting to get into a council house,' I protested. 'You know the heart-burning that goes on, every time a few are allotted to different families.'

'Ah!' said Mr Willet, nodding sagely. 'They all WANTS a council house—but not at the rents they asks for them.'

'Good lord!' I expostulated, 'the houses are subsidized now! They're living partly at other ratepayers' expense. They get the amenities they ask for cheaper than they would in a private house. What more can they want?'

'Take old Burton, that used to be shepherd. He used to pay three bob a week for that cottage. Now his rent's nearer thirty-three.'

'And how can you expect any landlord to keep a cottage in repair for three bob a week? I should have thought you'd have seen the sense in that!'

Mr Willet was not at all put out by my heat. He stropped his chin thoughtfully, as he replied.

‘ ’Tisn’t that I don’t see the sense. *Of course*, three bob’s not enough. *Of course*, thirty-three don’t cover the proper cost of one of them new council houses—I knows that. But, you think again. What is a chap like old Burton to do, on his bit of money? Where is he to live, if he’s to stay in Fairacre?’

I pondered this problem. Mr Willet, who had obviously given this matter much more earnest thought than I had ever done, spoke again.

‘If the council could build some real *little* places—nothin’ elaborate, mind you—as could be let fairly cheap, why, they’d go like hot cakes. That’s the thing—some real *little* places for us old ’uns.’

He switched to another aspect of rural housing.

‘Mr Roberts gave young Miller the rough side of his tongue evidently.’

‘Oh? What’s the trouble there?’

‘Well, you know his old dad is the main tractor driver and his old mum does a turn mornings for Mrs Roberts? That cottage has got four rooms, and when young Ern got married he hadn’t got no place to go, so home he comes, wife and all, to live with the old people. Mr Roberts told him flat he was to find somewhere—but you know how it is—he just never! Now the baby’s come, and it grizzles all night and fair drives the old folks dotty. Young Ern works up the atomic and gets good pay. He’s got no business in a tied cottage and he knows it. It’s been that awkward. Mr Roberts don’t want to lose his best tractor man, by being too sharp, and yet why should that young Ern live off of him?’

I said it was certainly unjust.

‘Looks as though this baby’ll settle things. The old chap’s getting proper fed-up and Mr Roberts told Ern he wasn’t going to have one of his best workers upset, because his son was “a selfish lout.” Ah! that was his words, miss! Ern says he ain't stopping to be insulted, so I reckons he'll sling his hook—and a good job too.'

He seized the broom he had leant against the wall, during this interesting gossip, and stumped off to resume sweeping the scattered coke in the playground.

'How all you ladies does run on!' he called wickedly over his shoulder.

The half-term holiday flew by, and a week later Miss Jackson left the school-house to take up her new quarters with Miss Clare. I must say she seems very much happier, and has been remarkably punctual, despite her journey, each morning.

It was soon after her departure that Amy called to insist on taking me to a play, being performed nightly at the Corn Exchange in Caxley, by a repertory company.

'But it's so cold in the evenings,' I protested weakly. 'All I want to do after school, is to settle in here by the fire and doze with Tibby.'

'*Exactly*!' said Amy vehemently. She was back in her old dictatorial form, I noticed, quite unlike the unhappy Amy who had told me of her mythical friend's matrimonial sorrows, on an earlier visit.

'You live in this *backwater*'—here she waved a disdainful hand round my comfortable sitting-room, with such effect, that I could almost imagine the reeds standing in muddy water and the whirring of wild duck around us—'and dream your life away! This play will pull you up sharply, my girl!'

I began to say that I didn't want to be pulled up sharply, but Amy swept relentlessly onward.

'It deals with Problems of the Present. I admit it's Sordid and Brutal—but life's like that these days. Even the décor is symbolic. The first set shows a back alley in a slum. It could be anywhere, the Gorbals, or New Orleans, or Hong Kong

—and the windows are shuttered, symbolizing Blank Weariness. In the centre of the stage is a dustbin, symbolizing Filth and Hopeless Waste and Rejection.'

'You don't say!' I interjected, trying to restrain my mounting hysteria.

'If you are going to be *flippant*,' said Amy severely, 'I shall think twice about taking you, I haven't forgotten your disgraceful behaviour at that Moral Rearmament meeting!'

I said that I was sorry, and begged her to forgive me. She looked somewhat mollified.

'The actors speak in blank verse—the language is rather strong, naturally—but when the play is dealing with such things as rape, homosexuality, betrayal and lingering death, both of spirit and body—one must expect it!'

I said it sounded quite delightful, so fresh and wholesome, but that they were reviving *Genevieve* at the local cinema, and could we go to that instead? Amy ignored this pathetic plea, and was about to continue, when I capitulated.

'All right, I'll come,' I said sighing. 'But I warn you! If any old Father This or Brother That comes wailing on to the stage—as I feel in my bones he must—I shall walk straight out, stating in a clear, carrying voice that I am taking my custom to a nice, clean, cheerful entertainment at the cinema opposite!'

I gave Mrs Partridge a lift to Caxley on Saturday morning. I was off to buy some really thick winter gloves, despite the reproaches of my account book which makes gloomy reading. Mrs Partridge was about to buy Christmas presents for relatives abroad.

'Have you heard the good news about Mr Mawne?' she asked, as we passed Beech Green school. My godson, I noticed, was taking the air in his perambulator in the front garden of the school-house.

'I heard that he was trying to find a house,' I said guardedly.

'Well, it's all settled. He's renting Brackenhurst, where Captain Horner and his family were. He has been posted to Nairobi or Vancouver, or one of those places out East,' said the vicar's wife with a fine disregard for geography, 'and will be away for five years, poor dear. Still, it's very nice for Mr Mawne. Now, he really will be able to settle down in Fairacre, and look for a place to buy if he feels like it. He's a great asset to the village, you know.'

I said yes, I *did* know—the church accounts, for instance.

Mrs Partridge laughed and said that she didn't suppose that it was for the sake of the church accounts that Mr Mawne was making his home in Fairacre, and added that I was apt to belittle myself.

With this cryptic and uncomfortable remark still echoing in my ears, I drew up by the kerb, and allowed Mrs Partridge to alight.

As I made my way through Caxley's jammed High Street to the car park—which is ignored by most of the residents, who prefer to drive themselves mad by attempting to wedge their cars outside the shops rather than carry a basket for five minutes—I wondered how much longer I should have to endure Fairacre's romantic and ill-founded conjectures about my private life, in silence.

In the Public Library I was delighted to come across Mrs Finch-Edwards. She was looking through an enormous book, with plates showing eighteenth-century costumes. We had a sibilant but eager exchange of news under the SILENCE notice. Luckily, we were alone in the non-fiction department, and apart from a glare from a tousled young man in a spotty duffle coat who passed through, carrying an aggressive-looking book with a Left-Wing coloured jacket, we were undisturbed.

'We're making costumes for the Caxley Octet's concert after Christmas,' she whispered excitedly. 'It's to be a period programme. Eighteenth-century music and clothes and furniture. Isn't it lovely? Mrs Bond plays the viola and it was she who asked us to design and make the costumes. Isn't it fun?'

I said it certainly was, and that she and Mrs Moffat would be famous in no time, and that Mr Oliver Messel and Mr Cecil Beaton would have to look to their laurels.

'Oh, I don't think so!' protested Mrs Finch-Edwards seriously. 'I mean, they're *really* good. It will be some time before we can compete with them!'

On which satisfactory note we parted.

Mrs Pringle staggered in with a bucket of coke this morning, puffing and blowing like a grampus, and limping with great exaggeration whenever she remembered.

'If them as uses this coke so heavy-handed had to lug this 'ere bucket in, day in and day out,' she remarked morosely, dumping it noisily on a well-placed *People* by the guard, 'it might be an eye-opener to them! Flared up again, my leg has.'

I said I was sorry to hear that, and perhaps Minnie would help out again. As I had intended, this touched Mrs Pringle's pride. She drew in her breath sharply.

'What? And let her ruin my blackleading again? Not likely! I'll struggle on, thank you!'

She settled herself on the front desk, folded her arms upon her black woollen jumper, and embarked on a short gossip, before the school bell summoned the children.

'I hear there's going to be more changes in the village,' she began circumspectly. This, I suspected, referred to Mr Mawne's plans, but since our altercation over that gentleman, Mrs Pringle has been most careful not to mention him by name.

'That poor young Captain Horner's been took off to Siberia or Singapore—some place anyway—where the army's looking for trouble,' she continued. From her tone one would have imagined that the army had nothing better to do than stir up strife in a desultory way, with the ends of their bayonets, and solely for their own idle pleasure.

'So his house, I understand,' went on Mrs Pringle delicately, 'has been LET to someone!'

I said shortly that I knew that Mr Mawne had taken it.

'Oh, Mr Mawne is it?' said Mrs Pringle, feigning extreme surprise. 'There now, that will be nice!'

'What other changes are there?' I asked, leading her, I hoped, to safer ground.

'That empty cottage, where old Mr Burton used to live years back—that's being done up.'

'Who for?'

'Well, now, it's for a distant relation of mine. My old auntie married again, on the passing of her first husband to higher things, the second one being quite a young man, but steady. They had two children, pretty sharp, and this girl's the daughter of the second one. No! I'm telling a lie! He had but the two boys. Gladys was Tom's girl. Very refined she is—has her hair permed and all that, and speaks ladylike—and marrying a nice young chap at a baker's in Caxley. She was over last week. We had a nice set-down with the tea-pot and she told me all about him. "Auntie," she said, "he's wonderful! Love is the most important thing in the world!" '

Mrs Pringle's sour old face wore a maudlin simper which astonished me.

'And what did you say?' I asked, fascinated.

'I said: "Glad," I said, "you're right," I said, "it's only True Love that matters!" Don't you reckon that's right, Miss Read?'

Thus appealed to I found myself saying cautiously that

I supposed it was important, but agreed privately with the Provincial Lady's secret feeling that a satisfactory banking account and sound teeth matter a great deal more.

'Believe me,' said Mrs Pringle, rising from the desk to continue her labours, 'there's nothing like it! Let it come early, let it come LATE——' Here she fixed me with an earnest and slightly watery eye—'it's love that makes the world go round!'

Walking almost jauntily, and without a trace of a limp, she went, humming romantically, on her way.

The children came rushing in a few minutes later, in the greatest excitement.

'Joe Coggs, miss!'

' 'E's fell over!'

'Cut his head open, miss!'

I quelled them as best I could as I made my way into the playground, thinking, not for the first time, how very much I disliked that word 'OPEN,' added to these statements of injury. Somehow, 'He has cut his head,' sounds the sort of injury that I can cope with. Add that unnecessary and obnoxious word, and at once I visualize a child's head cloven in half, and looking like a transverse section in a botanical drawing. It is unnerving, to say the least of it, and I must admit that I am a squeamish woman at the best of times.

We met Joseph in the porch, surrounded by a crowd of garrulous well-wishers, who were almost tearing the clothes off his back in their anxiety to assist his passage. Luckily, the wound turned out to be a minute cut on his forehead, which was soon put to rights with a piece of adhesive bandage.

Prayers were over, and the children were just settling down to arithmetic, when the vicar called with the hymn list. He seemed disposed to chat and I brought another chair and set it by my desk.

He had just come from old Mr Burton's council house, where he had lived since giving up his regular shepherding.

'I'm afraid he's sinking,' said the vicar sadly, looking down at the leopard-skin gloves on his thin knees. 'It was a pity he ever left that little cottage of his. He's ailed ever since he went up to the council house. He was too old to uproot himself, you know.'

'It was jolly damp and uncomfortable in that cottage,' I replied, 'and the only water available was from that stand pipe out in the lane. I should have thought he would have been much more comfortable in the new house.'

'More comfortable in his body perhaps,' said the vicar slowly, 'but not in his spirit. In the first place he has little privacy there, in full view of his neighbours. And then, that little old cottage was like a snail's shell to the snail. He'd lived in it all his life, and it had vital associations. The mantelpiece, for instance, with its rest above it for whips, and the bracket below for his old gun, the peg on the back door where he hung his canvas lunch bag—it was an old A.R.P. gas-mask holder, I remember—the kitchen shelf still showing grooves where his wife screwed the mincer, and where his children had nicked the edges with their penknives—why, the whole place was a record of his life! Take him from that at the age of seventy-odd, and how can you expect him to flourish? One might just as well tear up a primrose plant from the wood and expect it to flower in concrete!'

I agreed and said that I'd heard he had become very morose lately and inclined to be querulous.

'Naturally,' went on the vicar, 'he feels lost and without value there. Have you read *Lucy Bettesworth* by George Bourne?'

I said that I had not.

'I'll lend it to you,' said the vicar, 'he sums up this problem so well in one of the essays in the book. "Whatever is agreeable and kindly in his nature"—I quote from memory —"is kept alive by the intimate touch of homely possessions. They are the witness of his life's work, and surrounded by them he still feels a man." So true, so true!' sighed the vicar, reaching for his biretta.

By this time the children were getting restless. I could see that Ernest had contrived a warlike weapon from his ruler and an elastic band, and was busy making ammunition with pellets of pink blotting-paper, which he was ranging with military exactitude along the groove of his desk. The next stage, I knew, would be to dip each pellet in the ink-well before letting it fly gloriously abroad, and I was anxious to see the vicar comfortably to the door before this last and lethal step was taken.

On the threshold he paused again, and said more cheerfully: 'Young Captain Horner is off to Malta, I hear, and has let his house to Mr Mawne. So that's quite settled. I have written to him, and my wife and I hope you will both come to tea as soon as he is back. I must say I shall be glad to see him. The Free-Will Offering Fund has somehow become inextricably involved with the Altar-Flowers and Church-Fabric Accounts—most mystifying. They're all together in a chocolate box, but I can't find enough money to tally with the three accounts.'

I said that he should have an Oxo tin for each. His mouth dropped open with admiration.

'What an excellent idea! I shall go straight to the vicarage and do it at once. Really, Miss Read, what a grasp of business affairs you have!'

Much cheered, he bustled off, and I returned in the nick of time to prevent the first ink-dipped pellet from being projected, and to direct that the entire arsenal be put forthwith into my waste-paper basket.

* * *

As tomorrow will be the first day of December, I settled down this evening with my account book.

I am delighted to find that I have £1 4s. 9d. left in the bank from this month's salary, and twelve shillings and fourpence in my purse. Greatest triumph of all is the fact that the dinner money and needlework money tins are untouched.

The account book makes depressing reading, however, for I really cannot see that I can spend less than I do, unless I cut out such pleasant items as 'Anemones—9d.' and 'Sweets for Children—2s. 3d.,' which I don't intend to do. If only I lived in the kind of exalted circles where champagne parties, two yachts, diamond dog-collars and so on are normal—if such circles still exist, which I doubt—I believe I could cut down a bit. Say, *one* yacht, and *topaz* dog-collars . . .

Meanwhile, remembering Mr Micawber's well-known maxim about expenditure, I feel exceptionally smug, and having decided to abandon my gloomy and tedious account-keeping, I threw the book on the back of the fire, and Tibby and I ate our supper by the light of its flames.

It was only when I was snug in bed, still glowing with thrift and virtue, that I remembered that the grocer's bill was as yet unpaid. Another of life's little tweaks!

DECEMBER

MISS JACKSON arrived at school this morning, pink-cheeked and starry-eyed, and clutching a bulky envelope.

'It's from Miss Crabbe,' she told me, her voice trembling with awe. 'A copy of the lecture she gave to a W.E.A. meeting somewhere near Middlesbrough. Isn't it wonderful?'

I said I had not heard it—but I expected that it was.

'Oh, not just the *lecture*,' said Miss Jackson, slightly shocked. 'I meant isn't it wonderful that she's sent me a copy? It's terribly enthralling!' Here she withdrew, with some difficulty, a wad of crumpled and flimsy typed literature, which bore the unlovely title of 'Some Psychological Interpretations of Play-Behaviour in the Under-Fives.'

'And in her letter,' continued Miss Jackson, sorting among the litter feverishly, and finally abstracting a grubby piece of paper, covered with large angular writing in green ink, 'she says that she wants me to read her notes with particular attention, as she hopes one day to start "an enlightened school of her own" based on her studies, and perhaps I may like to help her with it, when I have had a little more "work-a-day experience with the hum-drum." Doesn't she express herself well?' sighed my assistant ecstatically.

The school bell, lustily pulled by Ernest, now reminded us that the children would be with us almost at once, and I said that the future looked most hopeful for her, but would she mind reverting to the hum-drum present for the moment, and go outside into her lobby where a vicious and strongly-worded fight appeared to be going on.

So exalted was Miss Jackson this morning that this request was met with a happy smile, instead of the scowl and flouncing with which she so often obeys my behests, and Fairacre School was lapped in bliss and peace all day, thanks to Miss Crabbe's benign influence from afar.

'Heard about poor old Burton?' asked Mr Willet at playtime. 'Went early today. His son and daughter was up there with him. Nice old fellow—be missed he will. Knew all there was to know about sheep, and did some lovely carving too.'

I said I had not realized that he was so clever.

'Ah! Them pew ends in Springbourne church—they're his work; bunches of grapes and hops and that. A fair treat. Those old chaps was good with their hands. Miss Clare's father now—he was a wonder with straw. You should see the straw ornaments he made for his ricks; birds and little old men and women, 'twere wonderful! My missus said last night "These young chaps don't seem able to make like their fathers." And Mrs Partridge said the same, only yesterday. " 'Tis a pity to see the old crafts dying out, Willet!" I told 'em both the same!'

Here he paused, pursing his lips up under his ragged moustache, and I took up my cue.

'And what was it you told them?'

'I said to 'em both: "There's no one disputes that 'tis a pity the old crafts is dying, but you never hears people say how clever the youngsters has been picking up all the new ones. I bet old Burton couldn't drive a combine-harvester, or a tractor, and dry the corn or milk the cow by electric, like his boy can!" That's true, you know, Miss. There's new skill taking the place of the old, all the time, and I don't like to hear the youngsters becalled, just because they does different!' said Mr Willet sturdily.

He looked across the playground and raised his voice to a formidable bellow.

'Get you off that there coke! Let me catch one o' you little varmints on that pile again, I'll give 'ee a lift under the ear that'll take 'ee clean over the church spire!'

Notices have been posted at strategic points in the village for the last fortnight announcing a meeting to discuss the possibility of reviving the annual Flower Show, which has not been held in Fairacre for a number of years.

Evidently, before I came here, the Flower Show was an event of some magnitude, and people came from miles around to enjoy a day at Fairacre. It was usually held in the field at the side of the Vicarage.

It was a frosty starlit night, and the muddy approach to the Village Hall was hard and rutty. I had decided to go, as the children, I knew, used to play quite a large part in this village excitement, in earlier days, and there was a number of special classes, such as wild flowers, pressed flowers, dolls'-house floral decorations and so on, included in the programme, for their particular benefit. Also, fired by Mr Annett's horticultural efforts at Beech Green, I had been considering for some time, a modest school garden of our own, and this village show should give our efforts an added fillip.

By the time I arrived there were about ten people already in the hall. The vicar was in the chair, Mrs Partridge in the front row, talking to Mr and Mrs Roberts from the farm, and Mr Willet, Arthur Coggs and a few other men were warming their hands over the rather smelly oil stove, which was trying, inadequately enough, to warm the room. There was a strong smell of paraffin, mixed with the smoke from shag tobacco, and a few black smuts, trailing gossamer threads behind them, floated across the scene.

The meeting was called for seven-thirty—a most uncomfortable time in my private opinion—as it successfully throws the evening into confusion and plays havoc with one's evening meal. By a quarter to eight, only fifteen people had arrived. The vicar looked at his watch, then at his wife, and having received a nod, rose to his feet.

'I think we must begin,' he said, turning his gentle smile upon us. 'If you could shut the door, Mr Willet?'

Mr Willet shut the door with such firmness, that the oil stove belched forth a puff of smoke which reinforced the army of smuts already abroad. The vicar gave a brief little speech about the past glories of Fairacre's Flower Show, and his hopes that it might flourish again.

'Perhaps someone would propose that the Flower Show be revived?' he suggested. There was a heavy silence, broken only by the shuffling of boots from the bench at the back.

All fifteen of us, I noticed, were elderly. John Pringle, Mrs Pringle's only child, must have been the youngest among us, and he is a man of nearly thirty. It was John who, at last, sheepishly answered the vicar's plea.

'I'll do it,' he said. 'Propose we has a Flower Show, then.' He sat down, pink and self-conscious, and the vicar thanked him sincerely, his thoughts, no doubt, fluttering about his postponed supper.

'Could we have a seconder?'

Again that painful silence. It was as though we sat in a trance.

'I'll second it,' I said, when I could bear the suspense no longer.

'Good! Good!' beamed the vicar. 'Those in favour?'

All fifteen raised hands unenthusiastically. To look at our faces, an outsider might reasonably have thought that we were having the choice of hanging or the electric chair.

Slowly the meeting ground on. It was uphill work for the chairman, as indeed it is for any chairman at Fairacre's public meetings. Eight o'clock chimed from St Patrick's church, and then eight-thirty. The vicar by that time had squeezed from his reluctant companions that they were in favour of reviving the Flower Show, that it should be held in the Vicarage meadow next July, and that there should be classes for outsiders to enter as well as for Fairacre folk, and a number of special classes for the children.

'Well now,' said the vicar, in an exhausted tone, 'are there any questions, before we close the meeting? Do please speak out now so that we can have a discussion while we're all together.'

This sensible appeal had its usual effect of casting everyone into utter silence again. Mr Willet coughed nervously, and we all looked at him hopefully. He looked unhappily at the ceiling, and fingered his stained moustache. Mrs Roberts made a slight noise as she moved in her chair, and the vicar turned courteously towards her.

'Yes?' he enquired hopefully.

'Nothing—oh, nothing!' replied Mrs Roberts in near-panic, and looked as unhappy as Mr Willet at this publicity. The pall of silence fell upon us again. No one dared to move in case our chairman should suppose us anxious to spring to our feet with brilliant suggestions for the success of the Flower Show—which would have been unthinkable.

At last the vicar rose to his feet again.

'That seems to be all that we can do, at the moment then. I suggest that we call another meeting before Christmas, when we'll hope to see more people with us, and perhaps some of the younger generation. We'll leave the setting-up of a Flower Show committee until then. Thank you so much, everyone.'

Like so many released birds the men on the back bench hastened through the door. Once outside, in the fresh air, under the stars, they seemed to breathe more freely, for they gathered there and wagged the tongues which had for so long remained locked behind sealed lips.

The vicar collected his papers, and he and Mrs Partridge and the Roberts left the hall amid a chorus of cheerful 'Good nights' from the knot at the door. Mr Willet and I remained in the building.

From the wall glowered the long-dead footballers, flanked by a copy of the Scout Rules. Mr Willet turned out the oil-stove, which gave a last malicious belch before it expired.

'That the lot?' queried Mr Willet looking round the hall, and rubbing a smut across his nose thoughtfully.

'Looks like it,' I replied, as we made our way to the door.

'HAVE YOU SWITCHED OF THE LIGHT?' asked that maddening notice severely.

'Us has now!' said Mr Willet, snapping the switch in

answer to this silent enquiry, and plunged the hall into darkness.

He locked the door behind us, and we all set out for our own hearths again.

Mr Willet and I proceeded homeward, a few steps in front of the backbenchers, who were now as vociferous as they had formerly been tongue-tied.

'I don't hold with outsiders coming in on our Flower Show. We gets it up—has to pay through the nose for a marquee and that—and then, like as not, some foreigner gets the prizes!' said one.

'Ah! You're right there!' agreed another energetically. Little sparks, struck from the flinty road by his metal-tipped boots, accompanied this statement. All Fairacre meetings really start in the lane after the official meeting has been formally closed.

'And another thing,' said Arthur Coggs morosely, 'where's all the youngsters tonight? Don't know what'd become of the village if us older chaps didn't take an interest.'

'Never seems to care if Fairacre goes hang, does 'em?' commented the spark-maker. 'Why, when I was a boy, it was us young 'uns that turned up to all the meetings, and helped to get this ol' Flower Show up every year, and a Glee Club in the winter, and them tableaus for the Red Cross, and a Nativity Play every Christmas in the church——'

'Ah! We made our own fun then! Fairacre always had something going on. But look at the young 'uns today! Take tonight—not one of 'em interested enough to turn up to this meeting and speak out like the rest of us!'

I remembered the abysmal silence of a few minutes before, and was glad that it was dark. Mr Willet spoke beside me, throwing his words back over his shoulder at the dark figures behind us.

''Course we made our own fun when we was young. 'Twas a case of have to, with no buses to Caxley, and no wireless or telly. We'd have gone plumb crazy setting about twiddlin' our thumbs. But times is changed. You can't expect young folk to want what we did. They've got all the world to amuse 'em now, and if you asks me they're a sight more civilized that we was! I ain't forgot the gangs of lads that used to lounge outside the "Beetle," kicking their heels, and not above chucking mud at folks passing, and swearing at any strangers as dared to come into Fairacre! You don't get them louts about now in this village, say what you like. They've got something better to do!'

By now we had reached Tyler's Row and Arthur Coggs wished us good night before kicking open his ramshackle gate.

'Well,' he said unctuously, 'I suppose us old stagers 'll have to put our shoulders to the wheel again for this 'ere Flower Show!'

We proceeded through the village, the lighted cottage windows throwing a homely flicker across our path.

'That Arthur Coggs!' burst out Mr Willet testily. 'He fair gives me the pip—un'oly 'ypocrite! Great useless article! Why the Almighty saw fit to put waspses and adders and Arthur Coggs into this world, is beyond me! Good night, Miss Read—see you bright and early.'

Preparations for Christmas are now in full swing. For weeks past the shops in Caxley have been a blaze of coloured lights and decorated with Father Christmases, decked trees, silver balls and all the other paraphernalia. Even our grocer's shop in Fairacre has cotton-wool snow, hanging on threads, down the window, and this, and the crib already set up in the church all add to the children's enchantment.

It has turned bitterly cold, with a cruel east wind, which has scattered the last of the leaves and ruffles the feathers of the birds who sit among the bare branches. The tortoise stoves are kept roaring away, but nothing can cure the fiendish draught from the sky-light above my desk, and the one from the door, where generations of feet have worn the lintel into a hollow.

Yesterday afternoon the whole school was busy making Christmas decorations and Christmas cards. There is nothing that children like more than making brightly-coloured paper chains, and their tongues wagged happily as the paste brushes were plied, and yet another glowing link was added to the festoons that lay piled on the floor. All this glory grows so deliciously quickly and the knowledge that, very soon, it will be swinging aloft, above their heads, among the pitch-pine rafters—an enchanting token of all the joys that Christmas holds in store—makes them work with more than usual energy.

In Miss Jackson's room the din was terrific, so excited were the chain-makers. The only quiet group here was the one which was composed of about eight small children who had elected to crayon Christmas cards instead. Among them was the little Pratt boy. I stopped to admire his effort. His picture was of a large and dropsical robin, with the fiercest of red breasts, and very small and inadequate legs, as there was only a quarter of an inch of space left at the bottom for these highly-necessary appendages. His face was solemn with the absorption of the true artist.

'It's for Miss Bunce,' he told me. 'You knows—the one at Barrisford what took me to the hostipple to have my eye done. She writes to me ever so often, and sometimes sends me sweets. D'you reckon she'll like it?'

He held up his masterpiece and surveyed it anxiously at arm's length.

I told him truthfully that I was sure she would like it very much, and that all sensible people liked robins on Christmas cards. With a sigh of infinite satisfaction he replaced it on the desk, and prepared to face the horrid intricacies of writing 'HAPPY CHRISTMAS' inside.

The afternoon flew by amidst all this happy turmoil, and we were clearing up hastily when Mrs Partridge arrived. She stayed with us while we sang grace, and helped to tie scarves, and button up coats, before sending the children out into the bleak world. I wondered vaguely why she had called, for she is such a direct and bustling person that it was unusual for her not to have stated her business on arrival. I invited her into the school-house for tea.

Miss Jackson was wheeling her bicycle across the playground, and Mrs Partridge asked her how she was faring at Miss Clare's.

'It's lovely!' said my assistant with enthusiasm, 'I'm absolutely spoilt and she lets me do a little cooking if I want to, and we gossip away about school and the children——' It was the first time that I had seen her genuinely happy, and I thought how shrewdly Dr Martin had summed up the position when he had meddled so successfully in the affairs of Fairacre School.

Mrs Partridge seemed ill at ease as I made up the fire and put on the kettle. She followed me into the kitchen as I set out cups and saucers, and she began to pleat the dish cloth that hung along the sink's edge.

'Gerald asked me to call,' she began, her eyes fixed on her handiwork. 'He felt that I should have a word with you.'

'Well, I'm very glad to see you,' I said cheerfully. 'Was it about the hymn list?'

'No, no. Nothing to do with the school!' She left her pleating abruptly and asked if she could carry anything. I gave her the biscuit barrel, picked up the tray, and followed my unhappy guest into the dining-room.

After a few sips of tea, she made a second attempt to broach this painful subject, of which I was completely in the dark.

'We've had some very unsettling news,' she said at last. 'About Mr Mawne.'

I said I was sorry. I hoped that he wasn't ill? Mrs Partridge gave a heavy sigh.

'No, he's not *ill*——' she said, and stopped.

'Perhaps he's decided not to come back to Fairacre?' I said, trying to help her, and thinking that perhaps she was worried, on my account, about this matter.

'Yes, he's coming back. That's partly the trouble,' said the vicar's wife, stirring her tea meditatively. 'Gerald had a letter this morning from him.'

'I should think that's good news,' I said. 'I know he's an enormous help to the vicar.'

'But, my dear,' Mrs Partridge broke out in anguished tones, 'I really don't know how to tell you! To be blunt, he's bringing his wife back with him!'

The relief which this thunder-burst brought to me cannot be described, but Mrs Partridge looked so distraught that I could hardly let out a cheer and caper round the room, when she had suffered so much on my behalf. I did the next best thing.

'Believe me,' I said earnestly, 'that's the best news I've heard since Mr Mawne came to live here. Now I hope I shall be left in peace!'

I wished that I hadn't added the last sentence, when I saw poor Mrs Partridge wince.

'We've all behaved insufferably,' said she, 'and I hope you will forgive us. Really I've been greatly to blame. It seemed such a very good thing——' She faltered to a stop.

'I'm delighted to know that he still has a wife,' I told her, 'and to be honest, I rather suspected it from the first. So you see I am not at all upset by this disclosure—in fact I am greatly relieved. He was sorely in need of companionship.'

Now that the first breach had been made Mrs Partridge's words rushed out in spate.

'They separated about two years ago evidently. That was why he took John Parr's flat, and his wife went to relations in Ireland. There was never any question of divorce, I understand—which makes me feel that if any overtures were made to you, he behaved very badly.'

'I can assure you,' I said, 'that I never for one moment imagined that Mr Mawne had designs on me; and if he had been free to offer marriage I should not have hesitated to refuse him. I am—quite honestly—much happier as I am. Fairacre's romantic heart is the only one that is going to be broken when the news leaks out.'

Much relieved, the vicar's wife accepted a second cup of tea, and our conversation turned to less painful topics. It was only when she departed that she returned again to the subject.

'You've taken it so well,' she said. 'You put us all to shame. I shall never be able to forgive myself for being so thoughtless, and such an old busybody.'

I assured her again that she was forgiven, and that I felt as though a great weight were lifted from my back.

I closed the door behind her, and waltzed gaily back to the kitchen, cutting the caper that had been pent-up for so long.

Tibby was not amused.

On Saturday morning I met Amy in Caxley. She was busy shopping for Christmas presents and had already accumulated half a dozen neat little parcels.

'I'm buying small things this year,' she said, 'that are easy to pack. Costs so much less in postage too.' I thought, not for the first time, how efficient and sensible Amy was. My own presents included a large cushion, and an adorable, but fragile, fruit set, and I was already beginning to wonder how on earth I was going to prepare them for the post.

'Let's have some coffee,' I suggested, shelving this problem for a moment, and we entered the doorway of 'The Buttery.'

A blast of hot thick air, and a noise like the parrot-house at the Zoo greeted us, and we settled ourselves comfortably among the oak beams, settees, warming-pans, chestnut roasters and other archaic domestic utensils which have witnessed the shredding of many a Caxley reputation. The coffee, as usual, was excellent, and over it Amy told me that she wanted a particularly nice present for James this year.

'I usually give him cigarettes,' said she, 'but he's had rather a worrying time lately at the office and I think he needs cheering up.'

I said I hoped that all was well now.

'Oh yes,' answered Amy, lighting a cigarette, and keeping her gaze carefully upon the flame, 'he has had to get rid of a number of his staff; and things should go much more smoothly. He's buying me a garnet bracelet that I've wanted for some time, and so I'd like to give him something rather special.'

'Cuff-links?' I suggested vaguely.

'We went through the cuff-links stage when we were courting,' said Amy, somewhat impatiently, 'and talking of that—is Mr Mawne back yet?'

'Mr Mawne,' I said, with relish, 'is coming back almost immediately, and is bringing his wife with him!'

'*Never!*' said Amy, dumbfounded. Then she began to laugh. 'Snooks to Fairacre, I suppose you think—you heartless hussy! Well, it's best as it is!'

I agreed wholeheartedly, and Amy returned to the pressing business of James's present.

'There's a rather nice paisley dressing-gown next door.

Let's go and look at that.' We gathered our parcels together, while Amy continued.

'James said last night that he thought it would be fun to go away for Christmas this year. It's been pretty hectic at the office, I gather, and as he said, we haven't seen much of each other lately, with so much business to attend to.'

I said that a little holiday would do them both good. Amy seemed to be far away in her thoughts. She stood in the crowded restaurant, amidst the chattering Caxley folk, and an impatient waitress tried in vain, to pass her with a loaded tray.

'He said,' she said slowly, oblivious of her surroundings, 'that old friends were best!' She looked very happy, and much as I remembered her twenty years ago. The waitress gave a final heave to her tray, and struggled past.

'Let's go and buy that dressing-gown,' I said.

The news of Mr Mawne's early return, and of his married state, has now leaked out in Fairacre. That it has been a shock, no one can deny, but I have been amused—and also touched—by the sympathy and staunch support which have been shown me, in the most delicate and unobtrusive manner.

Mr Willet took a long time working round the subject to try and find out if I knew yet of Mr Mawne's perfidy. At last I took pity on him and told him that I hoped to meet Mr Mawne's wife before long, and that it would be pleasant to have new people settled in Fairacre.

A great gusty sigh blew from under Mr Willet's stained moustache.

'Ah! Well now—glad you've heard about it! My old dad used to say "Speak the truth and shame the devil," so here goes! I never took to that chap Mawne myself, and I don't know as I ever shall. But there, we must all shake down together, I s'pose—so "Least said, soonest mended!"'

He plodded off across the playground comforting himself

with this homely philosophy of well-tried tags which serves him so well. In fair weather or foul, in joy or adversity, Mr Willet can always find an age-old snatch of country wisdom to guide him in his wanderings. His conversation is sprinkled with salty maxims, adding not only savour, but support, to his daily progress.

The first intimation I had that Mrs Pringle had heard the news was the discovery of a small parcel, wrapped in greaseproof paper, on my desk.

The classroom was empty, for it was only twenty to nine, but Mrs Pringle was already moving ponderously about her dusting, behind the closed door of the infants' room. I recognized her handwriting on the parcel.

'To Miss Read,' it said, in careful copperplate, and smudgy indelible pencil.

I undid it carefully, and found inside a partridge, trussed and dressed ready for the oven, even to the refinement of two fat streaky rashers lashed securely across its dusky breast. This gift, I realized, was a tribute of sympathy, and I was more touched than I should have cared to admit.

Sitting alone, in that quiet classroom, with only the tick of the wall-clock and the faint shouts of my approaching pupils to be heard, I felt, perhaps more keenly than ever before, just what it means to be a villager—someone whose welfare is of interest (sometimes of unwelcome interest) to one's neighbours—but always to *matter*. It was a warming thought—to be part of a small, living community, 'members one of another,' so closely linked by ties of kinship, work and the parish boundaries, that the supposed unhappiness of one elderly woman affected all.

The opening of the partition door disclosed Mrs Pringle looking sombrely upon me. I thanked her, most sincerely, for her present.

'My John had a brace from Mr Parr's week-end shoot,' she said, 'I thought it'd make you a bit of supper. It's a change from butcher's meat.'

She bent down, corsets creaking, to dust the rails of the front desks. With her face thus hidden from me, she spoke again.

'You've heard the news, I don't doubt?'

I said that I had heard about Mr Mawne. She puffed along to the last desk and then straightened up cautiously.

'Wild horses wouldn't drag that name across my lips after what's been done between us, Miss Read, as well you knows! But in all fairness, I must say that I wasn't the only one in Fairacre as thought he was hanging his hat up to you. He ain't thought much of in the village, I can tell you—and him having the sauce to come back and live here too!'

Her face was red with indignation. She sat herself heavily on the front desk, arms folded majestically, and gazed grimly at me over the brass and mahogany inkstand.

I felt laughter welling up inside me, which would not be checked.

'Mrs Pringle,' I said, 'you can let it be known discreetly, that I'm as pleased as Punch about the news. Believe me, a heart as old as mine takes a lot of cracking!'

Her belligerent countenance softened, and a rare smile curved those dour lips. For a moment we sat smiling across the inkstand, and then Mrs Pringle heaved herself to her feet.

'Ah well! That's done with!' was her comment, and she retreated again to the infants' room, to finish her dusting. I could hear her singing a hymn in her usual gloomy contralto.

It was only when I had repacked my partridge, and looked out my register and red and blue pens for marking it, that I realized she was singing:

Let us with a gladsome mind
Praise the Lord, for He is kind!

By right and ancient custom at Fairacre School the last afternoon of the Christmas term is given up to a tea-party.

The partition had been pushed back, so that the two classrooms had been thrown into one, but even so, the school was crowded, with children, parents and friends. Mrs Finch-Edwards was there, showing her baby daughter Althea to Miss Clare. Miss Jackson, who had dressed the Christmas tree alone, was receiving congratulations upon its glittering beauty from Mrs Partridge. Mr Roberts's hearty laugh rustled the paper-chains so near his head, and the vicar beamed upon us all, until Mrs Pringle gave him the school cutting-out scissors and reminded him of his responsibilities. For it was he who would cut the dangling presents from the tree before the party ended.

In the quiet of the school-house across the playground my godson slept peacefully, too young yet for the noise and heat engendered by forty-odd hilarious schoolchildren. Mrs Annett was with us, busily discussing clothes with Mrs Moffat, her former landlady. Mrs Coggs and Mrs Waites had walked up together from Tyler's Row, and now sat, side by side, watching their sons engulf sardine sandwiches, iced biscuits, sponge cake, jam tarts and sausage rolls, all washed down with frequent draughts of fizzy lemonade through a gurgling straw. Mr Willet, at one end of the room, had the job of taking the metal tops off the bottles, and with bent back and purple, sweating face, had been hard put to it to keep pace with the demand.

It was a cheerful scene. The paper-chains and lanterns swung from the rafters, the tortoise stoves, especially brilliant today from Mrs Pringle's ministrations, roared merrily, and the glittering tree dominated the room.

The children, flushed with food, heat and excitement, chattered like starlings, and around them the warm, country voices of their elders exchanged news and gossip.

After tea, the old well-loved games were played, 'Oranges and Lemons' with Miss Clare at the piano, and Mr and Mrs Partridge making the arch, 'Poor Jenny sits a-weeping,' 'The Farmer's in his Den,' 'Nuts and May' and 'Hunt the Thimble.' We always have this one last of all, so that we can regain our breath. The children nearly burst with suppressed excitement, as the seeker wanders bewildered about the room, and on this occasion the roars of 'Cold, cold!' or 'Warmer, warmer!' and the wild yelling of 'Hot, hot! You're REAL hot!' nearly raised the pitch-pine roof.

The presents were cut from the tree, and the afternoon finished with carols; old and young singing together lustily and with sincerity. Within those familiar walls, feuds and old hurts forgotten, for an hour or two at least, Fairacre had been united in joy and true goodwill.

It was dark when the party ended. Farewells and Christmas greetings had been exchanged under the night sky, and the schoolroom was quiet and dishevelled. The Christmas tree, denuded of its parcels, and awaiting the removal of its bright baubles on the morrow, still had place of honour in the centre of the floor.

Joseph Coggs' dark eyes had been fixed so longingly on the star at its summit, that Miss Clare had unfastened it and given it into his keeping, when the rest of the children had been safely out of the way.

The voices and footsteps had died away long ago by the time I was ready to lock up and go across to my peaceful house. Some of the bigger children were coming in the morning to help me clear up the aftermath of our Christmas revels, before Mrs Pringle started her holiday scrubbing.

The great Gothic door swung to with a clang, and I turned the key. The night was still and frosty. From the distant downs came the faint bleating of Mr Roberts' sheep, and the lowing of Samson in a nearby field. Suddenly a cascade of sound showered from St Patrick's spire. The bell-ringers were practising their Christmas peal. After that first mad jangle the bells fell sweetly into place, steadily, rhythmically, joyfully calling their message across the clustered roofs and the plumes of smoke from Fairacre's hearths, to the grey, bare glory of the downs that shelter us.

I turned to go home, and to my amazement, noticed a child standing by the school gate.

It was Joseph Coggs. High above his head he held his tinsel star, squinting at it lovingly as he compared it with those which winked in their thousands from above St Patrick's spire.

We stood looking at it together, and it was some time before he spoke, raising his voice against the clamour of the bells.

'Good, ain't it?' he said, with the utmost satisfaction.

'Very good!' I agreed.